Praise for

Hood

"A strong plot and carefully drawn characters with classic motivations." —*Publishers Weekly*

Praise for

Thong on Fire

Winner of the African American Literary Award for Erotica

"Noire delivers a captivating page-turner that will be hard to put down. *Thong on Fire* is not just a book but a literary journey that goes beyond the sheets."

—APOOO BookClub

"*Thong on Fire* is compelling and engaging, the kind of story that once started, is hard to put down."

—RAWSISTAZ

Praise for

Candy Licker

#1 Essence Magazine Bestseller

"Raw, in your face, and straight from the street. Urban erotica has never been hotter!"

—NIKKI TURNER, author of *The Glamorous Life*

"[*Candy Licker* is] completely absorbing. . . . [The book] delivers everything that lovers of this emerging micro genre—black urban erotic chick lit—are coming to expect: cribs full of music, sex, drugs and criminality; many dollars flying by; and an honest, often-abused girl just trying to make it through."

—*Publishers Weekly*

"Noire skillfully mixes gritty, in-your-face urban drama with a healthy dose of raw sexuality. *Candy Licker* proves that Noire is a force to be reckoned with in the urban erotic genre."

—Urban-Reviews.com

Praise for

G-Spot

#1 Essence *Magazine Bestseller*

"*The Coldest Winter Ever* meets *Addicted*!"

—JAMISE L. DAMES, bestselling author of *Momma's Baby, Daddy's Maybe*

"Freedom comes with a price in Noire's sexy, gritty urban melodrama. Noire's heady brew of lethal realism and unbridled sexuality should spell 'hot and bothered' for erotic fiction fans."

—*Publishers Weekly*

Also by Noire

Novels

Hood

Thong on Fire

Baby Brother
(co-written with 50 Cent)

Thug-A-Licious

Candy Licker

G-Spot

Edited by Noire

From the Streets to the Sheets:
Urban Erotic Quickies

Hittin' the Bricks

NOIRE

Hittin' the Bricks

An Urban Erotic Tale

One World | Ballantine Books | NewYork

A One World Books Trade

Published in the United States by One World Books, an imprint of The Random House Publishing Group, a division of Random House, Inc., New York.

ONE WORLD is a registered trademark and the One World colophon is a trademark of Random House, Inc.
ISBN 978-1-60751-559-3

Printed in the United States of America

Book design by Laurie Jewell

This book is dedicated to some of the creative geniuses
who worked their asses off to lift my characters off the
pages and bring them to life on the screen:

Alexandra Merejo
Texas Battle
Ness Bautista
Enrique Almeida
Millie Ruperto
And introducing . . . Reem Raw!

And to Ken Atchity, Chi-Li Wong, Mark Sullivan,
Adria Lang, Michael Kuciak, and Brian Jaynes for bringing
us together and making the magic happen!

Acknowledgments

All things good are attributed to the wise Father above. I give Him thanks for keeping my hopes and dreams big, and my ego and my head . . . very small. Nisaa, Black, and Reem . . . y'all the most righteous peeps in the universe. Thanks for keeping this urban erotic train rolling steady down the tracks.

STAY BLACK

NOIRE

Lights, Camera, Action!

The past three years have been crazy busy for me! After writing seven urban erotic tales and editing a hot collection of urban erotic quickies, I was able to do something that for the longest time I had only dreamed about: I wrote a movie!

It was a crazy good experience. I loved working on it from the first word until the last word. All writing is not the same though, and doing big things with a screenplay designed for a film is a whole lot different than writing a sheet-soaking bestselling novel, but it was a challenge I was ready to meet.

Film is a highly visual medium, but even when I'm writing books I can actually "see" my characters as they venture down those grimy back alleys of life. Most readers say my urban erotic tales really grab them and "put them there," thrusting them into the scene so much that they visualize, experience, and feel the drama, so maybe that's why making the transition from book to film writing was so much fun for me.

But writing a movie was a lot of hard work too, so I studied up and learned the ins and outs from the professional scriptwriters on my management team, and at the end of the day I discovered I was able to express my creativity in visual ways that just aren't possible when your thoughts and ideas are confined to the pages in a book.

This was also my big chance to get some Noire Music Group artists involved in a gully production, and we rolled out the amazing Reem Raw for his first film performance where he not only spit on the mic and worked magic on the stage, but starred as himself in a character role. As a music artist, Reem wrote the lyrics for several songs used in the film, and he also helped actors perfect the art of rapping, while they helped him perfect the art of acting. Everybody was so real and everything came together so tight, that we couldn't have asked for better chemistry and love on the set.

I always knew I'd go hard with my first movie project, but I knew I'd need room to put my own unique thing down on it too. That meant I was gonna require the freedom to switch up and do me in ways that might be different than somebody else might do them. One innovative thing I wanted to do was flip the face of some of my film characters and make them different than the characters in the book. To do this, I took the theme of my urban erotic tale, which is really a common theme across a lot of cities in urban America, and I shifted the lines of neighborhoods and ethnicities to see if the tale would play out the same way across cultural barriers.

Man, the actors and actresses who turned out really put it down on the movie set. They took my story from being a straight-up gully urban erotic tale into a multicultural street film that proved that there are no concrete territorial lines to be drawn when it comes to crime and drama in the hood. Whether you live in the ghetto or *el barrio*, whether you get down on fried chicken and collard greens or *arroz con pollo*, whether you're Black, Latino, Asian or some other subculture in the multimix of urban America, the street's sagas are all the same, the struggles are all the same, and above all else, the dire and sometimes deadly consequences . . . are the same.

I know ya feel me. So get tight with ya girl Eva as she struggles to survive on the cold streets of Harlem. Savor this urban erotic cautionary tale that shows you what real life can be like on cruel city streets. Then check out the film *Hittin' the Bricks* starring Texas Battle, Alejandra Merejo, Reem Raw, Enrique Almeida, and Ness Bautista, and holla at me and show the film cast some hot gully love for bringing their multicultural flow game to my urban erotic mix.

Look for a code to get a Special Edition pre-release DVD of *Hittin' the Bricks* available to loyal readers at the back of this book!

NOIRE

Noire@AskNoire.com

Warning!

This here ain't no romance
It's an urban erotic tale . . .
Little Eva's got a monkey
And her body's up for sale
Daughter of the ghetto
Abused by friend and foe
Eva's got a secret
It's gonna cost her don't you know?
A deal went down on Rikers
Of that there is no doubt
Eva was the trade-off
Someone special sold her out
Dreams of fame and big success
Little Eva has no wins
Fiyah does a bid for her
She's gonna suffer for her sins
Lies, deceit, and power
Reign supreme on ghetto streets
It's an everyday struggle
Just to stay up on your feet
Schemes and fiends and playas
Cut deeper than a knife
The next man's thirst for glory
Could cost Eva her life
So this here ain't no romance
We 'bout to stop and hit the bricks
'Cause on the streets of Harlem
The good ones take the licks

NOIRE

In the Beginning ...

Have you ever been betrayed by those you love? Violated and abused in the worst kind of way? And no matter how hard you tried to fight your way out of a trick bag, no matter how tall you tried to walk, did the cold streets of life lead you right back to your grimy destiny? Have you ever lived with fear? Crying out in the darkness as it charged through your veins and numbed your spirit in the middle of the night? Did you damn your own soul as you despised your fear, because deep inside you knew you adored it too? You there? You feel me? The boot of life been on your neck before? Suffocating you and holding you down? Well, if you've ever felt the pain of treachery, then walk with me for a minute. Let's hit one of the hottest nightclubs in all of Harlem. A cutthroat joint called Bricks. A place where dissin' a shot caller could get a bitch bodied real quick, and wicked fear reigned supreme. Let me go on and break it down for you. My name is Eva Marie Patterson. I fought my fear in a club called Bricks, and this is how my end began . . .

Hittin' the Bricks

Black Girl Lost

The Brooklyn housing projects were deserted as Eva Patterson took a shortcut through the buildings, trying not to get drenched in the pouring rain. It was unusually cold for early fall, and all she had on was the corduroy skirt and Salvation Army sweater she'd been wearing when Rasheena kicked her out of their tenement apartment, but the temperature was the last thing on her mind as her eyes scanned the crime-ridden buildings in search of a safe place to go.

"Sheena, please . . ." Their neighbor Iris had butt in on the earlier drama as Rasheena cursed her daughter out like she was a grown woman. Iris had puffed out her cheeks and held her breath between tokes of weed. "Stunt, stop fuckin' trippin'. Eva's a good girl. And young as she is, I know you ain't . . . putting her out in the . . . street this time of . . . night."

It was a Grey Goose night, and Rasheena drunk was somebody altogether different than Rasheena high. The high Rasheena would have been sitting in a corner somewhere. Getting her nod on and leaving Eva the hell alone. The drunk Rasheena had stood over her daughter giving her a grimy look that said Eva could kiss her ass.

"What?!?" Rasheena had turned to Iris. "Fourteen is *grown!* Sheeit . . . my ass was on the ave gettin' tricked when I was twelve. Who the fuck took care of me?"

Rasheena slurped a mouthful of Goose straight from the bottle, then chased it with a long swig of cranberry juice and explained. "Look, I. If you lie you steal, and Eva is a thief. A *goddamn* thief. There's two things I ain't 'bout to watch in my own goddamn house. My duji and my dick! Ya feel me? Eva grown enough to fuck with my man and dabble in my shit? Then she grown enough to let the doorknob hit'er in the ass on the way out!"

"Well *damnnn*," Iris toked the blunt and muttered under her breath. "Y'all the ones who got her started on that shit in the first place . . ."

Eva had just sat there crying inside and looking forty instead of fourteen. She *had* tried to dip in Rasheena's stash, but she'd been sick all day and couldn't go out and make no money. Eva hated stealing from her mother. These days she hated taking anything from anybody, but she had a hungry monkey on her back. And Iris had it right. Eva wasn't responsible for putting herself on the gutter path to drug abuse, but neither did she have what it took to get off of it. She hadn't gotten a hit all day, and just thinking about having to get out on those cold streets was enough to bring her jones down even harder.

"*Don't worry I got you,*" Eva's stepfather Jahden put his hand up to his mouth and whispered. He winked and grinned as Eva slunk into the tiny room she'd once shared with her cousin Fuego, whose street-translated name was Fiyah. Eva missed her cousin real bad. But Fiyah's mother had gotten out of rehab a couple of years earlier and he'd gone back to Harlem to live with her. Even with all the grimy things they'd done together Fiyah was down for her through thick and thin, and Eva wished she could have escaped to Harlem with him.

"And don't you take a damn thing outta here that I bought you!" Rasheena screamed from the kitchen. Eva sighed. The only thing she was interested in taking from the room was the most important thing.

Her works.

Jahden grabbed her thin arm as she headed out the front door.

"Hold on, baby. I said I got you." A mid-level drug dealer, Jahden specialized in pushing smack while most trap boys were busy trading that rock. His hand slid around Eva's narrow shoulders then fell to the small of her back. Eva stiffened as his fingers crept down the lump of her ass and massaged her cheeks. A cold sweat broke out all over her skin. *If my real father was here Jah wouldn't be touching me like this,* she cried inside. *This nasty pervert woulda been bodied by now.* Eva bit her tongue, trying not to throw up. Jahden liked to cold sex her. He would do things to her that Eva's young body just wasn't ready to handle. There was no end to his twisted demands, and earlier in the day he had forced Eva to sit on the floor and watch him fuck Rasheena from the back while Rasheena got in Iris's pussy at the same time.

"Check me out, Eva baby!" he had panted as his ass cheeks gyrated and pumped like a steam engine. Eva shuddered. Her mother was rotating her head in circles and lapping nookie juice like that shit came in thirty-one flavors. Jahden laughed at the look of revulsion on Eva's face, then screamed on her as she closed her eyes and tried to escape the horrible scene playing out in front of her. "Bitch open ya goddamn eyes! You betta be a student and pay attention, dammit!"

Eva had just sat there and cried. She was traumatized and sickened. She wanted to stick a knife in Jahden's neck. The same way he'd stuck a fearsome needle in her neck a year ago and turned her into the scared, humiliated shell she was today.

Although Rasheena had starved her child almost to skin and bones and done things to Eva that even the lowest dog-mother would never consider, Jahden was the real reason her life was so fucked up and Eva hated him for it. Every other day she'd promise herself that she'd kick dope cold turkey before she let him rape her *or* get her high again, but her greatest fear had become her greatest joy, and Eva was helpless.

Rasheena, who had held Eva down the first time Jahden shot her up, and who had then stood by and watched as her boyfriend busted her young daughter's cherry, had been acting real jealous. She got mad whenever it looked like Jahden would rather fuck Eva than fuck her, and she put her foot down and demanded that from that day on Eva had to pay for her skag with cold hard gwap just like every other fiend-head customer.

Desperate, young Eva had taken to the streets to earn her drug money the only way she knew how. On her knees and on her back. She'd been beaten by strange men, raped, stabbed, and almost strangled. She had cried out to God for help, begging to know what she had done to deserve such a dark, treacherous life. But as usual, there were no answers for Eva. There was only more destitution and misery. Only fear and more pain. And right now, standing next to Jahden while he rubbed all over her ass, she was hurting. Real bad. Hurting and scared.

Seeing the disgust on her face Jahden grinned and reached in his shirt pocket. He passed her a tiny foil-wrapped package and squeezed her fingers when she tried to take it.

"I got what you need, baby girl." He cupped his dick and licked his lips. "See how cool I am? Tonight I'ma let you get it for free."

Eva burned with rage, but he was right. She feared what he had, but she needed it too. She snatched it greedily and fled.

Downstairs, Eva's nose was runny and her entire body ached. A deep pain gripped her as she was leaving her building, and it wasn't just from anger or from her mother's cruel behavior. Rasheena had once been a top clothing model for a highly successful designer, but these days she was a common needle fiend who put her man, her drink, and her drugs way ahead of her only child. She had also been an extremely beautiful and intelligent black woman who could have gone far in life. Tall and shapely, with skin the color of brown sugar, she had wide eyes, stunning lips, and hips like sweet chocolate milkshakes. Back in the day she used to be known as the finest chick in Brownsville, but a fast life and a series of grimy men had proven more than Rasheena could handle. She'd traded her exotic beauty for one too many heroin trips, and these days she scrambled with the low-life Jahden because he not only paid her rent, but he also kept her head right.

Having a junkie for a mother was bad enough, but the drunken rages Rasheena flew into always cut Eva deep. Juiced, Rasheena would wrap an extension cord around her fist and whip her daughter until Eva's skin split open and she passed out from the pain. Eva's starving body was a canvas of thick, ugly scars and fresh bruises that she'd picked until they were oozing, infected sores. Her stomach, ass, and back would be so cut open that her wounds bled through and pussed over and glued her undergarments to her skin. Her arms and legs had their fair share of crisscrossed cuts and welts too, but Rasheena had learned to chill on those areas after the school social worker got on her case and told her she'd make sure her black ass got locked up the next time she saw Eva with a fresh belt mark.

It was hard for Eva to admit that she would rather see her mother mainline heroin than guzzle vodka and gin, but that was the way it was with Rasheena. Besides, Eva understood duji. She respected that shit. Liquor was something else though. A smack head could find any old corner and cop a quiet nod, but a drunk usually got loud and abusive. Drunks liked to bully the weak, and that was Rasheena to a tee.

Eva dodged rain puddles and hunched her narrow shoulders against the cold. It was after midnight, and the sixteen-story concrete towers of Howard Houses Projects were a mixture of illumination and darkness. Rain curled Eva's silky hair and drenched her down to her bruised skin. Shivering, she tightened her grip on the tiny package she'd gotten from Jahden, then ducked her head and moved down the walkways as fast as she could.

She was close to building 420 when the same pain she'd felt earlier slammed into her again. This one hurt so bad it snatched her breath and doubled her over in her tracks. She tried to pant quick and deep and get past it, but the agony clawed at her gut and she fell to the wet ground, busting open a partially healed sore on her knee.

"*Please, God,*" Eva begged. Her nose was running freely now, and she was totally sick. "God, please help me." Rainwater mixed with tears fell into her mouth. Eva was scared. She felt like a train had hit her and she needed to find someplace safe fast. The wind screamed and she clenched her fist tight, holding on to her precious package. She crawled over to a seesaw and rested her cheek on the painted wood. Her knee throbbed and her stomach felt pressurized, like she needed to take a real big shit.

Eva fought the urge, and as the wind screamed all she could think about was getting someplace dry where she could get herself right. She was a young girl but experience had taught her what would happen to her if she went up in one of the regular drug dens to do her thing. Like a lot of chicks, she might come out of one of those joints either raped or beaten, if she made it out at all. She gripped the small square of foil in her fist and pressed on. She was alone and afraid, jonesing in the night, and moments later she stood staring up at the windows of building 420. She knew people there. Her girl Sherri from junior high lived on the third floor with her crippled grandmother. Eva had come up on the streets with Sherri and a real cool dude named Reem Raw, a true friend who would fight any niggah in the street who so much as looked at either one of them wrong. But Reem had moved up to Harlem, and Sherri . . . Eva gazed at her friend's window where a light shone from a bedroom. She saw movement. She took a step toward the building, but then remembered. Sherri was clean now. She'd washed her hands of all the shiesty things she and Eva had done together. Eva moved closer and the curtains fell closed. A shadow retreated from the window and the light went out.

Friendless, Eva glanced around, searching for a spot. She was tempted to take her chances and run up in a project stairwell and get right real quick, but on a night like this there would be more predatory winos and pipe heads on the stairs than there were people living in the apartments. She would probably go into a nod and come out of it dead.

A large basketball court was on her right and a parking lot was on her left. Eva thought about breaking into a parked car, but she didn't have the strength. She didn't have the time neither.

Suddenly she thought of something better.

Drunk Mister James.

Drunk Nasty-Ass Mister James.

Clenching her silver package, she scurried along the side of building 420. Her sleeve scraped against the building's rough brick exterior. She hesitated at the mouth of the ramp that led down to the underground laundrymat and decided to take her chances. Sometimes Drunk Mister James was too lit to lock up on the weekends. Closing time would come and go, and the old man would be off, who the hell knew where, sipping on his cheap wine.

With her dope safe and dry in her left hand, Eva's bony fingers skimmed the rain-slick banister as she descended deeper down the ramp. Step by step, terror crept over her. Pitch blackness waited for her at the bottom, and probably a piper and a stray cat or two as well.

"*Oh . . . my God . . . please help me,*" Eva moaned. Another pain seized her and she almost peed right there. She pressed her knees together, feeling hot and nauseous. Like she needed to shit and throw up at the same time. Determined, she moved deeper down the ramp, the wind kicking her in the ass. If she could just get someplace dry, she would be all right. She didn't really care about the pain. She lived with pain on the regular. It was the dope sickness that was killing her.

A sudden surge of vomit splashed at the back of her throat and Eva flung herself down the ramp. Her jones was riding her *bad.* Desperation wiped away her fear and she was ready to fight. If something bad was waiting to hurt her at the bottom of the ramp then it better be jonesing harder than she was.

She stepped deeper into the darkness and stood before the closed door. Her hand slipped on the wet knob as she twisted it frantically. She almost couldn't believe it when the door swung open and she was inside an empty foyer that was as big as her apartment. She was greeted by the smell of bleach and laundry detergent mixed with the moldy aroma of rank old piss. Drunk Mister James was a lazy ass. The Housing Authority paid him to keep the place clean and swept up, but even in the dark Eva knew the walls and pipes were covered with years' worth of residual lint particles that spewed out of the ancient clothes dryers.

She walked into the main room holding her hands out in front of her, willing her eyes to adjust to the lack of light. The shadows were still as the wind raged outside, and Eva's eyes darted over the large, spacious room. The project laundry was supposed to be used by the residents only, but Eva had been coming over here by herself since she was eight. She used to envy the project kids as she watched them from the fourth-floor window of her raggedy tenement. They had plenty of heat and hot water over there. And windows that closed all the way in the winter. Eva's apartment building didn't have a laundry room or much of anything else, so she would venture across the street and through the tall buildings to use the project laundry that Drunk Mister James ran. Rasheena didn't even have to make her do it neither. At the age of eight Eva knew it was either cross the street so Drunk Mister James could sneak her in the storage closet and feel her nubby titties to see how big she was getting, or walk around in dirty clothes every day.

The far left wall was lined with fifteen front-loading washers. At a dollar fifty a pop and ten minutes of lukewarm water, they were just another ghetto rip-off. Three large wooden tables stood in the center of the room. People often fought for folding space on these tables, and Eva's eyes had adjusted well enough to make out several towels and shirts and other items that had been discarded or left behind by their careless owners.

On her right were the clothes dryers. Eight of them. They were jumbo. Industrial-sized.

Eva approached a middle dryer and pulled the metal handle on its large Plexiglas door. She stood trembling and wet as she gazed into the giant blackness. Her sickness rose again, and Eva leaned forward. Pain throbbed in her lower back and there was no room in her head for thought or fear. Every fiber in her being needed this. She climbed into the dryer and settled her small frame between its grooves. The metal was cold against her wet skin. Her teeth chattered as she scooted backward, pushing herself deeper inside.

Eva sat cross-legged. She uncurled her fist and gazed at her fearsome package, then reached under her shirt and into her dirty bra. She pulled out the plastic baggie containing her works. Excitement surged through her the moment she held it. Her skin was slick with anticipatory sweat despite her rain-drenched clothes. She took off her panties, then removed the belt from her skirt and looped it around her bruised upper thigh. The bulging vein and scabbing track marks in her groin didn't bother her. Nor did her hunger pangs. Neither did the warm liquid that had begun to seep from between her legs. She took out a spoon and hummed as she flicked her lighter, then cooked and made her preparations. Fast music played in her head and her stomach cramped again. Hard. Eva ignored it and held the thing she feared out in front of her. She flicked the tip with her middle finger. Twice.

Anticipation had her head spinning. Soon she'd be in a place where there were no beatings, no hunger, and no pain. She withdrew the plunger then pressed it back in slowly. Liquid dribbled from the tip. Wrapping one end of the belt around her hand, Eva bit hard on the other end and jerked her head. Yanking it tight. Drool slid from her mouth and trickled down her chin. She sat there, head bent and gap-legged. Straining against the belt, Eva slapped the crease between her pelvis and her thigh. The sound echoed in the darkness as her body yearned. It was gonna feel *sooo* good. Her fear was turning into joy, and it was beautiful. The sharp tip glistened silver. She pressed it into her flesh like a pro, piercing a worn vein.

Pure love shot through her. Her skin was on fire and her nipples tingled. Eva pumped the plunger in and out, sending pleasure waves from her vein straight to her brain. She rode those waves until her mouth went slack. The needle fell from her hand and her chin dropped to her chest. She had no idea how long she stayed like that. Nodding. Emerging briefly from the fog, just long enough to pick at the pus-filled sores on her arms and legs, and then dive back in again. Eva's lips spread in a half smile. Music was in her head. In her stupor, she danced. She felt happy there. Safe. Eva would have loved to stay in her nod forever, but a pain so bone-grinding and graphic moved through her midsection that it blew her high and sent a scream flying from her lips.

"Mommy . . ." she moaned, loosening the belt as a huge gush of water soaked her lower body. Eva was gripped in a tide of pain that arched her back and ripped at the soft area between her vagina and ass. She patted her pussy, horrified as a hard mass bulged right there inside of her.

What the . . . ? The mass was forcing its way out. Making her push. Eva gripped her thighs and fought with her pelvic muscles. She pushed down three times and screamed into the darkness. Four pushes later it was in her hands and she lay back in the dryer, moaning. She could hear it, but she was too scared to look. Minutes later another wave of agony tore through her. Eva cried out and pushed again, then got freaked out by the hot glob of tissue that just seemed to roll out of her.

She panicked. Crawling over everything she'd just pushed from her body, Eva jumped out the dryer and staggered over to one of the large folding tables. The back of her skirt was saturated and a trail of fluid splattered the floor behind her.

Shock tried to paralyze her, but her panic was too great.

"Oh shit, oh shit . . ." Eva cried out, her fear-filled words mingling with the small cries coming from the clothes dryer. She grabbed a discarded shirt from the table and pushed it between her legs. Her mind raced. Where in the hell had this thing been hiding? She was too skinny to hide a damn baby! She touched her stomach. It hadn't even gotten big! Her period? Shit, she shot so much smack she couldn't tell you the last time she'd had one. She had started her period at thirteen. Jahden had started getting her high and messing with her even before that. Eva held on to the table and took deep breaths, trying hard not to freak out.

The soft cries were becoming demanding.

Shut up! The noise was killing her. It sounded like a kitten was in the dryer. The mewing was pitiful and it scared the shit outta Eva and added to her confusion. *What if I just leave it there? Ain't nobody gotta know it was me . . .*

She crept back over to the clothes dryer. Her heart was jumping around in her chest and her head was spinning. The crying was louder, making her dizzy, like she wanted to black out.

Run, stupid! Get the fuck outta here! Don't nobody hafta know!

Eva peered into the clothes dryer. Arms and legs waved in the air as the baby wriggled, naked on the cold metal. It was a boy. Eva's hand found the door handle. She pushed against the dryer door . . . closing it. The baby's cries grew fainter.

Seconds later she flung the door open again. Eva reached out for it despite the voices that were screaming out warnings in her head. The baby was slippery in her arms. Soft and small. It was hers.

Eva wrapped everything in the abandoned towels from the folding table. Drunk Mister James would be opening up at daybreak. Saturday was the busiest day of the week. Plenty of project folks would be lining up to fight over the washing machines, extractors, and dryers.

Holding tight to her bundle, Eva stumbled weakly back to the folding tables. She had just lifted up her knee when a wave of exhaustion washed over her that was more draining than anything she had ever felt before. Crying, Eva scooted her weary body onto the table. She curled up with her baby cradled against her chest.

Outside, the rain had stopped but the howling wind still screamed through the project buildings. Eva was bleeding bad and she knew she didn't have much time. *Just for a quick minute . . .* she told herself, holding her baby close. She was weak and her young muscles felt like jelly. *I'ma rest just for a minute.* In tears, Eva kissed her baby's forehead and slept.

Chapter 1

"**F**uck 'em up, Papi!" Eva's girlfriend, Alex, screamed as they watched a skinny Puerto Rican cat swirl around on the stage. He was packed out. Dude had titties, cleavage, ass, all that. He wore a purple mini-skirt and a skimpy white tank, and his bronze skin glowed under the stage lights. Holding tight to the glistening gold pole, he spread his pretty legs, arched his spine, and then threw his head south until it almost touched his phatty ass.

"*Pop* that thang! Pop it, Papi! You workin' it, boy!"

"Sssh!!" Eva elbowed Alex in the ribs. "Why you gotta bust Georgie out like that? If these cats find out what he really is you know what'll happen to him."

Alex was laughing. "Yeah, I know. They'll take his

prissy ass upstairs and beat him until his balls grow back." She grinned. "Don't worry about my brother, Eva. All them hormones got him puffed up real nice. Nobody would ever guess he's got a little sausage hidden between his legs. His booty looks better than mine."

They were sitting in the front row of Club King. Eva had moved to Harlem four years ago, and loudmouth Alexandra Mercado was one of her closest friends. Alex looked over to the far wall where the lap dancers peddled their asses, then tapped Eva's leg furiously, squealing under her breath.

"Oooooh! Eva! That chick is over there ridin' that niggah's dick! They ain't supposed to be doin no *real* fuckin' in this damn club! Somebody's ass is gonna get *fired*!"

Eva looked over where Alex was pointing. Her girl was right. Some long-legged chick was straddling a dude and they was getting their gushy on for real! The look on dude's face was indescribable. He had the ugly fuck-face going on like a real pro, and it was clear that the girl on his lap had some real good pussy. Eva and Alex watched with their mouths wide open. That chick was dancing in his lap all right. Her little short skirt was up around her waist and she was impaled on his long steel dick while the guy gripped two handfuls of her phat round ass. Every time he lifted her in the air his thick wet rod was visible going in and out of her snatch. The chick had her head thrown back and was bucking on him faster and faster, going after her nut full force like the last damn thing in the world she was worried about was a fuckin' club job. Dude slammed her down hard a few times and then she fell forward on him, her head lolling over his shoulder. If the club management was gonna fire her then now would have been the time because girlfriend looked fucked totally out!

Eva shook her head as Alex laughed like crazy. Eva was all for some good hot sex with the right man, but after the trauma she'd suffered at Jahden's hands, it had taken her a long time to get to that point. Her sexual healing had come along in stages, and there were still times when she felt guilty and self-conscious about her past.

"I'm ready to go," she said, standing up. She sucked a cube of ice from her glass of Sprite and crunched it down to liquid. "You checked on your brother, Alex, and he's looking good. Now can we get the hell outta here?"

Alex grinned. She was a pretty redhead with a blessed body. Her family lived across the hall from Eva's aunt Milena, and Alex had dreams of singing and dancing and becoming a big star one day.

"Where we going next?"

Eva pretended to think for a second. "How about that new club called *Shakez* on the Lower East Side?"

Alex gave her a slick grin as they headed out the door.

"Oh, I'm on you, heffah! You tryna scope out that guy we saw on 125th Street. The cute one who was selling bootleg CDs, DVDs, incense, musk and polka-dot socks, two pairs for three dollars."

"*What* damn guy?" Eva laughed.

"Oh, bitch don't front! The cat who was slobbering all over his damn table when you walked by! The one who had that big-ass camera hanging around his neck and took your picture! The one who told you he was gonna be rapping at *Shakez* this weekend and gave you those two free VIP laminates. That's what fuckin' guy!"

Eva laughed again. Dude did have his mouth open as he checked her out. She had smiled as he took her picture, then laid some smooth words on him real quick, and by the time she strutted away, not only didn't he have her number, but Eva had gotten another free laminate out of him for her girl India too.

Even after four years of healing and nurturing it was still hard for Eva to believe that she looked as good as a lot of men seemed to think she did. She'd escaped from her nightmares in Brooklyn and found a home in Harlem with people who really loved her, but deep inside she was still that beat-down, bony little girl. The little girl who had been so abused that she stayed high, stayed hungry, and stayed hopeless and helpless. Life was different for Eva now. From the moment she arrived in Harlem she had hoped and dreamed for a better future. But old memories were hard to erase, and like always, she found herself checking out her arms self-consciously. The scabbed-over needle marks and extension-cord bruises had long since healed and were fading away. Whereas she used to walk around looking strung out and starved, Eva now had the kind of body that was a show stopper for real. Gone were the nasty sores and the festering boils from track marks in her groin. And gone was the pain and fear that Rasheena and Jahden had inflicted on her when she was too young and too scared to protect herself.

"Oh, *that* guy?" Eva asked innocently as she switched her vicious hips past the bouncer and out the door. "Rappers ain't all they got going at *Shakez,* Alex. They have talent shows and dance contests too, remember? But yeah, I might check that guy out if ain't no other fine dudes up in there."

"Beeetch!!!" Alex's happy self was all in her ear. "I *know* you, Evita! You wanted that guy. You was all up in his incense! Tryna spin his fuckin' illegal CDs! Shit, I wanted his ass too. Dude was *hot!*"

"Well cool ya red tail off. We gotta swing by the building and pick up India first, okay? That's if Saint's gonna let her hang out tonight."

Alex's wide smile disappeared at the mention of Saint's name. He was a cold-blooded drug dealer who'd been wrecking shit all over Harlem for the past two years. He'd started out as a runner and a look-out, then worked his way up to handling trap as a corner boy. It wasn't long before he was running the local drug game. Alex's younger brother had gotten robbed and killed in a crack spot last summer, and word on the streets was that Saint and his crew had orchestrated that shit.

"I hate that Saint mothafucka," Alex said as they jumped into a taxi and gave the driver directions to their crib. "I don't know why India don't just drop his homo thug ass and find a real baller."

Eva nodded in agreement, but deep inside she knew exactly why India couldn't leave Saint. Eva had earned herself a street degree, and she knew some shit didn't change whether you rested in Brooklyn or Harlem or even in the Bronx. You didn't just bounce or walk away from a gangster like Saint just like that. You could end up shut the fuck down.

Their cab pulled up to a traffic light where a big crowd had gathered in an alley outside of an elite club called Bricks. There was a big record shop in front of the club that stayed crowded all the time, but Eva had heard it was really just a front for all kinds of illegal activity. All the real action was going on beyond that, where the hottest artists, ballers, and professional athletes in the nation hung out in a converted loft in the back.

Eva looked out the window with wide eyes. People were standing out there waiting to get in like it was a free liquor giveaway. It wasn't like Bricks was some chic or ultra modern uptown club or nothing. It was in a grimy area of Harlem where niggahs and bitches was hood as hell, but all kinds of people stood in line for hours tryna be seen up in there. And not just anybody could walk up to the door and get in, either.

A murderous-looking security crew kept things on lock outside, and if you didn't have a VIP pass from an insider, or your name wasn't on the guest list, it didn't matter if your ass was Tupac or Biggie Smalls. You wasn't getting past security and you wasn't getting in.

"*Dayumm!*" Alex squealed as they eyed the crowd. "It's about to be banging up in that spot tonight! I wonder who's performing? Forget about *Shakez* and India's ass too! Tell Mister Cabbie to pull over. Let's jump out this bitch right now! I can text India and tell her to meet us inside Bricks!"

Eva shook her head. "Come on, Alex. We ain't dissin' India like that. And besides, you said you wanted to sing at *Shakez* tonight. This could be your big chance to get in that contest and blow it up. Nah," she said as the cab pulled off, "we ain't going to no club without India anyway. The way that girl shakes her ass?"

The Harlem walk-up they lived in wasn't much different than the tenement Eva had lived in with Rasheena and Jahden in Brooklyn, but at least it felt like a real home. Eva's aunt Milena was her papi's older sister, and even though Milena had taken a bad stumble with drugs herself, she was one of those addicts who had gotten back on her feet and tried to be somewhat of a mother to her child. Eva's papi had been two years younger than Milena, and they used to be real close when he was alive. Eva's grandparents were Dominican and had come to New York as teenagers to find work and a better life.

Eva's papi's name was Marco, and him and her aunt Milena had the same silky black hair and coffee-colored skin of their parents. When Eva's mother, Rasheena, was younger she had had the kind of body and good looks that could devastate a club full of gay men. Papi had been wide open on Rasheena from the day they met at a mutual friend's card party in the

Bed-Stuy neighborhood of Brooklyn. Eva had inherited the best from both of her parents. Her skin was dark cocoa and real smooth, just like Rasheena's. Once she stopped getting high and started eating regular meals it was clear that she had gotten Rasheena's stacked body too, maybe even a better version, but Eva's hair came mostly from her father. It was jet black and silky when she blow-dried it, but let that stuff get wet. She'd be walking around with a thick mass of puffy curls that hung halfway down her back. It was something that Eva both liked and didn't like. Black folks acted like she thought she was cute because of it, and Dominicans all over Harlem called her nappy-headed and screamed on her to get a damn perm!

"Your mami is a queen," Eva's papi used to say all the time. There were stars in his eyes each time he looked at Rasheena. "My beautiful black queen."

Papi had moved to Brooklyn to get next to Rasheena, and not too much later they had Eva. But destiny just wasn't on their side. Life seemed to shit all over Eva's family no matter which way they turned. Her grandparents were burned to death in a suspicious house fire. The police thought it mighta been a crackhead trying to stay warm in the basement of their building. After that, her aunt Milena got messed up behind some worthless baller who had hand problems and liked to beat on her. The guy had a big problem with Fiyah, so Papi used to go get his nephew from Harlem and bring him to their crib in Brooklyn all the time. Eva and Fiyah were only a year apart in age, so they hung out together and became close.

But life took a fucked up turn for both kids when Eva's father died. Papi used to work construction for this Italian family in Brooklyn. He didn't get like, trained in school or nothing, but he was a fast learner so they put him on and paid him decent doe under the table. It was a hot day in August and Papi had been doing roof work out in the sun for ten hours straight. When it was time to get off work he went down to the portable showers his bosses kept on the site and started washing all that sweat and sticky tar off of him.

Eva was only eleven when it happened, but even at that age she could tell that the people Papi worked for were shiesty. One of Papi's co-workers had called Rasheena and told her that something real bad had happened. Papi had gone in one of the stalls to take a shower, and as soon as he turned the water on they heard a loud thud. Immediately his friend said they started smelling a real nasty burning odor.

It was Papi's hair.

They had to break the door down to get to him. Papi was burned all over his body, but not from hot water like you might have expected. Eva's papi had been electrocuted. Fried. Somebody on the site had messed up and didn't ground the water heater the right way, and the water that sprayed down on her papi was charged with high-voltage electricity.

The co-worker who called Rasheena from the hospital had been the first one to reach Papi. He had tried to drag Papi out of the stall and had gotten some real serious burns himself. Rasheena was crying on the phone as the man told her that Papi was still alive when he got to him. He hadn't died right away. Eva's papi had suffered some horrible-ass agony first, and even though his heart was still beating when the ambulance got there, the condition of his body was enough to know that he wasn't gonna make it.

Ghetto-lawyers were hanging all out the project windows telling Rasheena how she should sue those damn Italians for every dime they had. They had her counting all that phantom money in her head for days before she got the news that Papi's death wasn't gonna bring her and Eva nothing but grief.

For one thing, them Italians were slick. They had real lawyers on their side. Not the kind that had picked up some law lingo while doing time in jail, but the kind who had actually gone to law school and studied that shit. Those big-time attorneys-at-law sent Rasheena a letter saying there were no personnel records on file of a Marco Perez working for their firm. They said as far as they knew, Papi had been sneaking onto their property trying to steal copper wires, and it was tragic and unfortunate that he stumbled into an area where he didn't belong and got himself killed.

"But what about Papi's friend?" Eva had asked Rasheena. "He knows Papi worked there! He tried to save Papi and almost got killed too!"

By the time those bosses got through with him, Papi's friend was deaf and dumb. He couldn't remember ever working with a smooth Dominican cat named Marco, and besides, he said he couldn't have witnessed nothing because he wasn't even there. He had been on a whole nother construction site way across town when he accidentally burned himself while trying to ground a water heater.

That was it for Eva and Rasheena. They were left out there in the cold with no Papi and no money. It wasn't long after that when Rasheena let that slimy-ass Jahden move in with them, and that was the moment when stark fear crept into Eva's life and all her nightmares began.

Chapter 2

Eva ran into the building with Alex and held her breath as they dodged piss puddles and jetted up the steps. They sped past the second floor, pinching their noses as they got close to the stanky incinerator room. The chute had been sealed closed for years and the room was always full of bags of putrid, rotting garbage. Alex and Eva both lived on the second floor. Alex lived with her parents and her cross-dressing brother Georgie who shook his ass in the club, and Eva stayed with Aunt Milena and Fiyah. They ran up two more flights to the fourth floor where India rested. India had been living upstairs from them for the past three years. She was the type of sistah who looked just like her name. Tall, tan-brown with exotic features, and just beautiful from every angle. India had a vicious body on her too, and dudes chased after her like mad. She liked to dress nice and her long straight hair stayed buttered up. While Eva would be walking around with her natural bush in a halo of thick curls, India's hair looked like she relaxed that shit every other day, and even through some of her roughest times Eva had never seen her girl with one hair on her head looking raggedy.

But while Eva and Alex dreamed ghetto dreams of singing and modeling urban gear in sexy magazines, and dancing on stage with artists like Diddy and Jay-Z, India was finer than both of them. Plus, she had bigger dreams. India wanted to use her brain and go to college and become a surgeon one day. A pediatric surgeon who healed sick kids.

But dreams were just dreams in their hood, and reality was a real bitch. India shared a one-bedroom apartment with her little sister, Rosa, and her disabled father, and she had already fallen a year behind in high school because she was always busy trying to taking care of all three of them.

"Who is it?!?" India barked when Eva knocked on the door.

"It's me," Eva said, wondering what was up with all that hostility in her girl's tone.

"Me *who*?"

"Me, *me*! It's Eva, stupid."

There was a pause, then India asked suspiciously, "Who's out there with you? You by yourself?"

Eva turned and gave Alex a what-the-fuck look.

"It's me and Alex, Indy. Why you trippin'? Open the damn door!"

She opened the door, but only a crack. She left the chain on and peeked through the slit.

"What's up?" Eva asked, puzzled.

"Anybody behind you?"

Eva shrugged over her shoulder. "Just Alex."

Alex started wilding as she eyed India through the crack in the door.

"See there, Eva! This chick ain't even ready! I told you we shoulda dipped into Bricks and then texted her ass later!"

Eva ignored Alex, but when India opened the door and yanked them inside, she knew something was wrong. India's father was sitting right there in the living room with his head slumped over in his wheelchair. Eva could feel the tension in the air. What she had taken for a shitty attitude in India was really fear. Her girl was scared. Shook down to her low-rider shorts that were cut damn near down to her pussy.

India closed the door behind them and locked both locks. Then she put the chain back on the door and stuck a kitchen chair up under the knob.

For the first time ever, India looked a busted mess. Her hair was wild and her T-shirt was mad dirty and looked like she had dribbled red Kool-Aid all over it.

Alex gasped. "India! Your shit is fucked up!"

"What's wrong?" Eva cried. Her girl was *un-the-fuck-done*!

Tears rushed to India's eyes. "It's that niggah Saint. He's gunning for me, y'all! He gave me a package to take to Jersey this morning and I fucked up. I got the drop address wrong and lost three of his bricks. He sent me a text when I came back without the money that said, 'You stupid black bitch, kiss ya whole family good-bye 'cause you gone be bodied before the sun comes up.'"

"He gave you a *package*? I thought you said Saint didn't involve you in none of his drug business. What? You riding for him now?"

India nodded, looking miserable. "I've been riding for about a month," she admitted. "Kapp usually makes the Jersey runs 'cause he didn't have no record. But he got knocked for handing off to a narc. Saint needed somebody to take his place, so he sent me. It was only supposed to be for a minute."

Eva couldn't believe the bullshit she was hearing.

"Indy! You over here with your father and sister depending on your ass and you let yourself get caught up in some dumb shit like this?"

"I know," she whispered, and she was really crying now. "I don't know what the fuck he's got planned for me, but I know it ain't good. I heard him talking on the phone before I left early this morning. He's got another drop to make later on tonight so I think I'm cool for right now. But his boys have been riding past the building all night. Tone and Vasquez was calling me out the window earlier, telling me to come downstairs. Them fools was waving gats in the air! I closed the curtains and made Rosa get in the closet. I didn't know what else to do."

"Call the fuckin' cops!" Alex demanded. "I'm tired of these drug-slanging bastards! Yo, if Saint is gonna be somewhere making a transaction tonight, why don't you just drop a dime on that niggah and let the narcs take him down?"

India shook her head. "I take him down, and what about his posse? When I lost that dope I lost their money too. You think they just gonna roll over and let me slide with that?"

"You got Rosa in the closet?" Eva asked quietly. She thought about all the days she had spent locked in small spaces when she was younger. Rasheena would leave her alone in the closet so long that she'd be gasping from hunger. She learned to hide a roll of toilet paper underneath all the trash her mother kept in there. When she got real hungry she'd tear off one square at a time and chew it good enough to swallow it. She didn't even care that it made her stomach hurt and poke out like a starving kid from Africa. At least she was full off something and wouldn't starve.

"Yeah. She's still in there," India cried. "I didn't know what else to do!"

Eva marched into the apartment's only bedroom and yanked open the door. Poor little Rosa was sitting cross-legged on the floor. Her round eyes were big and scared.

"C'mon, baby," Eva said, reaching out to her and smoothing her braided hair. Rosa was already six and too big to be carried around, but Eva picked her up and balanced her on her hip anyway. Rosa clung to her. She was trembling, and as Eva held the child close she felt moisture seeping into her clothes.

Rosa was wet. The poor little girl had sat there in the closet and peed on herself. Tears came to Eva's eyes. She knew how it felt to be locked up and confined in a closet when you had to go. She used to fight against her bladder for hours. And when she lost, as she usually did, she'd have to piss right there on the floor and then scoot into a corner and try not to sit in it as she inhaled the rank aroma for hours until Rasheena felt like letting her out.

Eva turned to Alex, who loved kids just as much as she did. "Do me a quick favor," she said, passing Rosa to her. "Take Rosa downstairs and see if my aunt Milena is still up." Eva's aunt took care of Rosa while India went to school every day, and Eva knew she wouldn't mind getting up to take care of her now. "I think Rosa would probably dig a bubble bath too, Alex." She turned to Rosa. "You wanna take a bubble bath in my tub, baby girl?"

Rosa nodded with big eyes and a serious face. Eva was glad when Alex kissed the child's cheeks, then cuddled her in her arms and carried her out the apartment as India double-locked the door behind them.

Eva sat down on India's bed and pulled India down beside her. There was a look of terror and deep shame on her friend's face.

"I fucked up, Eva. I fucked up."

Eva tried to comfort her. "You made a big mistake, Indy, but it don't have to be a fatal one. You gotta get away from Saint, though. You gotta do whatever it takes to get away from that mothafucka."

"Eva, you don't really know. It ain't that easy to just bounce like that. Saint owns Harlem. Where I'm gonna go?"

"India, listen to me," Eva said forcefully. She put her arm around India's shoulder and pulled her close. "It don't matter where you go. Just *go*! Don't you have some friends out in Queens? Jet up outta here and go chill with them for a minute. Saint got too much product flowing in Harlem to worry about following you. Go lay low with your friends for a few. He'll forget about you the minute the next cute chick with long hair and a big ass walks by. For real."

India didn't look convinced. She just looked miserable.

"What about Rosa? And my father? I got responsibilities, Eva! I can't just run away and leave them here to make it by themselves."

"Don't worry about your family, India. Your life is on the line. Between me and Aunt Milena, Rosa will be well taken care of. She's downstairs with us all the time as it is anyway. Everybody in my house loves Rosa like she's our own family, so it won't be no problem. And we got your papi covered too. I'll bring him something to eat every day, and I'll get Fiyah to help him take a bath and change his clothes. We can handle this shit, India. What we can't handle is you sticking around here and then Saint taking you out. Nah, none of us can handle that."

"Saint put me in an impossible spot. He told me I had to make them fuckin' runs and I was scared not to! What the fuck was I supposed to do, Eva? It ain't nobody here for Rosa but me and my father, and he's stuck in that damn wheelchair. If Saint takes me out, my father sits there and dies. If he fucks with my sister or my father, then I'll die. You don't know what this shit is like! I'm on my *own*, Eva. You got Fiyah and your aunt to help you. And your moms is right downtown in Brooklyn if you need her. Saint would straight body me if I crossed him," she cried. "Who the fuck do I got?"

Eva stared hard at India but she didn't have any words for her. Eva had been in Harlem for four years but the memory of Brooklyn still haunted her every single day. Nobody knew what she had been through back in Brownsville except her one trusted friend, Reem Raw. Milena and Fiyah knew Rasheena and Jahden had beaten her, yeah. They knew about the drugs too, and it was Aunt Milena who took Eva to a drug treatment center so she could get clean. She was totally beat down back then, but a big part of her head was still real clear. Eva wanted off the drugs and she was willing to go cold turkey to do that shit, but the people at the clinic wouldn't let her. They said she was too sick and too malnourished. Her iron was real low and her blood count wasn't right. They said kicking cold turkey would probably kill her, so they put her on a quick detox course. Fourteen-year-old Eva was sedated and given the powerful drugs that would get her off of heroin, and by the time she woke up her body's neuroreceptors had been so programmed to reject skag that even if she shot up for the next year she wouldn't have felt the high.

India couldn't even imagine how much of her situation Eva understood. Eva knew how it felt to be alone with nobody to depend on but herself. To be cold on the streets and jonesing for a fix. To have her young body sexually battered by grown men, and to leave the most precious part of herself behind in the midst of all that trauma.

"You just don't know, Eva," India moaned.

But she was wrong.

"I do so know," Eva began in a shaky voice. "I know what it's like to feel trapped by a situation," she said, and then, because Eva really loved India and she wanted her girl to see that it was possible to overcome anything in life if you truly wanted to, she told India about her baby.

Chapter 3

It was hard going back to that last painful night that she'd spent in Brooklyn, but Eva did it. She told India everything, and she didn't leave none of it out. Not even the parts that she was ashamed of and that made her look bad.

"Me and Fiyah used to steal anything that wasn't nailed down," Eva admitted miserably. "We didn't have no kinda parental supervision and nobody gave a damn about feeding us neither. Even back then, as young as we was, Fiyah decided he was never gonna have a real job. He was into making music and looking good on the streets, so he was willing to steal in order to finance all that. He swore he was gonna be down with the ballers and the shot callers who flossed the platinum chains, mixtape CDs, and all the latest gear. But I never cared about that kinda stuff. I went along on all them grimy capers mostly so I could eat, but I got real good at my criminal activities, and by the time Fiyah left Brooklyn and Jahden turned me out, my ass was a pro.

"I used to dip on ballers, get up in the bed with them and wear them out, then sneak out the room with their doe in my pockets while they was sleeping. I was so strung out that it seemed natural for me to be hoeing and sucking dick at the age of thirteen just to get a fix. I would fuck all day and all night to get high. When my pussy got too sore I would give head to playas in the projects for five dollars a pop. I'd let 'em do me on the dirty stairs, up on the roof, in the back of abandoned cars, wherever . . . It didn't matter. I learned to do anything I had to do in order to get high, Indy. I was only thirteen years old and already I was a ho and a fiend. I hadn't even gotten my first period yet, but I was out there fuckin' like a grown woman."

India looked crushed when Eva was done. She was full of sympathy for her friend.

"Eva . . . I'm so sorry you had to go through all that. Nobody would ever be able to look at you and tell you'd done all that. I can't even imagine you sticking yourself with a needle."

Eva shrugged. "I had to. Jahden started me off mainlining. Smoking heroin off a piece of foil with a stem didn't really get me high. I needed that direct hit just to feel right."

"Why the fuck would he wanna get a little girl high off smack?"

"So he could fuck me any way he wanted to. He was a freak, Indy. A funky-nuts fuckin' freak. He dealt the brown, so he had plenty of it to spare. The first time he shot me up I thought I was gonna die. He caught me in the middle of the night and Rasheena helped him hold me down. He hit me in the neck and I flipped out. I was terrified. The high was horrible to me. I felt like bugs and shit was crawling all on me and my whole body got dragged down in slow motion. I was in school then, so at first he only did it to me on the weekends if he wanted to fuck me without a fight. After a while he didn't care about me having to go to school. He stopped shooting me in my neck and started injecting me in my groin, and that way nobody could see that I had track marks. By the time Rasheena started getting jealous they didn't have to hold me down no more. I was strung out with a monkey on my back so I just gave the pussy up. Before long my moms didn't want him fuckin' me for drugs no more so she made me get out on the streets and earn my own money. I would turn tricks half the damn night and bring my money home to Rasheena. Then she'd let Jahden sell me the dope he had gotten me strung out on in the first damn place."

India shuddered. "Girl please tell me that muthafucka is in jail right now!"

"Nope. His ass is still right there in Brooklyn. With Rasheena."

"But what about the baby, Eva? You somebody's moms, girl. You got a son!"

Eva smiled slightly. "Yeah, I do. I have a son."

Then India's face changed. "You ain't just leave him in that laundrymat alone, did you, Eva? Where's your baby at now?"

"I did leave him, but he's doing fine. He's still in Brooklyn. I send him money and go down there and try to see him whenever I can. I was so weak and scared after delivering him that it was hard for me to think straight. I knew the old man who ran the laundry would be there when the sun came up, so I stayed with my baby boy as long as I could. As soon as it got light outside I put him in one of them cloth laundry carts. You know the ones you use to carry your clothes from the washer over to the dryer?"

India nodded.

"Well I put him in one of those and pushed it right inside the doorway. I took an empty bleach bottle out the garbage and used it to prop the door open, then I walked back up the ramp and sat on a bench to wait for Drunk Mister James."

"What did he do when he came to work and found the baby there?"

Eva shook her head. "He didn't find him. I don't even know if his drunk ass ever showed up. God musta been watching over me and my baby because a lady named Mrs. Threet got there first. I was in the second grade with one of her foster daughters named Jocelyn, and that little girl used to sit with me at lunch and share all her food. One winter we was in the middle of a bad snowstorm and all I wore to school was a little red pleather jacket with no buttons. Miss Threet was dropping her kids off, and when she saw me she asked where my hat was. I told her I didn't have one and she looked at me like I was crazy. That afternoon she was waiting for me when school let out. She had brought me a long down coat, some gloves, and two hats. She was just nice like that.

"Anyway, I saw Miss Threet pulling two shopping carts full of clothes toward the laundry and Drunk Mister James hadn't showed up yet. Miss Threet took in a lot of foster kids back then, so she would always have two and three shopping carts' worth of dirty clothes to wash. I can remember when I used to do laundry for me and Rasheena and I was too small to reach the quarter slot on the dryers. There would be all kinds of grown folks sitting right there watching me struggle on my tippy toes, but Miss Threet would always come over with a kind word and help me put my money in. She'd touch my face and tell me, 'Smile, baby. Life only hurts until it starts feelin' good,' and that's why as soon as I saw her I knew my baby was gonna be all right. Like I said, I believe God sent that lady down to the laundry early that Saturday morning. I stayed long enough to watch her go inside, and when she came right back out again holding my baby in that raggedy towel, I took off running and never looked back. I didn't have to. My baby was with Miss Threet, and that meant he was gone be straight. I felt like God was telling me that this was the right thing for me to do. I got outta Brooklyn right after that. I called my aunt Milena and she told me to sneak under the turnstile and take the train to Harlem, and I been here ever since."

India had tears running down her face. She put her arm around Eva and kissed her on the cheek. "You been through a lot, Eva," she sniffled. "I didn't even know you had all that hurt inside you. You can't even see it from the outside."

Eva shrugged. "Everybody has pain, I guess. Like Miss Threet said, life can only hurt until it starts feeling good. Well, I'm feeling good now and I feel pretty lucky too. I got away from my mother and I know where my son is. He turned four this year, and every now and then I take the train down to Brooklyn. Sometimes I'm lucky and I can spot him playing with the rest of Miss Threet's foster kids right outside of building 420. You should see him, Indy. He is *so* cute. He has the same kind of birthmark under his chin that I have under mine, and he looks just like me."

India shuddered. "I feel bad for you and your son, Eva. Somebody shoulda kicked your mother's fuckin' ass. Letting her niggah do all that crazy shit to you. Foul bitch!"

India was right, but a part of Eva still had a hard time separating herself completely from Rasheena. "She had a lot of pain in her life too," Eva defended her mother. "I think it fucked her up real bad when my father got killed. It seems like she just lost hope after that."

By the time they were finished talking about life, the streets, drugs, and misery, both of them were exhausted and they still had their drug-lord problem.

"That's why I hated it when you started fuckin' with Saint, India. I would come up here and take Rosa downstairs a lot because I can't stand drugs, or drug dealers. Anybody who's ever around them, even a little bit, is bound to get fucked up. And that's another reason you gotta leave too. India, you gotta get outta here before you get fucked up too."

"You really think I can get outta Harlem without Saint and his boys getting hold of me?"

Eva nodded. "Yeah. I do. Saint is gone be out handling business tonight, right?"

"Uh-huh. He's supposed to be meeting his man at a joint near Taft at two a.m. That's what I heard him telling his boy Hassan this morning."

"Good. He's probably on his way over there now. All we gotta do is call a cab and get you outta Harlem before he gets back. I try to save all the money I can get my hands on, you know, so I can send it to Mrs. Threet for my son, but this is an emergency, India. I don't have a whole lot to offer, but whatever I have you can get it. Every dime I've got in the world is yours."

India got a look on her face that was full of hope and gratitude. She was young and beautiful, and she really wanted to believe that she could get away from Saint without being killed. Eva helped her pack a few clothes in a white Donna Karan tote bag. She took a few pictures of her dead mother and Rosa off her mirror and stuck them down in her pocketbook, and Eva frowned when she saw what else her girl was packin' in there.

"You holding heat now too?" Eva said incredulously. She musta really been sleeping on India's game because suddenly her girl was into shit that Eva didn't know nothing about.

She shrugged. "I was out there riding dirty. I'd be scared outta my mind on those upstate runs. You never can tell what you might run into on the road."

"Um," Eva said sarcastically. "How about you might run into the goddamn state police? Don't you know it's a mandatory one-year sentence for a gun charge in New York? Where'd you get that shit from anyway? I know Saint didn't give you no tool that you might turn around and use to cap his ass with."

India shook her head. "Nah. I bought it off a dude I know over on Saint Nick. I heard he was the best person to buy from in Harlem because all his tools are clean."

India slung her pocketbook and her tote over her shoulder and they prepared to sky up. Then she walked into the living room and leaned over the wheelchair and kissed her father's cheek.

"Bye, Daddy," she said softly. "Eva's gonna take care of you and Rosa. I promise, I'll be back soon."

Mr. Jackson came out of his fog long enough to whisper something and pat his daughter lovingly on the hand, and when India turned back toward Eva there were tears on her cheeks.

"Let's go," she muttered, and Eva knew how hard her friend was fighting to be strong. India didn't wanna leave her family, but she didn't wanna *leave* her family either, ya know?

Eva was walking just ahead of India and their heels were click-clacking down the stairs when they got bum-rushed. That big niggah Saint was a huge blur as he ran up the steps toward them, knocking Eva down and catching India about halfway down the flight.

"You lost my shit?" he menaced, but before India could answer him that maniac started swinging.

India screamed. She held her hands out and went into a squat. Saint swung her by the hair and slammed her face into his knee. India's nose busted. Blood squirted out in an arc. Her bag and purse rolled down the stairs and she went tumbling after them.

Eva's body went into survival mode. After years of abuse back in Brooklyn it was second nature for her to try to save her own ass. Cursing and screaming, Saint followed India down the stairs, and Eva followed Saint. He stopped at the bottom to continue fucking her up, and Eva ran past both of them as fast as she could. By the time she realized that she had abandoned her girl, Eva was already on the second floor.

Breathing hard, she forced herself to turn around. India was screaming and crying at the top of her lungs and Eva wanted to go back and help her girl, but . . . she had gone halfway up to the third floor, and she was begging her feet to go up the rest of the way when a loud *cap!* rang out.

Instantly, India went silent.

Survival was a motherfucker!

Eva turned back around and started running back down the stairs again.

Saint cursed and she knew he was coming after her.

There was no time to dig in her purse for her apartment key, and if she managed to make it out the building he'd shoot her down like a dog in the streets. Without hesitating, Eva dove into the incinerator room and wormed her way under a whole slew of plastic bags overflowing with rotting garbage.

She could hear Saint's footsteps. He was looking for her, and he was gonna give her some of the same damn thing he had just given India. Eva was breathing hard and her heart felt like it weighed a hundred pounds. She was suffocating under heavy bags of stank, putrid garbage, and the foul smell was making her choke and gag.

Eva squeezed her eyes closed and made herself go limp. It was a trick she used to use when she lived with Rasheena. It was almost like going into a nod without being high. It was Eva's self-protection. It calmed her down and helped her escape the insanity of everything outside of her control.

Saint stormed up and down the hall. He was looking for her. Eva heard his footsteps fading, like he was going back up the stairs, and then they got louder again. Closer. Like he was coming back down. She lay there quietly in her self-protected world as his footsteps got even closer. And then they stopped.

He was standing outside the incinerator room.

Eva heard him breathing hard as he stepped inside. He grunted and kicked at a few bags. He picked one up from the top of the pile and Eva felt a rat run across her thigh. She was terrified. Frozen. But she was protected in her own mind. He couldn't get to her. She was limp, so he couldn't even see her.

He stood there for hours it seemed like.

Eva heard an apartment door open somewhere upstairs and a woman laughed in a high-pitched voice. Saint moved then. His footsteps were fast and heavy. They retreated toward the stairs and got fainter and fainter, until she couldn't hear them anymore.

The high-pitched laughter turned into a scream, and Eva fought her way up from the mounds of garbage and staggered out of the dirty room. She ran up the steps as fast as she could, and what she saw hit her in the stomach and boggled her mind.

India lay crumpled on her side. Eva knew it was her, but it didn't look like her. She was unrecognizable. Her face had been kicked all the way in. Her eyes were open and a pool of blood was fanning out under her head.

"Indy . . ." Eva moaned. She sank down to her knees beside her girl. Eva was scared to touch her because she didn't want to hurt her, but in her heart she knew India was already way beyond pain.

A sob came from the top of the stairs and Eva looked up.

"Call an ambulance!" she shouted at the old Mexican prostitute who lived next door to India. The old lady covered her mouth and fled toward her apartment. Eva turned back to India, soft cries escaping her lips. The smell of blood sickened her. It gave her flashbacks.

"You poor baby," Eva whispered and cried. "You poor, poor baby . . ."

She bent over to kiss her friend good-bye, but there was no part of India's beautiful face that wasn't covered in blood. Eva took her arm and settled for a spot just above her elbow instead, then rose to her feet, grabbing India's pocketbook as she stood.

"I'ma handle that mothafucka!" Eva vowed, slinging India's purse over her shoulder. She took one last look at the lifeless body of her best friend, then ran back down the stairs as fast as she could. Pausing outside her apartment door, Eva heard the faint sound of police sirens in the distance. She took out her key, said a quick prayer for Indy, then went inside and called the 28th Precinct, and dropped a big fat dime on that black-hearted sinner they called Saint.

Chapter 4

India's murder marked one of many turning points in Eva's life.

She had always held on to her dream of having a legitimate career and doing something positive with her life because she wanted to reclaim her son someday. But now, after India's death, everything was different. It seemed like time wasn't on her side anymore. Eva truly understood the old saying "Life is short." Suddenly she was in a rush to do everything and to do it all immediately.

The first thing Eva needed to do was get a job. Money was real tight in their house and picking up a temp job here and there wasn't getting it. Aunt Milena had agreed to take Rosa in with them, but in reality the little girl was just one more mouth to feed. The only thing Fiyah cared about was scribbling in his songbook and rapping into the mirror like somebody important was about to discover his ass, and it pissed Eva's aunt the hell off that he wasn't out there earning money on a job instead of wasting time talking shit into a microphone.

Eva loved her auntie and she knew Milena loved her too, but she was a real bitter woman who carried too much of a load. She'd gotten off drugs and had taken care of both Eva and Fiyah, but Milena had expectations of her son that he just wasn't ready or willing to meet.

"Get a fuckin' job!" she would scream whenever he grabbed a mic and started blasting his beats. Fiyah would be all up in the living room acting like he was on a stage. All the little Catholic saint statues that Aunt Milena collected would be his audience. They'd sit there staring back at him like his flow was the shit for real.

Eva found a job in midtown working as a receptionist for a printing company. They processed blueprints for architects, and since she was straight outta high school with no skills or nothing, the pay was shitty but it beat having nothing at all.

Sometimes Eva felt like a burden in her house. Don't get it wrong. Aunt Milena never did or said anything to make her think that, and Eva and her had a good relationship, but always in the back of Eva's mind she felt the need to pull her own weight. She wasn't Aunt Milena's child—she was her niece. Milena didn't owe Eva shit. She'd taken her in and helped her get clean because Eva was her brother's only child and Milena loved her. But still . . . Eva had a mother out there who shoulda been doing all the stuff that Aunt Milena was doing for her. She felt guilty when Fiyah got screamed on for not working and bringing money into the house, when it was *his* house. Eva and Rosa were taking food out of *his* mouth. And even though Fiyah never once complained or nothing, Eva made sure that each week when she got paid she gave Aunt Milena the majority of her check. She tore off some to send to Mrs. Threet for her son, she held back a little bit for a MetroCard, and she broke Fiyah off a few ends, but the bulk went straight to her auntie.

Eva was at work sorting through the mail one day when her cell phone vibrated in her pocket. It was her old friend Sherri from Brownsville, the one Eva had introduced to heroin when she was twelve. They had reconnected a couple of years back through their boy Reem Raw, not too long after Eva had moved up to Harlem and gotten clean.

Reem and Sherri used to go together back when they were kids, and when Eva ran into him in Harlem he'd given her Sherri's telephone number. That same day Eva had reached out to Sherri to apologize for dragging her into her drug-induced nightmare, and Sherri had forgiven her. Sherri's grandmother still cursed when she heard Eva's name, but Sherri was still her girl.

"Yo. Your moms is in the hospital."

Eva's heart stopped. As bad as Rasheena had done her, there was still a place inside Eva that had love for her mother.

"Jahden tried to kill her. He burnt her ass up. That niggah made her strip naked, then he poured boiling water all over her."

"No . . ." Eva moaned. A hot wave of pain rolled through her body.

"That ain't all he did neither," Sherri said. "That twisted motherfucker dragged her outta the house and made her walk up and down Mother Gaston Boulevard. Butt-naked and burnt up."

Tears fell from Eva's eyes and she couldn't even speak.

"Now, I know you might not give a fuck about your moms, Eva. And you got a lot of good reasons to tell her to kiss your ass. But you her only family and I thought you should know."

Eva ran out the office and jumped on a train heading uptown. By the time she got up to Harlem she had killed Jahden a thousand times in her head, and in a thousand different ways.

Fiyah was feeling good as Eva walked up to their stoop. He'd just dished off some electronic items he'd stolen from a store on 125th Street, and had used the money he'd made to buy some jewelry. He jumped up the moment he saw the look on Eva's face and the tears in her eyes.

"What happened?" he demanded, looking down the block suspiciously, like Eva's troubles were right behind her. "What the fuck happened?"

Eva fell against his chest crying. He could see she wasn't bleeding or nothing, so he just held her and let her get it out.

"R-r-rasheena—" she finally managed. She started crying again and Fiyah's eyes narrowed in concern.

"What's wrong with her? She cool?"

Eva shook her head and Fiyah looked scared. "Tell me what happened," he said, and Eva repeated to him what Sherri had said to her.

"Can you ride with me down to Brooklyn?" Eva asked him. "I just wanna go see her and make sure she's all right."

Fiyah couldn't tell her no. They'd always been down for each other, even when they were doing dirt, and he knew if the situation was reversed Eva wouldn't be able to tell him no either. They were cousins, but they were also friends. Where one rolled, the other rolled too.

They didn't tell Milena where they were going. She wasn't feeling Rasheena at all, so she probably woulda said the bitch had finally gotten what she deserved. Eva ran into the apartment and changed out of her work clothes and into a pair of jeans and a T-shirt. She dug into the back of her closet and came out with the burner that India had been carrying the night she was murked. Eva wasn't sure if they were gonna run into that bastard Jahden, but if they did she wanted to be ready to pump a cap in his ass if he came at her.

Eva went into Fiyah's room. He had put on a hoody and was tying a bandana around his head. "I got a gat," she said, showing him the .22 that she had slipped into her purse. "Just in case Jahden rolls up on us."

"Girl, what the fuck you doing with that little-ass gun?" Fiyah asked. "Is that shit loaded?"

She nodded, passing it to him.

He checked the chamber, then looked at her and shook his head. "You the last one who needs to be packin', Eva. We get caught up in some shit out there and your crazy ass will prolly mess around and shoot me." Fiyah grinned and pushed the gun down in the back of his waistband. "Let's bounce."

They rode the train for an hour, then got off and took a city bus up to Linden Blvd where the hospital was. But when they got there Eva was told that Rasheena Patterson had signed herself out. Against her doctor's orders.

"Where you think she went?" Fiyah asked.

Eva shook her head. "I don't know. Probably back to the house. With no family or no money, where else could she go?"

They hopped on a bus heading toward Powell Street, and even before they got to Eva's old building she could see lights on in Rasheena's apartment. Eva started sweating and feeling sick just looking at the place. Sherri had told her that Jahden was selling big-time drugs now, and going in that apartment would be the closest she'd been to duji since the night she'd fled. A barrage of terrible memories made her stomach turn mushy and fear dried up all the moisture in her mouth. Music was blaring throughout the hallways and Eva and Fiyah gave each other a long look before climbing up the stairs.

Fiyah banged on the door three times. There was a round hole right above the keyhole where Jahden could pass his product out without opening the door.

Fiyah banged again, and Jahden said, "Whassup!"

"It's Eva," she squeaked.

Just the sound of his voice had her shook. But when he opened the door and Eva looked into the eyes that she'd seen floating above her face as he humped her young pussy a hundred times, her fear was gone and rage was in her instead.

"Yo, where my aunt?" Fiyah said, pushing his way inside. Jahden was caught off guard by the sight of them. There were about seven motherfuckers up in there. Drinking, smoking crack and heroin, and hanging out. Eva scooted inside behind Fiyah, and looked around for her mother.

Rasheena was stretched out on the raggedy sofa. That thing was so pissy and bug infested that Eva had stopped sitting on it when she was about ten.

"You okay, Auntie?" Fiyah said, crossing the room toward her.

Eva was stuck in one spot.

Rasheena was covered in bandages. Her body looked swollen. Bloated like a dead fish. There was a nasty smell coming off her that made Eva want to throw up, and she took a step backward without thinking.

Rasheena tried to say something, but she could barely talk louder than a whisper.

"You need to be in the hospital, Ma," Eva said. She looked at Jahden and her anger just came jumping out of her. "You grimy, stank-ass old bastard! They oughta lock your perverted ass up. Look what the fuck you did to her. And you was stupid enough to let her sign herself out of the hospital?"

Eva was feeling large because she knew Fiyah had a tool, but she wasn't prepared for what happened next. Instead of Jahden jumping bad and trying to shut Eva down, Rasheena drew forth all her strength and told her daughter what the fuck she could go do to herself.

"Mind your fuckin' business," Rasheena muttered. Her voice sounded like the graveled path of hell. Eva could tell her mother was in a lot of pain, but she was still the same old evil, crazy bitch that she had always been. "Get the fuck up outta my house telling me what to do," she rasped. "Who told you to bring your fast ass back up in here anyway? Jah show this trick where the door—"

There was a loud, horrible noise and Eva thought her heart had been kicked in.

But instead, it was the front door.

Everybody seemed to move at once except Eva and Rasheena. Eva stood frozen in place and Rasheena lay frozen on the pissy couch.

"Police!" Eva heard a male voice say. Narcotics officers dressed in dark blue swarmed through the apartment like roaches under a bright light. "Get your asses down on the ground good people, and don't nobody fuckin' move!"

Eva was miserable as hell.

The cops called an ambulance for Rasheena, then tossed the rest of them into a white van and transported them over to the 73rd Precinct. The precinct was only a few blocks away, but the ride seemed like it took a whole year. Fiyah stared at Eva the whole time. They'd found the gun on him that she had taken off India. Eva didn't know what was gonna happen, but it was all her fault that her cousin was in this predicament, and she felt like a stupid-ass little kid for putting him there.

This wasn't the first time Eva and Fiyah had been in this precinct though. They'd gotten knocked a few times when they were minors and out there stealing shit like the world was theirs. But the whole time the cops were taking their fingerprints and processing them in, Eva was racking her brain trying to figure out what she should do on this bust. Did she 'fess up and tell the cops that it was her piece? Or was Fiyah gonna do the unthinkable and snitch on her and tell them himself?

Eva didn't know what to think, but when they led them past each other to take their mug shots, her cousin whispered, "Keep your fuckin' mouth closed."

So that's what Eva did.

She was surprised like hell when they unlocked her cell six hours later and told her she was free to go. She'd never gotten out of jail this quick before.

"Why am I getting out?" Eva asked the question like they was trying to trick her or something.

The female officer shrugged. "We know who was dealing drugs in that house. That's who we came there for, and that's who we got. Besides, your name was on the lease, so we won't charge you with intention to buy."

Eva got excited. "Well, what about my cousin? Fuego Perez? He used to live there too. Me and him came in together and I can vouch for him. He wasn't copping shit because he don't do no drugs."

The officer shrugged again like she could give less than a damn.

"Perez ain't going nowhere except to Central Booking and

then on to Rikers. He had an illegal firearm on him. We'll be sending it to ballistics to see if it's dirty, but even if it comes back clean, possession carries a mandatory one-year sentence under New York law."

Eva was devastated. Fiyah was going to jail. All because he loved her and Rasheena and wanted to look out for his family. Milena was about to be straight pissed off. Fiyah wasn't gonna be getting no job and bringing home no money for real now. Her son was about to spend a year on Rikers Island, and the only person they had to blame was Eva.

Chapter 5

Rikers Island

Fiyah Perez lay on his jail bunk listening to the drumbeat that was playing out in his mind. He nodded his head as the tempo picked up and moved his lips as he spit his fire lyrics to an imaginary crowd. Jail was a muhfuckah. The judge had slapped him with a year, but his public defender said he would prolly be out in like eight months. His heart grew cold as he contemplated surviving his term of incarceration. Eight months was like forever on The Rock they called Rikers Island. This wasn't his first time dealing with the penal system, but it was the longest he had spent on lock. It was also the first time he was in for something he wasn't really responsible for.

Every other time he'd been knocked he had been just as guilty as charged.

But Fiyah wasn't sitting around having no pity party behind that shit. Evita was family. She was blood. And besides, she was a girl. What kinda sherm muhfuckah would snitch on a female? Nah, that wasn't him. This eight month bid was gone get done and get the fuck over with, and then he'd be back on the streets of Harlem scrambling for money and pushing his music even harder than before.

During his first month on The Rock Fiyah tried to do all the things he'd heard about on the streets: mind your own fuckin' business, keep ya fuckin' mouth closed, and watch ya fuckin' back.

But jail was just like the streets. There was always gonna be some come-up niggah who had to try you. Some kid who needed to make a name for himself. Or even some weak dude who had been flipped like a bitch and was being used as a pawn. Fiyah would see cats like that all the time. Bitch niggahs on their knees bobbing and slobbing down on some other man's joint. Slurping on that dick muscle like it was natural and shit. He didn't understand it. Some punk in the cell across from him had actually dropped his towel in the shower one morning, then bent over and opened his ass up wide for a big Italian cat. The big dude had gone in hard, right there in front of everybody, talking sweet shit to the gay dude like he was up in a soft wet pussy instead of some niggah's stank hairy asshole.

Fiyah vowed that kinda shit would never happen to him. He would die before he let some jailhouse plumber lay his pipe up in him. Fighting for ya manhood was an everyday thing in prison, and Fiyah had no problem with that. He was just as street as they came, and when some shady shit came his way, he handled himself like the G he was. He'd swung hard on the first fool who looked at him funny and didn't stop swinging until four or five cats pulled him off. He had six fights in his first three weeks on The Rock. If he wasn't earnin' a rep he was damn sure perfecting his technique.

"Yo, man," some Puerto Rican cat from Brooklyn told him after he'd come out of the hole for the third time. "You need to get with the Latinos, ese. These fuckin' goons in here they stick together yo, ya know?"

Fiyah had shook him off. "Nah, I'm straight, homes. I don't fuck with nobody but me."

"Okay." The cat shrugged. "But you see that big guy King Brody right there?" He pointed to a huge brown-skinned inmate who was about six-four and looked like he'd been lifting weights for decades. Fiyah had seen the cat on the streets of Harlem plenty of times before. He was a predator, and almost everybody knew about his rep. "Watch and see don't he brody your shit. He's a taker, man. Whatever he wants he strong-arms and he gets it. He got the COs on his dick. He brodied my cellie for his sneakers last week. Got 'em on his feet right now. He brodied another guy I know for his watch this morning. You better get some protection, man. You can't survive in here without it."

Fiyah had eyed the big guy they called Brody. He looked fresh and relaxed at all times. The COs didn't fuck with him and he had inmates hopping left and right at his command. Fuck the bars, Brody moved like a man who had power. And Fiyah knew how fast power could corrupt a muhfuckah. He didn't know when Brody was gonna decide that he wanted something that Fiyah had, but he knew it was just a matter of time before he did.

Determined to do his little bid and get back to his low-level crimes to support his lifestyle and his music, Fiyah wrote songs night and day. Eva had brought his songbook to him on her first visit and having it in his hands was almost like having his freedom.

Since he was a nonviolent offender he was able to sign up on a work detail. His job was to sweep and mop the tiers along with nine other inmates, and that was cool with Fiyah because it kept him moving.

The whole time he was pushing his broom he was also working on his grind. He chanted dope lyrics and spit the kind of shit that illustrated what was really real on the streets. A couple of cats would check out his flow game as he swept or mopped past their cells, and pretty soon inmates were lining up to check out his rhymes every time he walked by.

Fiyah loved the attention. He appreciated it when people dug the words that he strung together so artfully that they felt big enough to move mountains. There was always a slick reggaeton beat playing in his head. And although most times he laid his rap down in English, some of his songs were a fusion of English and Spanish verses that fucked everybody's head up, including Fiyah's.

It was in this manner that he spent his time and counted down the days until he would get off The Rock. Eva visited him every Saturday, and she brought him more notebooks when his old ones were full. With the money she earned from her little job she also kept his commissary tight, and Fiyah knew it was partly out of love and partly out of guilt.

"This shit is all my fault," she said over and over again. Each time she went off in that direction Fiyah would wave her off. The truth was, coming to jail had given him a lot of time to get serious about his music grind. It had taken his perspective from being just a simple street rapper to wanting to get a contract and cut his own CD, and it had given him the space he needed to tap into that creative pit in his belly and bring forth his best quality rhymes.

"It's cool, Evita" was the most he would say. He didn't wanna get into that mode with her, even though she was right. This was Eva's problem that she had made his, but some shit was just better left undiscussed, and that's how he felt about this bid. "Just take good care of Mami and Rosita, yo. I'ma be straight on this end."

And everything woulda continued to be straight too, except that some crazy dudes from his tier had cornered Fiyah going into the showers one morning and decided it was his turn to go bottom up.

"Hold him!" one of them had shouted as Fiyah fought back four to one. Despite the numbers he was holding his own. He cracked heads and busted lips. He bit and he scratched and he elbowed muhfuckahs in the eye. He was willing to do anything to anybody because he wasn't about to get his manhood took.

One of them caught him hard from behind though, and he faded left. Just for a second. But that was all it took. Them cats flipped him. He was laying facedown on the wet cement before he realized he'd left his feet.

"Yeah," somebody laughed over his shoulder. Fiyah craned his neck back and saw a buff dude holding a big erection. "Papi 'bout to get some of that man pussy!"

The little Puerto Rican cat from Brooklyn was down with them. He looked at Fiyah and shrugged. "I told you to get some fuckin' protection, homey."

Fiyah was fighting again. This time from the floor. But he was outweighed and outmanned, and to his horror they spread his legs wide and he felt a hard dick poking dead in his asshole. Fiyah screamed and bucked, trying to get free, and just when he realized it was useless and that he was about to get his cherry busted, a voice boomed out and the battle for his asshole came to a halt.

"Yo, break that dumb shit up."

Fiyah had been straining backward, his spine almost in a C. His legs were suddenly released and he slumped down to the floor.

"Fuckin' pervs . . ."

Fiyah turned his head. When he saw who it was that had rescued him his heart sank even further.

It was King Brody. That big niggah who strong-armed the weak and put fear in the hearts of the brave.

"Fall back, muhfuckahs!" Brody yelled, waving his massive, muscle-roped arm. "And get the fuck outta here!" Cats started scurrying out the shower like mad.

Him and Brody were alone. Fiyah rolled over and stood up. He was filled with fear and ready to fight again. Harder this time. If Brody wanted to fuck him it was gonna have to be on his feet.

"Here ya go." Brody tossed him a towel and walked away. Fiyah was stunned. He had a hard time believing he wasn't on the floor at that very minute. Getting deep-dicked straight up in his chocolate tube.

"Oh yeah," Brody said over his shoulder. He paused in the doorway and nodded. "I been digging your flow. You spit extra nice. I got a little music thing going on the outside. Shows, studio time. Contracts. All that shit. Might be able to put you on. I'll holla."

Fiyah stood there dumbfounded as the big mofo bounced out the door. He'd heard about the homo gangstas in jail, but he was a fighter. This shit wasn't supposed to happen to him. He felt lucky, but he was still scared. They didn't call that big niggah Brody for no reason. Cats like him didn't give up nothing for free. Especially their protection. Nah, they always wanted something. And it was always something big.

Fiyah reached back and touched his tight asshole with relief. He hadn't gotten deep-fucked today, but who knew? Tomorrow might bring something different.

Shit changed quick on the tiers.

Inmates looked at him different. Cats who used to grill him now cut a path around him or gave him a nod of respect.

"Yo, ese," the little Puerto Rican dude from Brooklyn told him. "We got no hard feelings, right? This is jail, meng. We was just having a little fun."

Fiyah dug what was up. Word had gotten around that he'd been tried. And word had also gotten around that he was off-limits too. Fiyah felt fucked in all directions. Without the protection of Brody and his crew, his asshole was open for anybody's interpretation. But living under Brody meant paying a mean piper, and Fiyah didn't know what the fuck it was he had that Brody mighta wanted.

The next Saturday afternoon he found out.

"Yo, man," Brody said, approaching him with a smile. Fiyah was cautious as they dapped and nodded their greetings. Visitation had just ended and they were heading toward the security area to be checked for contraband.

"So that's your chick, huh? That girl on your visit?"

Fiyah shook his head. "Nah, she's my cousin."

Brody whistled and grinned. "Yo, she's black and you're Puerto Rican? Is that like a *cousin*-cousin, where y'all got the same grandmother and shit, or one of them cousins you pick up as family 'cause when y'all was little they used to eat at your house?"

"Eva's my cousin. My real cousin. She's half black and I'm Dominican."

Brody shook his head with a look of pure delight. "That bitch is bad! She was killin' them shorts. I see her up here all the time. A ho like that ain't got no man?"

Fiyah bristled. He didn't like the look in Brody's eyes and he wasn't feeling the ninety questions about Eva neither.

"I don't ask her what she do, man. I just take care of her when I can."

Brody stopped walking.

"Like I take care of you, right?"

Brody's stare was colder than a blizzard. Fiyah felt his eyes held in a grip. He saw craziness lurking behind Brody's gaze and knew his life might depend on the way he answered.

"Yeah," Fiyah said carefully. "Like you take care of me."

Brody's eyes shot cold daggers for a second more, then he bust out laughing.

"Man, you all right, little shit. You cool with me." He threw his arm over Fiyah's shoulder as they headed back to the tier. "You know what, Fuego? You all right, my nig. I like you. Yeah. I like you. There ain't many idiots in here who got real talent, but you do."

Brody's arm was tight around his shoulder and every muscle in Fiyah's body was coiled and protesting. "I tell you what. You got, what? A few more months of easy time left in here? Well not only am I gonna make sure that time stays easy for you. I'ma give you the hook-up when you hit the bricks.

"I got a big operation going on out there on the streets. I'll put you on the trap when you get out. You don't even have to pull look-out first. You'll get straight on the trap action. How you like that?"

"I ain't a corner boy, Brody. I'm a rapper."

Brody stopped walking. The bulging weight of his arm on Fiyah's shoulder made Fiyah stop too.

"You know," he said, staring hard into Fiyah's face. "Usually when I offer somebody something they have like, a different reaction. I mean, I'm a pretty generous cat so I'm always giving. But usually when I'm giving a niggah something he accepts it and says some stupid shit like, 'Thanks man, that's whassup.' You know? Usually."

Brody started walking again, leaning on Fiyah and forcing him along.

"I tell you what!" he said moments later, his smiling face once again bright. "Since you got so much talent and shit, I'll make an exception this time. Don't tell nobody, though," he said, leaning close to Fiyah's ear. "I wouldn't want nobody to think Big Brody was getting soft or nothing, ya feel me? Besides, I got music connections too. You know about that club called Bricks, right?"

Fiyah nodded. Every fuckin' body knew about Bricks. But not every fuckin' body could get up in there. He'd heard mad stories about that place. Money wasn't nothing when it came down to that club. It didn't matter if you was a multiplatinum niggah. If you couldn't get inside of Bricks, then you really wasn't shit. Careers were born on that stage. Unsigned artists stood in line for hours tryna get picked to walk through those doors. Getting a chance to spit in that joint was just like paying for airtime on MTV or 106th and Park. That shit was priceless.

"I handle business outta Bricks, my man. You know the record shop in front?"

Fiyah nodded again. He was big-time impressed and he couldn't even keep that shit out of his eyes.

"That's me too. We got DVDs, CDs, mixtapes." Brody

grinned. "We produce a little triple X from time to time . . . So since I know you like to rap and all that shit, I'll put you on the VIP list when you get out. Cool? I'll introduce you to a couple of majors. You know. The power players that make shit happen in the music world. Dig?"

Fiyah's nose was wide open. He was nodding and grinning like a little bitch, and even though he knew it, he was so amped about getting a crack at Bricks that he couldn't help himself.

The next few months flew by. Fiyah composed hard Afro-Cuban drumbeats in his mind, and blended them with some funky reggae drops that could stank a club up. Eva visited him every weekend and he filled up notebook after notebook with song lyrics and still the words flowed like water in his head.

The little Puerto Rican cat from Brooklyn had gotten his walking papers. But not before Fiyah took advantage of the protection he enjoyed under Brody and his crew.

"Fuckin' fag!" Fiyah spit as he slammed his elbow across the bridge of his "ese's" nose. Blood spurted from the dude's face and he went down on one knee. "Tried to set me up, remember?" Fiyah kicked him in the face and the little dude fell over backward. "I should make you kiss this man pussy, you nasty fuckin' *puta*!"

Brody was scheduled for release a month before Fiyah was. He was only in on a probation violation so he'd served out the remainder of his time on Rikers and was now free to go.

"Don't worry, bro," he told Fiyah before leaving. "My arm is long and strong, my nig. You gone be straight in here even after I'm gone. And remember, I'ma be waiting to pick you up when they let you out. It's gone be lovely as fuck. Nothing but bitches and brew, ak. I'ma have so much pussy lined up waiting that you gone be smelling fish while you walking off the tier."

Brody gave Fiyah a dap that almost dislocated his shoulder.

"Now remember, man. We got us an understanding, right? You and me, we look out for each other, right? You been safe up in here. Ain't nobody fucked with you. I delivered on what I promised, and in a minute you gone hafta deliver on what you promised too? Ya dig?"

Fiyah nodded, fear gripping him low in his nuts.

Brody was a ruthless muhfuckah. Fiyah had seen and heard enough to know that clicking up with a capo like Brody came with certain risks. The problem was that Fiyah had made a deal with the devil, and on the mean streets of Harlem the devil always got his due. Fiyah understood that kinda thing. It was the way of the world. But this time the devil wanted more than Fiyah was prepared to deliver.

The devil wanted Eva.

Chapter 6

The scene was gully and 125th Street was popping. Eva was walking next to Alex and munching on a hot slice of pizza with extra cheese as Harlemites, tourists, and shoppers from other boroughs ambled down the streets in search of bargains.

Everything you could think of was up for sale. Corner boys lurked in doorways, then ran out to the curb to satisfy their customers, and African hair braiders stopped sistahs on the street with offers of crazy skills and cut-rate fees that would have your hair whipped into a million stylish braids in a matter of hours.

Eva pulled a long string of hot cheese from her pizza

and chewed on it. Even though her neighborhood was crime ridden and seeped in poverty, she loved Harlem. She loved the sounds and the pulse of the place. The hustle and the bustle, the pimps and the playas, and the flava of a group of die-hard survivors who truly lived in a New York state of mind.

It was hot, and Alex was busy sucking on a Blow Pop and shaking her cute hips as hard as she could. She was the type of fun-loving chick who kept a whole posse of niggahs on a long string, and she was always looking for another guy to hook with her charms so she could have him buying her jewelry and eating out of her hand.

"Don't look now," she side-mouthed to Eva with a grin on her face. "But dude up there in the KG jersey is checking you out." Alex giggled. "Fine mothafucka! I wonder can he fuck."

"Who?" Eva stopped chewing and looked around. "What dude?"

Alex sighed. "Dude up the block. I told your ass not to look."

Eva peered around. "You mean you can see way up the damn block and tell which niggah is looking at me?"

Alex raised her eyebrow and gave her girl a crazy look. "You mean you can't?" She shook her red curls and slipped her hands into her back pockets as her jelly ass rolled. "That's why you ain't got nobody and you ain't getting no dick, Eva. Shit, I can tell if a dude is scoping me from ten miles back. And I ain't bullshitting!"

Eva shrugged. Men checked her out all the time and most of them wanted to get with her. But she was choosey with her game. She liked to get her nasty on, but not with any old cat who wanted to bang her. But Alex was right, though. The guy in the KG jersey had left his customers standing there and come from behind his curbside table and was now standing in the middle of the sidewalk with his eyes locked on hers.

He was cute as hell and he looked kinda familiar too. It took Eva a minute to place him, but with all them damn bootleg CDs and DVDs flying off his table it didn't take her too long.

She turned to Alex and shrugged. "Girl, that's that dude, re-member? The guy who took my picture. We was supposed to hook up with him at *Shakez* one night." Just mentioning the night of India's murder sent vivid memories flooding through Eva's mind and they were painful as fuck. She'd been kinda dig-ging the dude and she had been planning to go check out his flow game on that fateful night.

O'boy musta remembered her too, because he had a big-ass grin on his face as she approached, like they was old friends or something.

"'Sup, pretty lady," he said, stepping to Eva and giving her a happy look as she walked by. "I think I know you. I'm Ice Mello. Remember me? I ain't seen you around for a minute now. How you been?"

Eva had looked into his pretty eyes and remembered exactly why he'd caught her attention the last time she'd seen him. He was just too damn fine, and he had a build on him that made a chick wanna see him butt-naked.

"Good," she said, her offhanded tone covering up the fact that just his brilliant smile had her wide open. "I been pretty straight. What about you?"

Mello laughed. "I don't know, girl. You had a brotha feelin' kinda rejected when you didn't call me. I ain't used to that 'cause I really wanted to see you again. You know, give you that picture I took. Maybe get a chance to take you out and let you enjoy yourself, ya know?"

Alex had stopped walking right along with Eva. She stood there with her hands deep in her back pockets as she checked Mello out from his tight braids down to his fresh sneakers. "I remember you too," she said with a devilish glint in her eyes, then she bust out laughing.

"Nah, for real though," Alex giggled. "My girl is kinda shy, that's why she didn't call you before. But I been working on her conversation skills and a lotta shit has happened since then. Trust, if you give her ya digits one more time, I promise she'll give you a call."

Eva had always known Alex was wild and off the charts, but Mello looked real surprised in the face as her freckle-cheeked girlfriend did something that just fucked her head up.

"While ya bullshittin'," Alex said, nodding toward the cell phone that was clipped to Mello's hip. "You ain't even gotta wait for her to call. I'ma bless you with her digits right now, baby. That way you can hit her up yourself."

Before Eva knew it, her and Mello were hanging hard. Movies, lunch dates, and long walks in the park—Mello treated Eva like she was the best thing that had ever happened to him. Eva tried not to play him close but she had to admit that she was feeling him just as much as he seemed to be feeling her.

Mello mighta sold CDs for Daddy Dre at Bricks, but he was a man of many talents and he was responsible for taking all the club pictures at Bricks for cats who wanted to flex with their honeys or throw up gang signs with their manz. Eva was even more impressed when she learned that Mello had parlayed his photography hobby into an even sweeter little part-time grind. For the past two years he had been working as a photographer for an urban clothing line called Birthday Cake, and when he told Eva his boss was looking for a new model and that he'd already recommended her for the job, Eva knew without a doubt that God had sent this man into her life for a reason.

"You think I can get a job like that?" Eva had asked, jumping up and down just like an excited little kid. "You think they'll like me?"

Mello had laughed and took her by the shoulders, turning her around so he could look at her ass.

"Do you know what kinda measurements you packing back there, baby girl? Anybody ever told you your waist-to-ass ratio? It's phat, baby. Deliciously phat."

Eva was floored. A man like Mello, who could love her like this? All she could do was thank God.

But nobody was perfect, and even though Mello had admitted to her that he used to be a trap boy slinging crack out on the corner, he had come to his senses early enough to get out of the drug game without causing any static. He told Eva that in high school he was a star basketball player and he took good care of his body. It wasn't that he didn't have the heart for the street hustle, he just didn't like what he saw drugs doing to the people in his own community. Mello said he didn't understand how anybody could pay money to put poison in their own bodies, and he said his conscience had fucked with him so hard that he had never slept through a whole night in peace the entire time he was out there slinging rock on the streets.

Eva's blood had gone cold hearing about Mello's past history selling drugs, but she forced herself not to hold it against him. He had been young back then and doing what he had to do to survive. She knew all about shit like that because she'd done shit just to survive too. And besides, he didn't owe her no explanations for nothing he was into before he met her.

That was then, and this was right now. The Ice Mello of today was everything she could have asked for in a man. Strong, hardworking, and a cat who commanded respect on the streets. He was known to be good with his hands, and the kind of hardbody Harlem boy who would scrap for his, pop a niggah off for his, do whatever it took for his. As a result, a whole lotta fools stayed outta Mello's range. He was a real cool dude who helped old people and loved kids, but who could also nut up on a niggah and go gorilla with the best of them.

But Mello had a real tender side too. A side that he didn't show to many people, and Eva felt special as he began to show it to her. He had sworn to her that he didn't have no babies or no baby mamas lurking in the alley waiting to jump out and ambush Eva's ass. Eva thought Mello would make a bomb father, though. Not a typical baby-daddy, but a real father. She wished her son could have been born to a man like Mello, if only fate would have been kinder to her and worked things out that way, the three of them could have been living like a real family.

So, with Fiyah locked up and Alex picking up singing gigs like crazy, Eva was grateful to have Mello in her life. She liked being with him and listening to his dreams of owning his own business one day and getting both of them outta Harlem. Mello's moms had died when he was sixteen, and although he had a little bit of raggedy family members scattered around, he had been hustling on the streets and earning his own way ever since.

Mello was a big kid who liked to discover all kinds of new things, and in a way, so was Eva. They went to movies and museums and fantasized about all their future dreams. They also discovered how to please each other in the sheets, and in his arms Eva learned to let go of her past demons and enjoy what she was being blessed with at the moment. Mello was a deep, but tender lover. He put his sex thang down on her in a way that was so hot and so perfect that Eva sometimes wanted to cry while he was up inside of her.

Eva's early introduction to sex had been so violent and trau-matic. It had taken her a long time to convince herself that the tinglings that went on between her legs were actually good and not bad. Because of what she'd been through she had naturally associated sex with fear and shame, but she'd come out of it slowly, and was finally able to enjoy her adult body without re-lating it to her childhood sins.

She had damn near blacked out the first time she saw Mello naked. They had gone to a movie, and afterward Mello had in-vited her to his room to eat peanut butter and jelly sandwiches.

Eva might have been beautiful, but she wasn't a spoiled diva. She looked for the size of the heart in a man instead of the thickness of his wallet. She knew Mello probably made good bank taking photos and selling his products on 125th Street, but she didn't care if he fed her lobster or if they just drank lemonade. Where some females woulda got swole behind a dude inviting them to a jelly sandwich, Eva got excited.

Both of them laughed while they ate in Mello's room, which was really more like a studio. It was clean and well organized, and Eva felt honored that he had allowed her to come up into his personal space.

They sat on his red leather sofa and kissed in front of the plasma TV. Mello had kept his hands to himself, letting his lips and tongue feel Eva out to see how much of him she wanted. It wasn't long before Eva let him know that she wanted it all. Breaking their embrace, she stood up and slowly began to un-button her shirt. She took her time coming out of it. She wanted him to see exactly what she had to offer, and she didn't want him to miss a damn thing.

Her bright yellow bra came off next, and Mello's eyes grew lidded as he gazed at her naked, majestic breasts. Eva had to squirm a little bit to get out of her jeans, but Mello didn't seem to mind. Of course she added a few extra sexy gyrations in there that had him licking his lips in anticipation. Finally she stood before him in nothing except a bright yellow thong. Her gorgeous brown curves were extra tantalizing. Mello was speechless as she peeled that off too, stepping out of it and leaving it there on the floor.

Mello had torn off his clothes in a fraction of the time it had taken Eva to get out of hers. It was her turn to be struck speechless by the perfectly sculpted man who stood naked and erect before her. Mello had a body that looked like it came out of a men's fitness magazine. His chest bulged with natural muscle and his arms were thick and strong. Eva's gaze had fallen to his tight, tapered waist. She stared at all that brilliant dick muscle that lay flat up against his pretty stomach, touching his navel, and sighed.

Just looking at him was enough to make Eva cum. They'd gotten freaky as fuck that night. Mello was one of them strong-backed brothas who could mash that shit up all night long. He'd licked Eva's tight brown body from the birthmark under her chin down to the tiny mole on her stomach. His lips had crawled over her breasts and gently sucked her nipples until Eva arched her back and felt cream dripping from her slit.

She had lain there panting like an old lady, but Mello was just getting started. He had tickled that sweet spot she had behind her knee, then lapped at the sweat that had beaded under her right breast. His breath hit her skin in short, hot bursts. Eva had moaned as he bent her knees and slid her legs back in the shape of an M. Her pussy was throbbing and leaking so bad she could smell her juices as they boiled between her legs.

Cupping her ass in his big strong hands, Mello had nestled down between her legs. Eva remembered freezing. Fear was crawling over her and sending her temperature down to a bitter cold zone. *He's gonna see your track marks,* the wounded part of her mind told her. She'd made sure to put makeup on her arms and legs, but it didn't make sense to mess up her panties with all that brown gunk. *He's gonna know what kind of person you really are.*

Mello musta noticed that something about her had changed, because he looked up at her with a concerned look on his face. "We can stop if you want to, baby. Just say the word. We ain't gotta do nothing. I'd be cool just holding you all night."

Those few words, spoken in such sincerity and tenderness, were enough to get Eva's blood stoked again. She shook her head no, then blocked out that fearful voice that came back to haunt her every now and then. She lay back and spread her legs even wider for Mello. She gave up the pussy without reservation as he kissed and nuzzled her thighs. Before she knew it, she was arching her back. Urging him to get to that hot spot even faster. Mello massaged the entrance of her pussy with his tongue. Then he dove deep inside of her. Like he was trying to drown himself in her wet tunnel.

Eva's clit had swollen up big and fat. It throbbed and ached as he lathered her pussy up. She sighed with pleasure the moment his lips touched the most tender spot on her body. Eva's hips moved on their own as he sucked that clit into his mouth. He spread her pussy lips open wider and Eva almost fainted. She held on to his head as Mello licked her from the bottom to the top. His lips moving constantly as he devoured every drop of cum that slipped from her body.

It was the experience of a lifetime for Eva. She had never opened herself up like this to a man before. Her body trembled as it roared toward an explosion. She squirmed all over the bed as he tongue-fucked her with short, erotic strokes. Eva whimpered and cried. She never knew anything could feel this good.

And when she reached that peak and wrapped her legs around Mello's head, driving her hips toward the ceiling, she screamed his name. Over and over, until the last sparks of fire slowly subsided in the pit of her pussy, and the muscles in her legs and stomach felt squishy with exhaustion.

Thank you, baby. Thank you.

But it wasn't just the sex that had Eva open on Ice Mello. He was a total package and he knew it would take more than good dick to win Eva's heart. Mello was sensuous and protective at the same time. He had this way of coming up behind her and holding her close that just blew her mind. He would reach down and scoop her up from her ankles all the way up to her tiny waist. His big strong arms would encircle her breasts as he sheltered her from behind, and this made her feel safe and sexy all at once.

For Eva, sex had finally come to mean love and security instead of fear and pain, and with a man like Mello giving up good dick and good loving, her body and her mind were both completely satisfied.

Chapter 7

Fiyah sat on his bunk waiting. He was amped, and every muscle in his body was ready for movement. He'd spent almost nine months waiting for this day, and when he heard the heavy footsteps of the COs on the tier, the sound was like music in his ears.

The guards' boots fell into a rhythm. A beat developed in Fiyah's mind and he nodded his head to it. His cell door slid open and that's when his mental music began.

Fiyah grinned inside. There were two types of time an inmate could do. Good time and bad time. Fiyah's time had been all good. Free from all the predatory shit that goes on in the pen, Fiyah had dedicated every spare moment to perfecting his grind. He had refocused on his goal as an artist and a performer, and he'd built up mad confidence that he had what it took to become a major powerhouse in the rap industry. He had the skills. All he needed was the means and the opportunity and the world would be his.

"Let's go, Perez." Two guards had come to lead Fiyah out, and both of them were rookies.

Stepping out of his cell was just like stepping off the edge of the world. Fiyah was entering a new universe. One that he was ready to completely own, and that shit felt good.

He walked down the tier harder than a muhfuckah. With the guards flanking him on both sides, Fiyah imagined that he was walking past the ropes at Bricks, and the COs were his personal bodyguards.

Fantasy images played out in his mind, blocking out all reality. Instead of cold-blooded criminals hanging out on the tier, he saw ballers chilling in booths. Phat-assed waitresses with jiggly titties. Delivering Cristal and Krug on silver trays. Down at the command station, Fiyah saw a stage. That shit was just a crawling with half-naked pole dancers. The fantasy intensified and Fiyah was up on the stage. Music was blaring and the crowd was wildin' as Fiyah spit some of the most prolific shit these industry insiders had ever heard.

"Sign here," said a requisitions guard. He passed Fiyah a brown envelope containing the personal property he'd had on him the night he got knocked. Fiyah felt like he was in a music video. He saw the guard as a bartender. Serving him a drink.

Reality hit him as soon as they opened the door. The bright summer morning hollered at him as he stepped on free ground for the first time in almost a year.

"You be good now," one of the guards told him before closing the gate.

Fiyah nodded. "I'm always good."

He rode a prison bus over the bridge from Rikers Island. Halfway over, he spotted another bus. It was full of inmates heading toward The Rock. Fiyah rubbed his eyes and sighed, happy as fuck that he was traveling in the opposite direction.

Fiyah got off the bus on the Queens side of the bridge and stood with the prison at his back. New York had never looked so fuckin' good. Walking along the sidewalk behind a couple of other cats who had just been released, he was about to look for a bus or subway and head to Harlem when a black extended-version Escalade with sparkling spinners rolled up.

Fiyah froze as the driver's-side window started inching down.

Some square-faced bitch who looked like a dude nodded at him and said, "What's good, ak?"

Fiyah looked past the dyke driver and his chest tightened when he saw who was in the back.

"Get in."

Goddamn! Fiyah's heart banged hard. He'd been hoping the one-month head start Brody had on him woulda dulled that niggah's memories but obviously it hadn't. Brody had been hyped about getting with Eva before leaving The Rock.

"Listen, man," he'd told Fiyah. "I got a whole lotta bitches on a long rope, but a chick like your cousin could be my queen. She's perfect, man. I wanna put her on a fuckin' pedestal and worship that phat ass, man. You get in her ear and make that shit happen, and I promise I'll make her a happy bitch. That's what's real."

Fiyah wasn't banking on none of that, but he'd figured once Brody hit the bricks there'd be so many fine-ass honeys strolling the streets of Harlem that he'd forget all about Eva and be gobbling up sweet young bitches like they was multiflavored Skittles.

He stared into the car. Brody's head was gleaming and his eyes were like ice.

"Get in, muhfuckah."

That shit wasn't a request. It was an order.

Fiyah opened the back door and got in.

King Brody was a large nig. His custom whip smelled like new leather and the interior had been redesigned so the middle row of seats faced the back row—like in a limo.

Fiyah slid into the middle row and sat facing Brody and two fine-ass chicks. There was a dude sitting on Fiyah's left. He nodded at the guy, and dude just grilled him. He was a big cat too, almost as big as Brody. Matter fact they kinda looked alike, and Fiyah figured they was prolly brothers or cousins.

He looked all the way left and saw another chick. A Latina. She was leaning against the window holding a frosty can of beer to her breast and looking whipped.

Brody grinned, and reached out for a dap.

"You done touched down, man."

Some guy sitting in the front passenger seat lit a blunt. Skimming Fiyah's head with the lit end, he reached over and passed it to Brody.

That shit had come way too close, but Fiyah forced himself to chill like his ear wasn't hot and nothing was up. "Yeah, it took a minute to get outta there, nah'mean? They quick as fuck to lock you down but slow when it's time to let you go."

"Yo." Brody grinned, touching his chest. "Who the fuck am I? I ain't no fuckin' body. I ain't got no problem waiting for the next Daddy Yankee, my man."

Fiyah had been hearing that Daddy Yankee comparison the

whole time he was locked up. Even under the present circumstances that shit still puffed him up with pride.

"Thanks, man," he said, his voice low.

"Nah," Brody said real loud, putting Fiyah's shit on blast. "That's the truth, man. Yo," he spoke to his posse. "This dude was spittin' crack when we was on that tier. His shit is airtight. That's what's up."

Suddenly Brody's mood changed. "Rolo," he ordered his female driver. Fiyah glanced back. The gay chick looked scary. Like she fucked from the top and slung big balls. "Get us the fuck outta here."

They rode through the streets of Queens, heading toward the highway.

"So what's poppin', son?" Brody asked. "What kinda trouble you tryna get into?"

Fiyah shrugged. "I'ma prolly try to get at a couple of dollas, hit some skin, get in the booth and lay a few tracks . . . Gotta fuck with my PO . . ."

Brody waved. "Fuck that PO shit. Don't stress about that muhfuckah. He gotta catch you before he can send you back. The gwap ain't a issue, neither. We put in work around here and we bank plenty of cheese. But your sounds, man, that's the key. That's what's gonna take you all the way, yo. And don't sweat that gushy neither. We swimmin' in women. You want some quick head, you can tap Charlene here. That's what this old bitch is for."

He turned to a girl in a yellow dress.

"Yo, how old is you anyway?"

She pushed out her big chest and sat up straight. "I just turned twenty-one."

Brody laughed, and mushed her back down in the seat.

"Damn! This bitch almost ready for a fuckin' wheelchair! Fuck all that. I like 'em young, bro."

Brody paused, then said quietly, "Eva's eighteen, right?"

"Eva?"

"Yo!" Brody exploded. "What the fuck is really good with that? They stuck your ass in the stupid cell when I left or something? We made a deal, muhfuckah! Five gorilla muhfuckahs and five big hard dicks! Ready to put in work rodding up your spic ass! Do you remember *that* shit!?!"

Fiyah was shook. He nodded, swallowing hard. "Yeah, I remember. Eva's eighteen."

"I thought so," Brody said, grilling the fuck outta him. That niggah was breathing hard and his muscles jumped like he wanted to do something.

"Don't fuck with me, Fiyah. You bring that young pussy straight to Big Brody, ya heard?"

Brody took a hit off the end of his blunt and blew that shit out in Charlene's face. She played her role, leaning her sexy little ass into him and breathing the smoke in like it was oxygen. With his eyes locked dead on Fiyah's, Brody untied a ribbon at the scoop neck of her yellow dress. Her titties looked bold and firm and Fiyah couldn't stop his dick from leaping in his drawers. But there was something else down the front of her dress too. At first he thought it was a tattoo, but when Brody held his fist out and laughed, Fiyah saw a bright red brand in the shape of a big B. It matched the platinum B on the oversized ring Brody sported on his middle finger.

Brody turned the other way. The skinny Latina girl in the red shirt was still leaning up against the window. Brody slapped the beer can out of her hand and it landed on the floor between their feet.

Fiyah knew what was up the moment he saw the dull gray blister standing out on the bulge of her breast. And Brody wanted to make sure he knew. He held his fist out and lined up his ring with the raw mirror image that was on her breast, then punched it into her so hard the girl yelped and slumped over, clutching her burned flesh.

Brody grinned. "Big B likes that fresh meat, yo. He likes it a lot."

Fiyah sat still. His face was like stone.

"Yo, Bullet," Brody said, nodding toward the guy who was his younger brother. Earn ya fuckin' keep, niggah! Crack that bottle, man. I wanna sip a little sumpthin' with Fiyah here because I got faith in this niggah now."

Bullet poured and Brody spoke quietly. "You in with *me* now. Dig? You my newest lieutenant." Bullet passed him a red laminate and Brody tossed it to Fiyah. "Show up at Bricks tonight. You been runnin' up a tab in the joint, muhfuckah, and now it's time for you to show and prove."

King Brody took a swig from his glass. "Yo. Charlene." He elbowed the chick in the yellow dress.

"Bitch find something to do. My man Fiyah just got outta jail, stupid. Go sit over there next to him and treat him right."

Almost nine months on lock was enough to make the strongest cat lose control. Fiyah tried to play that shit off. He sat there with his face as hard as stone. Moments later he was cursing inside for being such a weak muhfuckah. He wanted to be cool like he wasn't affected, but when mami in all that yellow got down between his legs and started yanking on his dick, he was done. Brody and his crew laughed, but Fiyah didn't give a fuck. Right then it wouldn't have mattered if his mother was in the back of that fuckin' Escalade. The way that chick slurped on his dick and massaged his balls? He pushed down on her head as he mouth-fucked her like it was just the two of them in the whip. Her tongue felt softer than butter. She licked his swollen head in tiny hot circles. It didn't take but three or four quick strokes before he busted his nut, but after dreaming about getting some for over eight months, Charlene's neck pussy was just what he needed.

"That should hold a niggah till we get to the crib," Brody laughed. He shook his head. "You coulda got ya dick sucked on The Rock. We gone swing by the house so Charlene can tear ya off real proper, aiight?"

That was cool with Fiyah. He stuffed his wet dick back in his pants, then sank back on the plush leather seats trying to catch his breath. Charlene smiled up at him, still snuggled between his legs.

Brody's joint was on Lexington Avenue and it was just as large as he was. The lobby had marble floors and smelled like lemon incense, and the mirrors and glass panels were sparkling clean.

Fiyah tried not to act too impressed when he stepped into Brody's crib, but that shit was so grand it was fit for a king. Every fuckin' thing in there was oversized and over the top, just like Brody. Granite pillars were spread throughout the house and mirrors trimmed in red velvet lined the walls.

Fiyah was thinking about Charlene's big juicy titties and how they had jiggled under her yellow dress as she sucked his nuts. He was already anticipating what it would be like to slide between her toned, sexy legs when Brody fucked up his fantasy by tossing him off a different bitch.

"Yo, Nakisha," Brody barked on one of the young girls who were sprawled out on his cotton-soft leather sofas. A whole row of them were dressed in colorful thongs and bras and just waiting for King Brody to give a command. Brody had seen the way

Fiyah was still digging Charlene, and he turned to the other bitches in his stable with a grin. "Nakisha, take my manz Fiyah in ya room and work him over." He looked at Fiyah like he was just another one of his bitches in a colorful thong. "Don't even sweat Charlene's old pussy. Nakisha is your type of bitch now, ya feel me?"

Fiyah looked the girl up and down. She was tall and skinny and had a body that looked like it had just started developing yesterday.

"Damn muhfuckah," Fiyah muttered as the girl grabbed his wrist and pulled him along behind her. Her little booty cheeks didn't even have no fat on them. They were all lean muscle. "How old is this chick, yo?"

King Brody laughed behind him and Nakisha laughed in front of him.

"Don't worry, Poppy," she said with a slick grin. "I'm old enough to fuck without getting stuck."

Age wasn't nothing but a number, and Nakisha had just shot to number one on Fiyah's list. The girl mighta been on the bony side, but she could swivel her long body just like a snake and she was wrapping herself around Fiyah's dick in a way that no other chick had ever done.

"Here, nasty," she said, holding out her first and middle fingers for Fiyah to lick. She had just finished fingering herself and her hand was dripping with young juices. Fiyah sucked them fingers up like they were made of platinum. He got all between the crevices tryna get every drop of that sweet liquid that she had just pulled out from her strawberry walls.

After almost nine months of smelling nothing but dick, balls, and crusty assholes, the scent of pussy was driving Fiyah crazy and he drooled as Nakisha swirled her fingers around inside herself again. His dick jumped to her sexy beat as she pressed down on her clit, then flicked it from side to side. Her feet slid up toward her ass and her knees fell apart, giving him the best possible view of her naked brown pussy with pearls of cream dripping from its center.

Fiyah went to work. He licked the insides of her thighs, which tasted just like sweet peaches. "Kiss it," she commanded as he hesitated with his face just two inches away from her beautiful snatch. Fiyah wasn't sure. He didn't know this chick from the next one out there, and eating strange pussy wasn't something he did just like that.

But that pussy was hot and sticky and the girl was demanding. Moments later he took the dive and buried his face all up in that shit. It tasted so damn good he wanted to holler as he sucked and licked and bit into her soft wet mound like he had never eaten pussy before in his life and might never get a chance to eat it again.

Nakisha bucked on the bed beneath him and urged him on. She had a real nasty mouth and Fiyah loved every fuckin' word that flew from her lips. "Yeah, you pussy-eating mothafucka!" she panted. "Lick my ass too, baby. Get busy on everything down there! Don't leave nothing out!"

She didn't have a problem with it when Fiyah flipped her over onto her stomach then pulled her hips back until her ass was aimed at the ceiling. He licked her mounds with his whole damn tongue and dug up in her from the back, sucking her out like a crazy man as she squealed and yanked at the sheets and bucked backward, gyrating her hips and rubbing her pussy all over his face.

That little bit of cum that Charlene had gotten outta him in the car was nothing but a memory now as Fiyah felt his nut steamrolling up from his balls and swelling up the head of his dick. He rose up on his knees and wiped sweat from his eyes as he plunged into her deeply, licking his sticky lips as he tasted her pussy and fucked it at the same time.

He was pounding into that ass with long, deep strokes. Nakisha wasn't talking shit no more. She was trying to take all that dick without screaming as she scooted forward on the bed and moaned and raised her ass as high as she could to meet his wet, shocking thrusts. Fiyah placed one hand on her lower back and held her in the right position as he backed out of her slowly, then slammed back in as hard as he could. He stuck his pointer finger up in her pussy, right along side his dick and wet it up. Then he pulled it out and rubbed it around the rim of her asshole, then jammed his finger inside her back tunnel to the same pace that his dick stroked the front. He was moaning himself now, whimpering too, when suddenly the door burst open and King Brody stood there bare-dick-naked with a big grin on his face.

Fiyah jumped so hard that his dick slipped out and Nakisha was left with both her holes wide open and gaped open at him.

"Yo, man! What the fuck you doin', Brody?!?"

Brody didn't say shit. He snapped his fingers three times and instantly Nakisha jumped out the bed leaving Fiyah on his knees as she rushed over to him. Without a word, the girl knelt down in front of Brody and started licking his dick.

Brody balled up his fists and placed both hands on his waist. He stood there looking like a giant African king as Nakisha deep-throated his dick and slurped at it noisily. Fiyah cursed inside as the girl jetted her neck back and forth, taking almost all of Brody's thick black dick down her throat as her hands moved like feathers over his hanging balls.

Brody groaned a few times, then gripped her by her neck,

freeing his dick and bringing her to her feet. He turned the girl around and bent her over on the bed, then rammed his wet penis up inside her so hard that she screamed in pain, trying to muffle the sound with the sheets. Fiyah was stunned as Brody dicked her ten times deeper than he ever could. He slung meat up in the young chick so hard that she started shivering and hiccupping with each stroke.

Then suddenly Brody pulled out of her and snapped his fingers three times.

Nakisha moved fast. She crawled up on the bed on her hands and knees. She scooted herself around until she was once again in the perfect position for Fiyah. Her ass was high in the air and her juices were glistening on her wet and ready pussy.

Brody chuckled as Fiyah looked amazed.

"This is Harlem, baby. *My* town. You can't even get no pussy up in this city unless I give the word."

Fiyah was stunned for several seconds even after Brody left and the door slammed behind him. What Brody had just done was real fucked up, Fiyah thought as he flipped Nakisha over and slid back up inside her warm pussy. He sucked a small titty into his mouth and pumped into her with quick, strong strokes, determined to blow his load and then get as far away from Brody's nutcase ass as he could.

Chapter 8

Fiyah stood outside of his building as the black Escalade driven by Rolo pulled away from the curb. He was fucked out. Brody's two women had drained every drop of backed-up cum he had in his nuts and now he was cool and could think straight. Pacing around in that jail cell he'd had a thousand dreams of coming back to this place, but now he wondered why. The crib looked even more run-down and dilapidated than it had when he'd left.

He looked up at his windows and spotted Rosa sitting outside on the fire escape. Her eyes were big and thoughtful in her pretty brown face. Fiyah grinned. He waved at Rosa and walked toward the stoop.

It was early, but already some of his neighbors were chilling outside. Mr. Ramirez was sweeping down the steps and he looked up as Fiyah approached.

"'Sup, Mr. Ramirez."

"Fuego," the old man said. "Glad you're back home."

Just inside the vestibule and out of the sun, a small group of older women sat on folding chairs and overturned milk crates as they smoked Newports and Kools. One of them smirked and said, "You see whose car he just got out of, right? Keep riding with that fool and he ain't gonna be home for long."

Fiyah just stayed quiet. These old ladies used to whip his ass when he was a little kid. If he gave them a reason they'd still fuck him up now.

He bounded up to the second floor and the door was snatched open before he could knock.

"Fuego!" Rosa jumped into his arms, laughing. "Aunt Milena!" she yelled. "Fuego's home!"

Fiyah's mother came out of the bathroom smoking a cigarette and drinking a beer. Slim and shapely, she had on a pair of tight jeans and a white shirt, and those who didn't know better often mistook her for Fiyah's older sister.

He held out his arms. "Hi, Ma. I'm home."

Milena walked right past him. "I got something on the stove," she said, her hips shaking as she went into the kitchen to turn off a pot. "Rosa, where's all my pot holders? Bring me a towel!"

Milena burned her finger and cursed in Spanish.

"Lemme get that, Ma," Fiyah said. Using his sleeve, he slid the boiling pot over to a cool burner. He bent down and kissed his mother on the cheek, and she turned her head away as soon as his lips touched her skin.

"I guess I'm right on time to eat."

Rosa came in and sat at the small table. She smiled at Fiyah and he winked back.

"Actually you're almost a year late, Fuego. But what the fuck. Who counts time when they're busy counting dollars?"

"What's wrong, Ma? You ain't happy to see me? Come on, they cut me loose early. Good behavior . . ."

"I'm happy to see you're back to help with some of these damn bills."

Fiyah watched his mother move around the tiny kitchen. He remembered the days when she was strung out, skin popping and picking up dudes off the street and bringing them home to fuck. Shit had gotten so bad that he had gone to Brooklyn to stay with Eva and Rasheena, but none of that had made him love his moms any less.

"We didn't have no heat this winter, you know," she complained. "The boiler broke and the landlord wouldn't do shit about it until Eva called the news hotline. If it wasn't for them showing up and blasting his ass all over the television we woulda froze to death in here."

She slammed a bowl down on the table in front of him, then sat down.

"Shit, you had it good out there on Rikers. At least they have heat in jail. There was a whole lotta nights where I envied you. I woulda switched places with you in a heartbeat just to keep my damn feet warm."

Fiyah stood up. He put his hands on his mother's shoulders.

"Ma, I'm home now. I'm about to get on my grind. I'ma be making music and making money. It's gonna get better, Ma. I promise you."

Milena smirked. "Yeah, okay. I'll believe that shit when I see it." She shrugged his hands off her. "Sit down, Fuego. Your food is getting cold and we sure ain't got no food to be wasting."

Fiyah sat back down. He got busy with his chicken and rice. Milena could burn, and this was the best food he'd eaten all year.

"Man, look at you," he said to Rosa. "You getting big, girl. You're almost grown up."

Milena touched Rosa's hair and agreed. "She is big," she said, bending over to kiss the little girl on her forehead. "In a minute she's gonna be wearing Eva's clothes."

"I went on the Cyclone," Rosa said.

Fiyah looked at his mother. "The Cyclone? In Brooklyn? At Coney Island? What was y'all doing over there?"

Milena pushed her plate back and lit another cigarette.

"My new friend Brody took her."

Fiyah froze. His stomach went liquid as he searched his mother's eyes.

"King Brody? He been coming around here?"

"What the fuck you lookin' at me like that for? He *helps*. Shit, we owe him."

"How much you owe him, Ma?"

"He took Rosa to Coney Island. I needed a break."

"How much, Ma?"

Milena shrugged. "Not a lot. He helped me out with the bills last month. Bought some food. He didn't have a problem with it, Fuego. Hell, I been sick. If it wasn't for him our asses mighta got put out on the street last month."

She lit another cigarette and took a deep pull. "Brody's got a job. He came through the door with cash money. You got a problem with that?"

The look on her face was straight nasty.

Fiyah fumed. "Nah, Ma," he lied. Hell yeah he had a problem. Brody hadn't waited for him to get off The Rock after all. Coming around the crib and taking Rosa out just so he could get next to Eva? That shit was foul.

"I ain't got no problems. I'ma handle it. Where's Eva?"

Rosa started grinning at the mention of Eva's name.

She got up and took a card off the refrigerator. On it was a color photo of Eva in a model's pose. She passed it to Fiyah.

"Eva Patterson for Birthday Cake? What's this?"

"Your cousin's out there doing her thing," Milena said. "She got a new job at some modeling agency downtown. All I know is between her new job and her new man, that ass ain't never home no more."

Fiyah took a close look at the card. He turned it over and saw an address on the back.

"Eva got a boyfriend? She working today?"

Milena shrugged. "How would I know?"

Rosa answered. "She works there every day from seven to five. Then she goes out with her boyfriend after that."

The little girl grinned at Fiyah and it twisted his gut to see how much she looked like India.

"Cool. Yo, Rosita. Can I hold this card?"

She nodded.

"I'll be back, Ma," Fiyah said, putting the card in his pocket.

Pulling deeply from her cigarette, Milena looked up at her son and rolled her eyes.

The Manhattan Parole Office was packed. Fiyah sat in the waiting room, slouched down in his chair. The room was overflowing with a bunch of black and Latino men who had the same bored look on their faces as he did.

He watched a fat white PO walk past with a frown on his face. The PO looked at the men like they were shit on his shoes. Dude carried a 9-mm tucked into his shoulder holster and Fiyah figured the piece was what made that lumpy cracker feel brave.

The guy spotted Fiyah scoping him.

"What the fuck you lookin' at?"

Fiyah just stared. He hadn't been out twenty-four hours yet and this cat was fuckin' with him. With music on his mind, he stared hard at the PO but kept his mouth closed.

"Yeah, that's what I thought. Got this place looking like a fuckin' social club for the criminally insane."

A few minutes later an overworked white parole officer in his mid-forties stepped into the waiting room and called out Fiyah's name.

"Fuego Perez!"

Fiyah came out of his slouch and faced the man. They grilled each other for a few seconds, then Fiyah followed the PO down a hall and into his small office.

Fiyah looked around as the PO skimmed his file. There were stacks of folders all over the place, and wanted posters covered the walls.

"It ain't your first time being locked up, but it's your first time on parole? Right. Just the first time you got caught by the right people. What kind of work did you do before your arrest?"

"I rapped. I'm a rapper."

"Yeah." He sounded bored. "You and every other wanna-be on a street corner. Here's the way it's gonna work, so listen up. I'm placing you on the intensive track. That means you get a job and report to me once a week."

"Every fuckin' week? What? I got caught with a toolie but I didn't shoot no fuckin' body!"

The PO slammed the file down on the desk, then pushed a

form at Fiyah for him to sign. "That ain't all. I'm gonna drug-piss you every fuckin' week too, and if you come back hot, I'll violate you on the spot. Your curfew is ten p.m., unless you ask for a work exception in advance."

"Ten o'clock? You gotta be bullshittin'—"

"Nine on weeknights. Don't fuck with me, though. I've got insomnia and can't sleep worth a damn, so I make bed checks instead. If you ain't in yours when I come creeping, that's another on-the-spot violation. Get three of those and I'll handcuff you and send you back to The Rock to complete the rest of your sentence and that'll be one less ex-con weighing down my caseload. Now, moving on. You're not allowed to associate with known criminals, so kick all your felonious homies to the curb. Don't leave the state without my permission, and don't spend the night no place other than your residence of record. You got all that?"

Fiyah was too mad to talk. He grilled the dude hard, then snatched the form and scrawled his name across it. Pushing back his chair, he stormed out of the office.

The PO held up a pair of handcuffs and called out at his back. "Three strikes and you're out! Tuesday is report day! You miss it, I click it!"

Chapter 9

"**Y**eah, baby," the lead photographer moaned. "That's how you turn a muhfuckah on!"

They were in the West Chelsea Photo Studio and Eva was working the shit outta the cameras. Standing on her cue spot, she swirled her hips and arched her back, and there was so much heat in the room the walls seemed to sweat.

Eva was in her element and digging that shit. No matter how scared or nervous she got in her real life, put her in front of a camera and she went the fuck off. She felt hot and sexy just hearing the shutters click. She was confident and her body was vicious. She got turned on like a mug, just from the sight of the lens, and her pussy would be slick and creamy by the time it was all over.

"I'm feeling you, baby," another voice urged behind her. Eva tooted out her phat ass and dipped her shoulder to emphasize the V in her waist. "Yeah, give it up to me, Eva," he laughed. "You got my shit so hard I can cut off one of my legs and stand up on this muhfuckah right *here*!"

Everybody in the room bust out laughing and the set director called a cut. They killed the lights and Eva strutted off the spot and walked into Mello's strong brown arms.

"Crazy ass," she said, laughing as he kissed her real quick. "You better stop playing like that on company time. You know the Birthday Cake campaign is way behind. They gone get mad and fire your ass."

Mello shrugged. "It ain't my fault the last model, Saucy, fucked around and threw everything off schedule. She was too hotheaded to handle her own success, but that ain't gonna happen to you. Besides"—he placed her hand on his bulging dick—"You feel this shit? It's hard as hell, Eva. It's hard for you."

Tingles zipped all over her body. Eva's nipples were already sticking out two inches through her red bikini top, and the juice that was collecting between her pussy lips felt hot and slippery.

Mello grinded up on her for a moment, then gently slapped her on the ass.

"Time to go, baby. The clock is running. But I got something I wanna slide up in them bottoms later, baby. Make sure you take those little red panties home so you can pose for me again tonight."

The next set called for her to get sprayed down with whipped cream. Eva was a little bit nervous about these shots because they'd hired a couple of male models who were supposed to lick her clean.

"You think the makeup is gonna come off?" she'd asked Mello earlier. Not all of Eva's scars had faded. The ones she had left still embarrassed the hell outta her and she was always scared that somebody was gonna find out the kinda life she'd lived and what she'd been through.

Mello had shaken his head. "The makeup is gonna work just fine, Eva. And nobody is gonna know anyway. But with or without the makeup, you're still beautiful, baby. Finer than any girl I've ever seen. A couple of old scratches on your body doesn't change that, baby."

Eva smiled inside. It felt so damn good to have a man like Mello. In just a few short months he'd taken every bad thing that Rasheena and Jahden had done to her and turned it into a positively good thing.

Before getting with Mello, Eva had always fucked with the lights off. She wore makeup to cover the crisscrossed belt marks on her arms and legs, but that shit would rub off on the sheets during some good fucking and embarrass her to death.

One time she was with a dude that Alex had set her up with. He'd been sweating her for about five months when Eva decided to give him a try. It was summer and she had patted concealer on her worst spots before going to his crib. But when they dipped into his bedroom and he got to licking her and they were sweating all over his sheets, it looked like all the color was rubbing off her body.

That niggah clowned on Eva hard.

"*Itch!* Uss all iss?" he said, sticking out his tongue. It was caked with makeup. Eva had never used that brand before and she must have spread way too much because his long pink tongue looked like he'd been licking mud. He wiped his tongue off on the sheets, but then saw that there was makeup all over them as well. "Get the fuck outta my bed!"

Eva had been so embarrassed she wanted to cry. Not only did dude get stupid on her, he told all his friends too. Alex had cursed him out when she found out what happened, but still. The damage had been done. Eva was real careful about how she got down after that. His trifling ass had taught her a real good lesson.

But with Ramel "Ice Mello" Williams it had been different. He seemed to love her even with all her flaws.

"Eva, that dude is sprung on your ass," Alex had told her late one night as they ate pizza and drank beer while Alex packed. Eva had been crying earlier in the day and she was still sad as fuck. Her girl was leaving Harlem for a while and Eva was gonna miss her. Alex had auditioned to sing in a play, and had blown the part up. The producers had hired her on the spot, and she was heading to D.C. in two days to begin her pre-production training. Alex had been born to sing and Eva was truly happy for her friend, but she loved Alex like a sister and she didn't know what she was gonna do without her.

Alex grinned and swigged her brew. "Between Mello and Reem, I'm leaving you in good hands, chica. For real. You got Mello open, girl." She laughed. "And not just because you got a big juicy ass, neither. Dude is into you. I mean really, really into you."

And it seemed like Alex was right. Everything about Mello felt good. The way he looked at her and really paid attention when she spoke. The way he seriously considered what came outta his mouth when he was talking to her, instead of just blurting out the first thing on his mind. He was thoughtful like that. He was generous and kind and not afraid to share his feelings and his dreams. On top of being sexy as fuck, Mello was romantic too. He gave her lots of small presents too, just to surprise her and make her happy. Once he was slow-fucking her with her legs spread open wide, and sucking her toes at the same time. Eva was shivering and trying to hold back on her nut, and didn't even realize that he'd had a diamond-crested toe ring in his mouth and had slipped it onto her second toe while he was sucking and fucking her. He'd brought it from Cartier and wanted to surprise her with it.

Eva dug that shit to the utmost. She dug everything that Mello put on her sexually and otherwise. She liked to lean back on him and tease his hard dick as he rubbed it between the crack of her soft, fluffy ass. He would breathe hard into her ear, his lips nibbling on her neck as he felt her up with both hands. Eva's soft moans would float into the air as her pussy leaked and warm cream slid from her crevices. The best would come next, when Mello would tease her nipples into hard peaks and send heat shooting through her body that felt like delicious fire-crackers going off between her legs. By the time they were both naked sweat would be covering their bodies and their mouths would be exploring each other's hottest zones. Mello was a heavy hitter and he was working with a package that was a cer-tified sexual apparatus. By the time he got through with his devastating foreplay, Eva would be begging for him to lay it on her, and Mello would be about ready to shoot his sticky semen as far up in her as he could get it.

All of her man's sexual virtues were on Eva's mind as Mello snapped photo after photo after photo. He urged her on with his beautiful deep voice. He whispered all kinds of sexy shit that he knew would turn her on. By the time the session was fi-nally over Eva was so horny that she'd had two silent orgasms for Mello, just from the sound of his voice.

"Check you out," Mello said a few minutes later as he showed her some of the early stills.

Eva peered at the pictures with a keen eye. She was her own worst critic and she could be so hard on herself. Besides, these photos were for a major campaign and Eva wanted them to be perfect.

"Yeah, I sure hate what happened to Saucy," Eva said as she studied her prints. She held out what she felt was the best picture, careful not to get whip cream anywhere near it, and sighed. Saucy Robinson had been the original Birthday Cake model, but that chick ended up being just as crazy as she was beautiful. Saucy had gone ballistic and dropped a dime on every cheating, scheming niggah she could think of in the entertainment industry, and in the end she'd messed around and lost her modeling contract *and* her life. Eva shook her head. "It was real sad how things ended up for her and all, but I'm damn sure glad they picked me to take her place."

Mello just shrugged. "Saucy was fire in front of the camera, Eva, but she had mental issues. Ain't nobody never seen her body so I don't think the psycho chick is really dead, but whatever. You're finer than her anyway, Eva. Way finer. You got a better body and a calmer attitude too. That's why Noire chose you to model her gear. You's a winner, baby. A straight winner."

Eva grinned, but she had to admit that he might have been right. Mello was just a part-time intern at the studio, but the shots he got of her looked better than what most professionals could do. Maybe it was because he was fucking her so good on and off the set, or maybe it was because Mello spoke the truth. Whatever it was, he was right. The photos were top-notch. Worthy of a high-end publication. They made Eva's ass look like it shoulda been plastered on billboards.

Back in her dressing room Eva wet a small towel and started wiping the whipped cream off her body. Mello came in behind her and put his arms around her, scooping her body up from her ankles to her waist. She loved it when he did that shit. When he wrapped his arms around her whole body like that.

"What a fuckin' day," he whispered, holding her and nibbling on her ear. "I'm done, baby."

Eva led him over to the couch and straddled him. She couldn't resist. Her coochie was popping like a firecracker and it was still soaking wet. She pulled his shirt up and slid her lips around on his stomach. Mello's skin was the color of peanut butter and his muscles were round and hard.

"Don't get too tired yet, baby. You still got work to do."

He responded by cupping her ass and squeezing her thick cheeks. "I ain't never too tired to get me some of this. He pulled the crotch of her little bikini aside and rubbed her clit. Eva moaned and he fumbled for his zipper.

"Hold up," she said, pushing off from him.

Eva didn't want no quickie. She wanted the whole experience. From head to toe.

"Maybe I should take a shower first. I got Cool Whip in a few places where Cool Whip ain't supposed to go."

"Don't worry," Mello whispered. His eyes had that sexy-ass look in them as he licked his lips and pulled her closer. "I know all your spots, baby. Even the secret ones. Wherever Cool Whip has gone, Ice Mello's tongue will follow."

He kissed Eva long and deep, and when he released her she got off his lap and slid out of her bikini nice and slow.

Eva sat back on his lap and kissed him hard. His lips were soft as he opened his mouth and fed her some tongue. Eva took it, sucking it like she wanted to swallow it. His dick was rock hard and her body was calling out for him too.

Mello let his fingers skim her neck and her shoulders. They

tickled her naked back. They slid around front and covered her breasts, and just as Eva moaned he opened his mouth and tugged one of her nipples with his teeth.

She almost melted all over him. It felt so fuckin' good! Chills ran through her body as he used his amazing technique to make the bud of her nipple grow even harder. Eva grinded her hips as she felt his dick digging between her legs. She rode that shit through his pants, humping shamelessly as her pussy dripped.

Mello stood up with her in his arms. He laid her gently down on the sofa and came up out of his clothes. Eva moaned as his dick leaped outta his pants. The Ice Man was fuckin' hung. He held it in both hands as he walked toward her with a crooked grin on his face. He guided his dick toward Eva's full, luscious lips. She touched the head with her tongue and it was his turn to moan.

Eva wet his dick up inch by inch. She gently sucked the head, then nibbled on the underside. She had been planning to tease that dick for a little while, but his scent was so fuckin' sexy that she lost her head and throated that whole shit at one time.

Mello gasped. His legs locked as he pumped into her mouth slowly. Eva let her throat go loose, like a trapdoor. He slid almost five of his eight inches over the wet satin of her tongue, and when the head collided with the back of her throat Mello shivered and whispered her name.

Eva felt pleasure waves boiling in her body. She loved sucking Mello's dick. She would have sucked it even if he didn't fuck her. It was just that thick and hard. Just that fuckin' good. She felt his hands in her hair and took him deeper. Bobbing faster, she timed his strokes as he got up in that throat pussy and loved it.

"Uhhhhh," Mello moaned and stuttered. His nut was

swirling around in his balls and racing toward the head of his dick like a tornado. His strokes became deeper and harder. His body broke out in a sweat and little gasps escaped his lips.

Eva prepared herself to drink long and deep. Mello always spurted plenty of hot seed, and nothing in the world tasted better to her. She milked his balls with love in her hands. She stroked the swollen vein that ran up the length of his dick. She felt his orgasm charging upward and she urged it outta him, hoping it was the best one he would ever have.

But then he flipped on her. He snatched his dick from her jaws and pushed her back on the couch. Grabbing her ass, he pushed her knees back to her chest. Right where he knew she liked them, and drilled his thick dick into her as hard and deep as he could.

Eva screamed in pleasure. Her nails raked across his strong, bucking back. Never had she felt anything so good. The sound of his balls beating up her ass turned her on to no end. She opened herself wider and tried to suck his dick up into her chest. He was pounding into her so good that her orgasm snuck her. Before she could hold back, it was right there. It tore another scream from her throat as Mello gripped her cheeks and slid his fat thumb inside her wet asshole. Eva felt another one coming over her. This one would be smaller, but just as fuckin' good.

Mello felt her chocolate pussy clenching. She held her breath and he pressed down on her hips and fucked her even deeper. This time, when Eva came, he came with her. His thick, sticky cum filled up her pussy and the overflow spilled out on her ass. Mello and Eva locked their lips together. They muffled their cries inside each other's mouths until both of them could only whimper the other one's name.

When they were finished Eva lay panting against his chest.

Mello had given it to her exactly the way she wanted it, and she felt energized and ready to roll.

Mello stood up and yawned. His pants were around his ankles and his fat, pretty dick hung limp against his thigh. He picked up the towel she'd thrown on the floor earlier and wet it again in the sink. Eva stood there like a baby and let him wipe her neck, between her titties, and down her stomach. He tapped her thigh and she spread her legs wide. He cleaned her pussy and her ass, then rinsed the towel in the sink and started wiping down his chest.

Eva had just finished dressing when she felt her phone vibrate in her purse. She had missed a text message a few hours ago, probably while she was in front of the cameras. She looked at the number. She didn't recognize it, but once she read the message a smile came over her face.

"Hey, baby," she said to Mello, still grinning. "I know it's Friday and all, but let's do Bricks tonight. My cousin Fiyah sent me a text. He got outta Rikers today. He's never been inside Bricks. You think you can get some laminates or put him on the VIP list so we can hang out?"

Mello grinned. Eva had told Mello all about her cousin. Mello understood that they were close and Eva loved him like he was her brother. Mello was even cool when on all those long Saturdays that he wanted to chill with her, Eva had to go make a visit with Fiyah on Rikers instead.

"He's out? Cool! That's what's up, baby. Yeah, we can swing by Bricks. It's reggaeton night so I won't be on the mic, but I'll still go. Besides, I heard ill Nino might be in the house, and I wanna meet him."

"I know. I ran into Reem the other day and he told me. That's why I wanna get Fiyah in there. Reem wants ill to meet him."

Mello nodded. "Cool. I wanna meet that ill cat too, but I

gotta do some editing first. I'll tell Speedy or Gita to leave you a couple of laminates at the door. You go 'head with your cousin and I'll catch up with y'all there later on."

Eva was hyped. She picked up her jacket from a chair and got her purse. Then she leaned over and kissed Mello on his lips. "Love me?"

"Hell yeah. You know I do."

"I love you too," she said, then kissed him again and bounced.

Eva had gone halfway down the block before she saw him. He was leaning on a parked car, grinning at her.

"Hey, chica! Whassup, you so hot now you iggin' your own cousin?"

Fiyah's arms were open and Eva jumped right into them.

"What you doin' here?!" she screamed. Fiyah's hair was curly and he was so damned cute. Eva kissed him all over his cheeks, leaving lipstick marks on his face. "You look good in street clothes, man!"

He stepped back and eyed her. "Nah, you the one who's looking good, baby," he said, checking out her hot designer mini-dress and all the matching accessories she'd gotten courtesy of the modeling agency. Eva knew she looked real different to him. Because of her job she no longer wore clothes from 125th Street. Her hair was pure butter, done by a professional stylist, and if you didn't know better you would swear she was the perfect picture of the Upper East Side.

"Dayyyyyum!" Fiyah couldn't take his eyes off her. "Evita, your shit is tight. Good thing you didn't wear no shit like this on none of your visits out on The Rock. There woulda been all kinds of clowns clocking for you then."

She laughed. "Boy, why would I get dressed up to ride that nasty prison bus? And I don't give a damn about impressing nobody on Rikers. Forget that joint. You're home now, Fiyah." Eva hugged him again. "All that shit is in the past. Come on," she said, looping her arm through his. Gimme a walk. I gotta go drop off some proofs."

They walked down the street together talking about things Fiyah had missed while he was gone. Eva still felt guilty about getting her cousin locked up, and she was truly glad that shit was over. It seemed like Fiyah had survived it okay, and that was a big relief to her. Eva could never have forgiven herself if something had happened to him on the inside just because she'd put him there.

"You been by the house yet?" she asked.

Fiyah nodded, then sighed. "Yeah. I went there. I ate lunch with Rosita and my mother. That shit was a trip, man. My moms seems like she got an attitude with me about something."

Eva shook her head. Milena had talked about Fiyah like a dog the whole time he was locked up and hadn't gone to see him once. She was still on that money tip, the same one she'd been on before he got locked up. Milena had really struggled to keep food in their stomachs when she got off drugs, and she didn't respect no man unless he was giving up the bank, not even her son. She thought Fiyah's big-time dreams of a career in music was a big-time load of bullshit, and she wanted him to put some money where his mic was.

Eva shrugged her shoulders. Things were different with her aunt these days. Eva figured she musta found a new boyfriend or something, because Milena had been spending a lot of time in her room with the door locked. Eva usually got home late, but a couple of times she thought she heard a man's deep voice coming from her aunt's room. And once Eva could have sworn she heard moans and fuck screams in the middle of the night. A few minutes later Milena's bed was creaking and rocking so hard that there was no way somebody wasn't in there tearing her pussy up. Shit, her aunt was still young and she had a pretty face and a real nice body. Why shouldn't she be getting herself some dick if that's what she wanted?

But Eva wasn't about to tell Fiyah none of that. "I don't know what's up," she said. "I leave early and get home late. I miss out on a whole lotta shit. Especially with Rosa. Your moms is good to take care of her for me the way she does."

"She don't do it just for you, Eva. She does it because she loves Rosa. She loved India too. We all did."

Eva nodded because he was right.

"So," Fiyah said, like he wanted to lighten up the mood. "Shit is finally about to happen for me, ya know. I got a lotta stuff that's coming together, Eva."

"Oh yeah?" Eva said. "Like what?"

"Like a lot of stuff. You know when I was locked up I stayed scribbling the whole time, man, the whole time. I got like, a whole album's worth of shit that I wrote while I was in there."

"That's what's up, Fiyah. You wanna spit some of that fire at Bricks tonight?"

He looked surprised. "At Bricks? What you know about that club, Evita?"

"I don't know a whole lot," she admitted. "But I know it's hot. My friend has a table on 125th Street. He sells CDs and DVDs for the guys who run shit in the record shop in the front of Bricks."

Fiyah shook his head. "Nah, I'm straight. I should prolly stay away from that joint. Besides, I went to see my parole officer before I came down here. That fool gave me a ten o'clock curfew on the weekends. I can't do nothing with that."

Eva frowned, disappointed. "All right. I was just asking because tonight is reggaeton night and I wanted to get you in there."

"Reggaeton night?"

"You been gone for a minute, cuz. Reem is hooked up tight over in Bricks these days."

"Reem Raw?"

"Yeah. Reem from Brooklyn. He got signed to a major label right after you got knocked. Anyway, they got a new jack set going on the weekends now in Bricks, and Reem hosts it. Saturdays are for new rap artists, and Fridays are for reggaeton. I heard ill Nino might blow in from Miami too, so it should be hot."

"ill Nino? Bottom Half Boyz, ill Nino?"

Eva nodded. "Yep. Reem just cut an album with him and told me they're looking to tour a new artist. Somebody fresh to warm the mic up for their opening act. I think Reem tossed out your name."

"ill Nino knows about me?"

Eva laughed. "He don't know every damn thing. Reem probably didn't wanna scare him."

Fiyah kissed her on the cheek. "I guess today is my damn day."

"Hell yeah," she said. "I guess so."

They had only walked a few more steps when Fiyah fucked Eva up.

"Know what? It's your day too, Evita."

"Oh yeah?"

Fiyah stopped and turned toward her. "Yeah. Look, you heard of that dude they call King Brody?"

Eva nodded. That dude had a rep on the streets of Harlem, and from what she'd heard he was shady and pyscho. Brody had gotten outta jail about a month ago. He was a big drug lord who made crazy bank on the illegal CD operation that was run out of Bricks's record shop. It hadn't slowed down at all while he was on lock, neither, and once he got back home he picked up right where he left off, running shit again. Mello didn't like the cat and that meant Eva didn't like his ass neither. Brody was into bogarting and pushing up on rivals for their drugs and their jewels, and Mello said he had a XXX video operation going on in some kind of bunkers behind the club.

"Well I got to know him on The Rock. He's running shit at Bricks and he's got mad connections in the music game too, yo. Your friend might can get you in the door, but Brody can get me put on wax. Shit's about to happen for both of us, Evita."

Eva's whole chest got swole. "You running with Brody? That drug-slanging bastard? You musta bumped your fuckin' head on Rikers, cuz. You sounding real stupid right now, for real."

Fiyah looked swole too. He grabbed her arm.

"Yo, what's up with all that disrespect, Eva? There was a time you woulda been happy to have me runnin' with a cat like Brody. I remember a time when you ran after cats like him yourself. You used to be out there dippin' in their pockets and sneaking out their fuckin' windows."

That was a low blow. It hit Eva right in the groin where she used to shoot her drugs. She was ready to curse Fiyah the fuck out, but she forced herself to chill.

"That was back then, Fuego. This is now. I was a kid back then. Today, I'm grown. Times have changed."

He shook his head. "Nah, baby. I just gave up almost a year outta my life for you. Times gone change when I say they change."

Eva gave him a crazy look. He was her cousin, not her fuckin' man.

"Yeah, whatever, Fiyah. You can go on with all that noise. You roll up talking all that 'me-me-me' yang. As usual you ain't thinking about nobody but yourself."

He shrugged and a set look came down on his face. "Look, Eva. Your shit is set up lovely. You been out here living phat and warm. I'm the one who was on the inside dealing with the cold, grimy shit. Now, my man Brody is feeling you. He seen you on a visit and he wants to get to know you a little bit. I ain't askin you to do nothing crazy. I just need you to get with the program for a little while, that's all. Spending a few minutes with a big willie ain't gonna kill you."

Eva smirked. Fiyah could kiss her ass.

"I'm getting with my own damn program, Fiyah. You should try it too. There are plenty of other ways to get on wax besides running with niggahs like Brody. I don't do drug dealers, *period*. I thought you knew that."

There was sadness in her cousin's eyes and he looked at Eva for a long time.

"You don't get it, Evita, do you? That's 'cause your ass wasn't on lock. Brody looked out for me on them tiers, girl. That cat watched my back and kept the goonies off while I did *your* bid, and now I owe his ass. *We* owe his ass!"

"I just don't wanna see you get in no shit, Fiyah! And I ain't available anyway so you can just tell Brody that. I already got a man."

Fiyah looked at her hard. "Who is he?"

Eva turned to walk away and said over her shoulder, "I'm chillin' with a dude name Ramel."

"Ramel, who?"

Eva kept walking. She didn't even answer.

She heard him walking up fast behind her.

"WHO? Who the fuck is a Ramel, Eva?"

She tossed two words at him over her shoulder.

"My *man*."

Eva kept it moving down the street. Even as she heard Fiyah yelling behind her like he was bonkers.

"Hey! *Hey!* Don't walk your ass away from me, Eva! Brody will fuck you and me both up! You better tell that fuckin' Ramel cat to step off, Eva! I ain't getting fucked up because of you!"

Eva waved her hand in the air, then walked on without looking back. Two seconds later she heard a loud thunk, then the sound of a car alarm blared in the air. She turned around and shook her head. Stupid ass. Kicking cars. If Fiyah was crazy enough to get in the gutter with a killer like Brody, then it wasn't a car that needed kicking, it was his ass.

Chapter 10

Fiyah rolled into Bricks around midnight.

From the outside he looked chill and confident. His gear was straight and he had his gangsta mug on. But on the inside he was shook.

He'd done a little asking around about Eva's boy. The kid they called Ice Mello. The streets of Harlem had offered up nothing but high praise about the cat. Fiyah had heard amazing tales about Mello's flow game and his reputation for dominance on the mic. Instantly, his competitive juices began to flow. Fiyah had been gone too long. Jealousy had washed all over him as cats whose opinions he trusted told him sagas of Ice Mello's lyrical game. Fiyah had spent all that time in jail because of Eva's ass, and while he was locked down her man had been on the streets making a name for himself, pissing on mics and marking his territory all over Harlem.

He'd caught up with Eva again at the crib. The way she had dissed him outside her job earlier was still burning him up.

"Fuck Mello!" Fiyah had said when Eva started making noise again about her man. "That cat is a *nobody.* He's selling hot CDs off a table on 125th Street, Evita! You gonna turn down a capo like Brody for some flea-ass chump like that?"

Fiyah and Eva had a bond, and they both knew it. There'd been a lot of times when the only person they had was each other, and it wasn't just love that flowed between them. There was loyalty too.

"I'm your *cousin,*" Fiyah had pleaded. Eva didn't know who she was fuckin' with. Fiyah was trying to save their lives. Brody was a killer, and he would murk them both without even blinking. "You gonna let this nobody niggah come between us?"

The look in Eva's eyes had been like a knife across Fiyah's throat. Yeah, the love for him was still there. And it was still just as strong. But Eva wasn't about to bend to his will. No matter what he said, Fiyah couldn't talk her off of her position.

"Mello is my *man.* And even if he wasn't I wouldn't fuck with a low-life like Brody. He don't rep what I rep, Fiyah. I don't think what he reps is your flavor neither."

She'd stormed into her room and Fiyah had wrestled with himself over coming out to Bricks tonight. The smart thing to do woulda been to stay his ass home and stroke his sore dick. He had a ten o'clock curfew from a PO who swore he checked beds. And even worse, Brody was expecting to get next to Eva tonight. Double-crossing a maniac like Brody was just as stupid as jumping in front of the number three train. But despite his fear, there was something else that had pushed Fiyah to stand in the long line outside and wait to have his name checked off on the guest list at Bricks. Eva had said ill Nino was gonna be in the house looking over prospects for next week's reggaeton competition. Fuck Brody, fuck a speeding train, fuck the world if it meant getting on with a baller like ill. Sometimes a certain level of risk was acceptable, ya know? If you wanted something bad enough then there were times when you had to be willing to put your dick on the chopping block in order to get it.

Fiyah took the risk.

Bricks was a banging club and a baller's delight. It was an Alizé, Patrón, Cristal and Krug set, and the sweet smell of Philly blunts and Game Dutch Masters was thick in the air. A cute Latina waitress sauntered past in a short skirt and high heels. She smiled and Fiyah grinned when he saw the blue glow tabs she was playing with in her mouth. The music was bumping, the beat was sick as shit. Fiyah knew he would piss Brody off by showing up without Eva, but despite his fear he was feeling the hell outta Bricks's atmosphere. He stood on the sidelines and checked out the pole dancers, the shot callers and some of the badass chicks who worked the underground XXX video circuit. Every female in the house was a stunna. His eyes got full on all the phat asses, high breasts, and flat tummies he could stand.

There were two bars in Bricks, on opposite walls. Fiyah checked out the pool tables, the booths and the love seats, then imagined himself up on the raised stage. Shitting all over the mic. He walked deeper through the club and passed a room where three ballers sat on stools with their pants down around their ankles. There was a naked chick in front of each one of them, down on her knees bobbing her head. It was a dick-sucking contest and cats was standing around waiting for their turn as they cheered the hoes on.

Fiyah backtracked his steps and went back to the main room. From his position on the wall he spotted the VIP area. It overlooked the packed dance floor where sexy-ass waitresses threaded through the crowd delivering drinks on five-inch heels. Fiyah found a spot at the bar and ordered a rum and Coke. He paid for it with some of the doe Brody had torn him off that morning.

"Fiyah?"

He turned left.

"Whassup, baby! *Que pasa, maricón?!*"

"I'm good, Sasha," he said, reaching for a hug. Sasha squeezed him close, rubbing up against him. His dick jumped bad and he ran his hand up her thigh. "What's up with you, girl?" They'd gone to high school together and had fucked a couple of times back then.

"Everything's up with me! Where you been, man?"

Fiyah shrugged. "Grindin', baby. Laying low and grindin' hard."

He tugged at her little skirt. Her toned legs looked luscious under her sexy sheer panty hose. "You a waitress now or something?"

"Yeah. I gotta grind too, you know." She picked up her drink order and smiled. "I gotta run, but it's good to see you. I heard you was coming home from jail, *meijo*. If you need some good pussy, you know where I stay."

Fiyah grinned and went back to his drink. A hardbody song by 'Hovah came on and he drummed his fingers on the bar, imitating the beat. He glanced around again, unable to believe that he was actually tossin' drinks down inside of Club Bricks.

But unbeknownst to Fiyah, a black Cadillac Escalade had just pulled up outside, and pretty soon his drink wasn't the only thing that was gonna get tossed.

Brody's whip slid up to the curb outside of Bricks with the music blasting. Rolo put the car in park, then jumped out of her seat and opened the back door for her don.

Two sexy-ass chicks slid across the seats, followed by Bullet and Anwar. The girls had just hit a few lines of coke and were now sucking on mini bottles of Cristal from tiny straws. The men were pressed out heavy in expensive urban gear. First to get out were the Latina girl, then Serena, and then Brody. Charlene lingered inside.

Where Brody was all man, muscular and thick, Serena had a small frame with sweet titties and a firm round ass that said her last name shoulda been Williams. They looked real good together and Brody knew it, which was one reason he kept her whiny ass around. Brody was expecting good things tonight and his mood was up, but Serena was starting to drag him down. Earlier, the dumb bitch had complained about the blister on her chest hurting, and before he knew it Brody had almost blacked out on that ass. That was why right now she was out at night wearing a ton of makeup and some oversized sunglasses. Her chest wasn't the only damned thing Brody had blistered neither.

"Hurry up and get the fuck out," he snapped. She slid across the leather seat like her big ass hurt too. Brody had put some fire on that shit, so he was sure it did. "Let's get inside and do the damn thing."

Tears swelled in her eyes. "Brody . . ." she said, moving like an old lady. "I can't move—please wait . . ."

"What?" he barked. "You wanna take your ass home?"

"No." The seventeen-year-old girl shook her head. "I wanna be right here with you, baby. But I'm feeling real dizzy. Like I can't—"

"If your ass is sick and you wanna go home, then step, bitch, step! You know the way!"

"I can't walk all the way back . . ." Her voice was a whisper.

"Then take the train or get in a cab."

"I don't have no money . . ."

Brody's voice was like ice.

"That's right, ho. You ain't got no money. You ain't got shit unless I give it to you, remember? So get the fuck outta my ride and hurry ya stupid ass over there in the club before I fly your fuckin' head again!"

Bullet and the rest of the posse were still standing on the curb. After hearing his brother's threat, he reached inside the whip and took Serena's arm and gently helped her out. She wobbled on her feet for a moment, then she pulled her shit together. Bullet looked down at her with sympathy in his eyes. Serena didn't look back. Instead she did just like Brody had said. She hurried her aching ass over to the entrance of Bricks, and along with the rest of the crew she went inside.

Up on the stage rapper Reem Raw was holding court with a couple of VIPs from Los Angeles. Reem was originally from Brooklyn, and had made big dents in the music scene in that borough before coming to Harlem. He'd toured with Robb Hawk, Hood, and the Bottom Half Boyz, and his top-ten Billboard track "No Regrets" was so gully and spoke such gutter truth, that it had become a ghetto national anthem.

Scanning the club, Reem nodded at Daddy Dre, who was

the owner of Bricks and an all-around Papa Cat to some of the young'uns in the hood, then nodded toward the front door where ill Nino and his small entourage were just coming in.

ill Nino was a slick and stylish reggaeton artist. The king of the Latino music set, he stepped inside of Bricks and immediately started getting mad love and props. His beautiful dark-skinned girlfriend looked like chocolate candy on his arm, and several Bottom Half Boyz were handling shit from the rear.

ill stopped in front of Dre, who looked him up and down.

"Man, ain't this some shit. I remember when you used to play stickball on Lenox Avenue with holes in your pants. Muhfuckah walking around here cleaner than Clorox now."

ill hugged his old friend and grinned. "Dre, man, don't be blowing my shit up in public, aiight?"

Dre laughed. "Welcome home, baby. Good to have you back on the set. Reem said the new album is hot. Y'all niggahs must be living right."

"Yeah," ill Nino shrugged. "Life is good, but CD sales ain't. But you already know that, Dre. When you gone stop pressing that pirated shit in them bunkers out back, man? Cats like you be cutting in on an artist's income. Between shit either getting leaked or downloaded on the Internet, and press shops frontin' as record shops like the one you runnin', ain't no real money in CDs no more. Me and Reem getting geared up to head back out on the road again. That's the only way to make some decent doe. Performing. We might take a new jack out with us this time. We'll see how that shit goes."

Dre laughed. He let ill's slick-ass remark slide by. He didn't give a fuck about all that bitchin' about pressing CDs. When there was money to be made, a businessman was gonna make it. "So what the fuck are you? Some kinda Puerto Rican Santa

Claus? You taking unsigned artists on the road, huh? You into charity work now?"

ill Nino shrugged. "Come on, Dre, you know me. I came up spittin' on these Harlem streets. Most of that shit they got rotating on the radio these days is garbage, man. The real talent comes off the streets. Outta the projects and off the tiers. That's the kinda music we looking for, man."

"Well I feel you, baby. A lot of these rappers that come in here could break out in a major way if they wasn't so busy slanging and bangin' and acting like a bunch of fooligans. The talent? They got that. The sense? Them niggahs is real short on that."

ill grinned and clapped Dre on the shoulder. "See? Ain't you glad you taught me better? All them times you had to knock me on my ass for doing wrong? I guess it worked."

"Man," Dre said, "I'm glad you got your shit straight, 'cause you were even worse than some of these fools are today . . . robbing old ladies and shit . . ."

ill laughed.

"Stealing candy from little babies . . ." Dre threw his arm around ill's shoulder. "C'mon over here," he said, leading ill and his crew toward a table in the VIP section. "The first round is on me. Name ya poison."

ill shrugged. "My baby likes Krug."

Dre eyed the fine-ass sistah holding on to ill Nino's arm and grinned. She had a fat little camel toe between her legs and he could tell that pussy was nice and juicy.

"Fine," he said, staring at her crotch. "Then Krug it is."

Chapter 11

Chapter 11

The night was sizzling. Reem Raw had taken the stage. A crowd of chicks were hanging off his dick as he performed a hot banga called "Twist Is."

Fiyah moved with the beat as Reem ripped the mic with his metaphorical flow.

> Shawty c'mere lemme feel how them lips is . . .
> The way them hips shift, I can tell you gifted . . .
> You know who the click is
> You know how we get biz,
> And I can put it down, whatevah ya twist is!

By the time Reem finished banging up the track the dance floor was rocking and the crowd was amped. Fiyah grinned as his manz jumped off the stage. Reem got mad props as both the chicks and the ballers made a path for him. Fiyah was so preoccupied digging Reem that he almost slept on the posse that was coming through the door.

"Oh shit," he muttered. He bumped a skinny girl outta his way and slid through the crowd toward Reem real quick. He tapped Reem's arm just as he got near the bar.

"'Sup, money."

Reem grinned and gave Fiyah a dap then a hug.

"Fiyahhhh . . . my niggah! What it do, baby?"

Glancing around nervously, Fiyah leaned in close.

"Yo, man. Lemme holla at you real quick." He glanced toward a side door. "Can we slide outta here that way?"

Moments later they were standing on the street behind Bricks.

"Yo, what's in them little things over there?" Fiyah asked, pointing across the street to what looked like garages encased in concrete.

"Them shits is bunkers," Reem answered. "That's Brody's property. They press all them bogus DVDs and shit back there. Ain't no guessing what else them fools be doing in there. Probably growing that crazy niggah a demented twin in a fuckin' pickle jar."

Fiyah shook his head. "I sure hope not. Let's walk," he urged, and led Reem around toward the front of the club. Fiyah stopped as they got to the corner. He peeped around, then leaned against the building in a way that allowed him to see the front door.

"Yo, man," Reem said shaking his head. "Welcome home, man! But you off the tiers now. You ain't gotta pull guard no more."

Fiyah grinned and played it off. "I'm cool, man. It's all good."

"If it's so fuckin' good why you holdin' a set out here on the street?"

"Sorry, man," Fiyah said. "But I'm on the clock, ya feel me? I gotta beat my PO to the crib or he's gonna violate my ass." He shrugged. "I'm tryna wait around for my cousin, though . . ."

"Who, Eva?"

"Yeah. She's supposed to be rollin' through."

Reem shook his head. "You got your nights wrong, homey. Eva's into the Saturday night set these days. She's rolling hard with a rapper they call—"

"Ramel."

"Ramel? Oh, you mean Ice Mello? Yeah. That niggah is live. He brings it hard on the rap beats the way you was bringing it with reggaeton right before you took that ride."

"Him and Eva into some shit, huh?"

Reem held his hands up, backing him off. "Don't talk that shit to me, man. I don't keep tabs on nobody's swerve."

"Yo, man," Fiyah asked, craning his neck to see around the corner. "That cat Brody. Did he just go inside?"

Reem laughed. "Niggah that's his one-of-a-kind whip parked right there on the curb! Ain't another one like it in Harlem. What the fuck is up with you, Fiyah?"

"I'm straight, man. Just tryna get back into this shit, ya feel me?"

Reem gave him the crazy look. "Then get ya ass back in it, man. You know how we do this shit. Get ya ass inside and spit some fire on that mic."

Fiyah followed Reem back into Bricks with his gut clenched tight. Eva was a fuckin' ghost and Brody was about to become a real big problem. There was a lot he could lose, fuckin' around in Bricks tonight. But a lot he could gain too. Fiyah knew his future was riding on him making a good impression. ill Nino was on the set and he was checking for fresh talent. Fiyah knew he had the mic skills to blow every reggaeton rapper in Harlem outta the box, and he couldn't wait until next week's competition. Not even a cutthroat like Brody could make him pass up what might be his best opportunity to shine.

"Check it," Reem said over his shoulder. "Go wait for me in the VIP section. And don't say I never gave you nothing. I wanna give ill a little heads up on what you can do. You know, a preview, so your shit is fresh in his mind next week when all the rest of them cats show up. ill is taking care of some business with Daddy Dre right now, but I'll pull ya coat when he's paying attention. Believe. Before the end of the night you gone be face-to-face with a cat who can elevate your shit in front of the entire world."

Fiyah made his way over to the VIP section. It was packed out with major power players from the professional sports world and some of the most recognized music artists in the country. The smell of chocolate dutchies was in the air. Decanters of cranberry juice and cans of Red Bull littered the tables.

Brody was sitting in the middle of the mix gripping an icy Corona in his hand. Waitresses hung around him ready to jump when he snapped. Niggahs was hard on his dick. Everybody in the joint knew he was a willie and a shot caller. His stark-white wife beater was tight over his huge shoulders, and his upper arm muscles bulged bigger than most men's thighs.

He looked up and spotted Fiyah, and his eyes locked in on him hard. Brody stood up and opened his arms up wide. He cracked a huge smile like Fiyah was his long lost manz from way back.

"Fiyah. The cat who stanks up the muhfuckin' mic!"

Brody reached for a dap. He fisted Fiyah so hard his wrist went numb.

"What up, boss," Fiyah said. He dapped out the rest of Brody's crew, including that man-ass Rolo, then stuck his sore hand in his pocket.

"Ya late again, niggah," Brody said, still grinning. "That's twice you done kept me waiting in one goddamn day."

Fiyah shrugged and tried to joke it off. "These fuckin' chicks, man. You know . . ."

Brody stared. "Nah, I don't know. What about 'em?"

"It's Eva. A closet full of designer shit and she still don't know what to wear. I had to bounce on her, man."

Brody's eyes narrowed. He stared at Fiyah deep, like he knew he was lying.

"But she's still coming out to ball with me, right money?"

"Oh hell yeah," Fiyah assured. "She'll be here, man."

"Cool." Brody nodded to a waitress. "Yo, bitch. Bring my manz here a drink. We 'bout to welcome this niggah home right."

Fiyah sat between Bullet and Rolo as he balled with Brody and his crew. Champagne tops were popped and the bubbly stuff flowed. Rolo had a pretty Latina grinding on her lap, and a thick-legged honey with little titties and a wide ass started dancing in front of Fiyah. She used her pretty legs to bump his knees apart so she could get closer to him. His sexual energy was intense, and even though his dick had already been sucked and fucked sore by Charlene and Nakisha earlier, Fiyah still felt like he had ten years worth of cum backed up in his nuts.

He grabbed her slim waist as she shook that thing at him. She laughed and put one leg up on the seat, and humped her ass in a million directions. Fiyah slid his hands up her thighs and under her skirt. Her butt was damp and sweaty and it jiggled in his palm. He found her pussy and rubbed it until his hand got slippery. The girl took it up a notch. She straddled him with her knees, then leaned forward and licked his ear.

"You can grind against it, but you can't touch it," she whispered. "Not unless you down to tear me off something in a back room."

Fiyah shrugged. As bad as he wanted to fuck her, walking away from Brody was outta the question. Besides, he probably wouldn't be able to cum anyway. He thrust his finger deep into her pussy and she yelped softly in his ear.

"Maybe later, baby," he said, pushing her gently off his lap. His dick was on rock like a muhfuckah, but before he could sweat it Eva showed up.

Fiyah's dick wilted with relief at the sight of his cousin.

Brody could back the fuck up offa his shit now.

Eva strutted toward them looking like a sweet black number-one stunna. She was wearing a pair of white Birthday Cake shorts and some kind of white top that showed off her toned brown stomach. Ice glinted and dangled from her pierced navel and her hips were knockin' niggahs out as she swayed across the room.

Fiyah grinned. Eva had really grown up. None of the grimy shit she had been through in her life was written on her. Her shit was polished and fresh. She carried herself with confidence and grace. Like she had come from the Nile and had been crowned its urban goddess.

"Goddamn," Brody said, standing up. His voice was thick as

shit. He cupped his dick as he watched Eva move. "Next time a shawty like her needs time to get ready . . . you just give it to her goddammit."

Every niggah in the crew had his eye on Eva. Brody's girls were watching her too. Eva shined and flossed as her long mane of curly hair flowed behind her.

She spotted Fiyah and strutted over to their table. Before she could reach her cousin, Brody stepped forward and offered her his hand.

Eva paused. Her beautiful eyes swept Brody up and down, then she smirked and put out her hand like she really didn't want to.

Brody grinned and raised her hand up to his lips. He made like he was gonna kiss it, but stuck out his fat tongue and licked all between her fingers instead.

"Damn!" Eva cursed. She pulled her hand away and wiped it furiously on her shorts. "What the hell was that about?"

Brody laughed. "It was about you. How you doing, baby girl?"

She nodded. "Brody."

The boss capo couldn't take his eyes off her. "You glossed up and shining real nice, baby. Straight shining. Can I buy you a drink?"

"Nah, that's all right. I'm good."

"Oh, I can see that. But c'mon. It's Fiyah's night tonight. Your cousin is celebrating. Have a little taste with us just for him, okay?"

Brody snapped his finger once and a VIP waitress scurried over with some champagne.

Eva accepted the glass with a shrug. "Cool. Since that's the only reason I came."

Brody raised his eyebrow. "Is that right? Fuck. I been waiting all night 'cause I thought you was coming out to get with me."

Eva gave him a crazy look. "Well you thought wrong."

Brody laughed, but Bullet and Rolo never changed their expressions. Fiyah swallowed real hard. His dick was all the way soft now and a hint of fear was on his face.

Brody spoke to Fiyah over his shoulder, although his eyes never left Eva's face. "Mami fine as hell, man. But she's wild. Untrained. But it's cool. That's how I like 'em. There's something hot as fuck about holding 'em down and breaking 'em in . . ."

Eva smirked. This gigantic mothafucka wasn't nothing but a bitch beater. She despised niggahs like him, and these days instead of scaring her, cats like him pissed her the fuck off. She took a closer look at the girls who were sitting with Brody's crew. Them chicks were high as hell. Duji'd down. They sat plastered up against the wall like they was waiting for instructions. Every one of them was pretty and was slinging mad jewels from their ears, necks, and fingers. They had nice bodies too. High titties and long legs. But these chicks were tore the fuck down inside. Eva could tell.

She nodded toward Serena, then looked up at Brody with big eyes. "Like you broke her in?" Even in all her fly gear and expensive jewels, the young Latina girl looked like shit. She had a big nasty blister on her chest and was struggling to sit up straight while holding her hand against the side of her head.

Brody shrugged. "That ho is yesterday. You tonight. Come dance with me."

"Nah, that's okay. I'll pass."

"Bitch," Brody growled. He grabbed her arm and squeezed it hard. "Who the fuck is askin' you? I'm telling your ass—"

"Hey *yo*!!" Reem stormed into the VIP section making noise

with ill Nino and his entourage right behind him. "Muhfuck-in' *Fiyah*!" He brushed past Eva, winking at her on the sly tip. "My *niggah*!" he said loudly, frontin' like he hadn't just been outside chillin' with Fiyah earlier. "Man, what the fuck it *do*?"

Reem dapped Fiyah and turned to ill Nino.

"Yo, ill. This the cat I was telling you about. He just got off The Rock but his shit is official, man. That's real."

Eva was forgotten and all eyes were on ill Nino, including Brody's. Eva sighed. Reem was her boy and always had been. He had diverted the attention away from her giving her a chance to slide outta Brody's grip.

"Yo," Reem said to Fiyah. "Niggah stand up and meet the great ill Nino!"

Fiyah couldn't tell what the fuck was running through him harder. Fear of Brody or awe because of ill Nino. He stood up feeling like a starstruck little bitch.

"'Sup, man," he said, trying to sound stable.

They dapped and ill Nino nodded. "What's good? Reem said you got a pretty decent flow game."

"Yeah," Fiyah boasted. "I'm nice wit' it."

"Yo," Reem said, "I hope you was busy scribbling while you was pressing that bunk, ak 'cause you bout to do it next week, aiight? We gone be assessing cats for a minute and whoever comes out on top is gone get a chance to jump on tour with me and ill, man. Maybe even get a contract. So be ready to get up there and give up ya best shit. Leave it all over the mic. Ya feel me?"

"I feel you, man."

"Cool," Reem said, turning to leave. Eva had dipped, so he could get back to the DJ booth. "Then that's what's up. I talked you up real large, muhfuckah, so don't make me look bad. You best bring that shit right."

"I got this, baby. I'm ready."

ill Nino dapped Fiyah again on the way past. "Welcome back to the world."

He looked at Brody. "Be good, man. Hit me up the next time you in Miami."

Searching the crowd for Eva, Brody nodded, looking like a killer. "I'll holla."

Chapter 12

Reem dipped through the crowd, his eyes on alert. He'd seen what was going down with Brody from the DJ booth, and had decided to go check for Eva. He knew Brody wasn't one to be fucked with, so he had to play it proper. Reem had seen firsthand what Brody could put on a bitch. Eva was from Brooklyn and she knew the streets, but she had been through so fuckin' much when they were shorties back in Brooklyn that he hated to see her getting close to a ruthless renegade like Brody.

Reem had been dominating the club set for years and he'd seen all kinds of corruption. But Bricks wasn't no ordinary club, and Brody wasn't no ordinary niggah. While ballers with big bank clamored to get in the doors each weekend, the underbelly of Bricks could be cruel and gutter, and Brody was commanding niggahs from the helm, calling big shots. Drugs, porn, pimping, murdering . . . Brody and his crew ran rampant with all that. Bricks, and the CD/DVD-pressing record shop where hundreds of artists got dicked outta their rightful royalties mighta belonged to Daddy Dre on paper, but everybody in Harlem knew who was really running shit. What Reem couldn't figure out was why a chick like Eva would be rubbing up against a monster like Brody.

He caught up with her as she was coming out of the ladies' bathroom.

"Eva . . ." He held out his arms. "Whassup, baby doll."

"What's up, Reem." Eva hugged him tightly, kissing his cheek. "I'm cool."

"Didn't look that way a few minutes ago." He nodded toward the VIP section where Brody was still wrecking shit. "Why you mingling with that dude? King Brody ain't the kinda guy you wanna be conversating with, nah'mean?"

Eva frowned. "Tell that to your boy Fiyah. Brody got him wide open."

Reem nodded. "I'll school him, baby. I damn sure will. You just stay outta that niggah's biting range, ya hear? I don't wanna have to call my goonies from Brownsville to come up here and light Harlem up."

The music changed and Reem winced as some wack rapper started screaming into the mic. Eva laughed and Reem could see why Brody was jocking her. The girl was fine. Her skin was gorgeous brown. Her teeth were bright white and her curly hair was glossy, silky black.

"You don't have to call the goonies, Reem, but you better go handle that."

"Hell yeah." Reem grinned walking away. "Amateur muhfuckahs gone mess around and run everybody the fuck up outta here."

Eva laughed. She was glad Reem had moved to Harlem. He was a solid friend from Brooklyn and somebody she had entrusted with her deepest secrets.

"You a cool-ass little man, Reem."

"You know it, baby. I'm a small stick of dynamite, and I *blow* the shawties up all night!"

Reem walked off and ran into an extra tall Latina chick whose hips and breasts were from another planet. His eyes traveled the thirty miles from her feet up to her amazing face and he whistled real loud. "Goddamn, muhfuckah!" he moaned, adoring what he saw. "I'ma need a ladder to get up on all that!"

Still thinking about her, he slid past a side room where chicken wings and French fries were being cooked and sold. There was a long line of tipsy niggahs waiting to get at some bones, and as he walked past somebody reached out and touched his shoulder.

"Reem, what it be like, man?"

Reem grinned and gave his boy some dap. Mello was one hardbody, hardworking muhfuckah. Reem had put in a good word with Daddy Dre and had gotten Mello on at the record shop a year earlier. Dre had assigned him to a floater table that had him traveling all over Harlem selling bootleg CDs and DVDs for five dollars a whop. The cat had grinded like he'd been born for the job. In no time Mello had worked his way up to a permanent sidewalk spot on 125th Street. Prized real estate. And there wasn't a niggah in Harlem who could out hustle him or outsell him.

"It's all good, baby. Whattup?" Reem nodded toward the Friday night reggaeton crowd as they broke up the dance floor. "This ain't your usual night. You still on for tomorrow's set?"

Mello nodded. "Oh, yeah. I'll be here tomorrow, that's real. I'm just chillin', man. I swung by to hook up with Eva. Her cousin hit the bricks and shit. She wanted to come out and show him around tonight."

Reem nodded. "Yeah. My dude Fiyah. I just seen that cat. He's got skills, man. I'ma put him on the mic at next week's competition. Let him show ill what he got."

"Show ill what?"

"Yo, we 'bout to go back out on tour, man. All them illegal units Brody got y'all niggahs moving on the streets be eating into an artist's profits, nah'mean? Performing is the only way to get ya paper up and stack ya cream these days. We gone take a new artist on the road with us. You know. Somebody nasty on the mic who can heat the crowd up before we come out and blast 'em."

"Yo!" Mello looked pissed. "What the fuck is up with that? Why y'all niggahs ain't doing that kinda shit on rap night?"

"Not my call." Reem shrugged. "ill asked for a reggaeton rapper, bruh. He wants somebody who can flog they asses in English and in Spanish."

Mello stood there nodding, taking it all in. He was still kicking it hard with Reem, but a steely look had entered his eyes. "Yeah. I hear you talkin' that shit, man. I hear you talkin' it."

Mello watched his baby crossing the room. She was dodging niggahs.

Stray hands were reaching out for her, trying to touch her and get her attention. She got hit on by two players he recognized from the L.A. Lakers, and by a screenwriter with big black glasses and thin lips. An old-head playa he'd seen pimping broads on the avenue invited her to take a ride in his rimmed-out caddy, and another dude who was dressed in a business suit told her he had a yacht down on Chelsea Piers that he knew she'd like to see. The offers for drinks, weed, dope, and dick were raining down on her as she killed her shorts and brushed off one baller after another, and Mello was proud of her for handling her bizz.

She acted surprised when he ran up behind her and covered her eyes with his hands, but then she relaxed. She knew those hands. He let her feel his wood and she laughed. She knew that dick that was poking her from behind too.

"Hey, baby." She turned around in his arms and let her body go soft. "I thought you mighta changed your mind about coming out tonight."

Mello grinned. "What? And leave the finest woman in Harlem alone in a room full of snakes?" He kissed her. "The music is hot. I'ma have to start coming out on Fridays more often." He saw a look on her face that concerned him. "You aiight?"

"I'm cool."

"Well Mello's here now. And it's about to get better. Dance with me, Miss Lady. I got some rhythm I wanna bump on you."

They moved out onto the dance floor where Eva started working her hips. Mello couldn't stop grinning. The Dominican in her was showing as she twisted it up on him and grinded her lower body until it looked like a worm.

Luckily, Brody was too preoccupied to notice. He was surrounded by three hot young'uns and had a tit in one hand and an ass cheek in the other. His fingers splashed in a pool of pussy as the young girl sitting on his hand humped her heart out.

Charlene and Brody's boys was drinking Moët and hitting lines, but Serena was damn near unconscious. Brody's brother Bullet sat beside her trying his best to help her get a grip and snap out of it.

Fiyah was balling. He had a chocolate babe on his lap and she was riding his dick through his pants. He had passed on the Chronic because he was scared his PO might drug test him, but he sucked down Krug like it was water from an open faucet. He had seen Eva fuckin' up heads as she danced on the floor, and figured the tall, good-looking guy leaning all over her was the cat they called Mello.

Fiyah was just juiced enough not to start no shit. Somehow he had to get Eva to drop that muhfuckah and concentrate on Brody, but right now he had a wet pussy sloshing around on his lap and he was concentrating on that.

He did take notice, though, when Bullet suddenly pressed his phone to his ear and stood up. Moments later Fiyah watched as Bullet left Serena's side then walked over to his brother and yanked the young bitch off his lap. He whispered something to Brody, who looked at his boys and gave them the silent signal that it was time to bounce. Fiyah was apprehensive as Brody looked at him too. He was waiting for Reem to give him the signal so he could get on stage and flaunt his shit. But Brody was looking crazy and his message was clear: get the fuck up, 'cause you coming with us.

Fiyah followed Brody and his crew outside to the whip. They hopped in and Rolo pushed the pedal over to Spanish Harlem. They pulled up outside of a small apartment building where a couple of young hoods were hanging out on the stoop.

"Man the muhfuckin' whip," Brody barked at his brother as they walked toward the doors.

Bullet balked. "Yo, bruh. That's what the fuck we got Rolo for."

Brody got swole. "I said stay with the muhfuckin' whip!"

Bullet turned around and headed back to the Escalade, but not before Fiyah saw a spark of rage in his eyes.

They walked toward a small door on the side of the porch, right under the stairs. Brody kicked that shit in with one foot. It was a dice game in an unfinished basement. Cats were playing C-low in groups, six and seven deep. Fiyah stood back as Brody and his posse went to work.

They grabbed a young Hispanic cat and dug in on his ass. Seeing that a notoriously brutal crew had rolled in, niggahs scooped up their dice and their doe and scattered. Fiyah watched the kid get his grill busted and his dome disfigured. He figured out by all the shit they were talking that the kid owed Brody some money.

"Come get you summa this!" Brody turned to Fiyah and demanded. He was bombing the kid with such devastating killer blows that there wasn't much left of the cat for Fiyah to get.

Fiyah got in there, though. He wasn't fuckin' stupid. He jabbed at the bleeding dude. The cat was so fucked up he was already sleep on his feet. If Rolo and two other dudes wasn't holding him up he woulda been out cold on the concrete.

As the rest of them fist-happy fools slammed the kid from wall to wall, Brody leaned close to Fiyah and whispered, "This is how I roll when a niggah fails to deliver on what he owes me. Ya heard?"

Fiyah nodded, then winced as a spray of blood flew from the Puerto Rican kid's busted mouth. He'd heard that muhfuckah all right. He heard him loud as a mug. And then he felt him too. Brody hit Fiyah so hard he thought his heart would stop.

Them cats were done battering the kid and now they were going for a chunk of Fiyah's ass.

Even while balled up on the ground and protecting his face, Fiyah knew Brody was in control. His boys were wailing on him, but they were also practicing restraint. Fiyah stayed down and rolled with the punches. He'd taken worse ass-kickings than this before.

When it was over, Brody put his foot on Fiyah's head and pressed down hard enough to get his full attention.

"It seems like you got a little problem, ak."

Fiyah didn't answer. He gritted his teeth as his face was smashed between King Brody's boot and the dirty ground.

"For some reason, your cousin didn't seem all that happy to see me tonight. What you tell her, man? What your cousin got against me?"

Fiyah gasped in pain. "It ain't you, man . . ."

Brody rolled his weight up onto his foot.

Fiyah squealed. "That's just Eva," he managed to squeak out. "You too big, Brody. Powerful. You control drugs all over Harlem . . . and Eva . . ."

Fiyah felt like his brain was gonna shoot out through his nostrils.

"Eva used to be a junkie. She used to shoot smack, man. Right in her neck."

Instantly Brody stepped off his head. Fiyah grabbed his temple and gasped from the pain.

"That fine bitch used to be a junkie?" Brody's tone was incredulous.

Fiyah nodded, praying this would be the info that would turn Brody off on Eva forever. Brody could have any chick he wanted. An ex-junkie prolly wasn't one of them.

"Yeah," Fiyah told him. "A long time ago. She was just a kid."

Brody thought for a moment, then reached down and grabbed Fiyah's arm. He yanked him up on his feet and brushed the dirt off his shirt.

"Cool!" he said, the happy grin back on his face again. "I like junkies!"

Chapter 13

Eva and Mello had turned shit out on the dance floor at Bricks, then gone back to Mello's rented room to chill for the night. The next morning was a gray and rainy New York City day, and Eva lay next to Mello with her eyes wide open as his snores rose into the air.

She had played shit off lovely the night before when King Brody had messed around and licked her hand, but the reality was that she was worried. About Fiyah. The fact that he had gotten in deep with a maniac like Brody meant that Fiyah hadn't learned shit after all those months he'd spent in jail. India's murder had forced Eva to see the light of reality when it came to her life, but Fiyah was still stuck in the same old mind-set they both used to be in back in the day when they were hustling on the streets together and cooking up schemes to do everything from snatching pocketbooks from old ladies to setting up and double-crossing unsuspecting johns who were willing to pay for a piece of Eva's prime young pussy.

With thoughts of Fiyah weighing heavily on her mind, Eva climbed across Mello as quietly as she could and got out of bed. Wearing a wife beater and a sky-blue thong, she walked over to his large window with the brick wall view and looked out as the rain came down heavily over the grimy city.

Her forehead rested on the cool glass as she thought back over her life and its many twists and turns. Fiyah had been right by her side for most of her journey, and the only thing he didn't really know about her was the fact that she had given birth to a baby. Eva knew Fiyah would still love her despite that horrible thing she had done in the darkness that night, but she also knew that him and Milena would press her to go get her son from Miss Threet and bring him into their world where family took care of family.

She just wasn't ready to do that. Her son was being well taken care of right where he was, and there was nothing Eva could offer him yet, not even the love of her cousin and aunt, that would take the place of what Miss Threet was giving him in Brooklyn. Sometimes Eva wondered, but there was no way she could guess the identity of the man who had fathered her child. She had always suspected it was her mother's boyfriend Jahden, but she couldn't prove it. Whoever the father was, it didn't matter to Eva and it didn't make her love her son any less. Her whole life was now geared toward getting her future together so she could one day go down to Brooklyn and get her baby and bring him into her life. But first that life had to be a worthy one. A life that was fit for a child to enter and to be nurtured and cared for the way he deserved to be. Eva was hoping that life might one day include Mello and that their love thing would last forever and Mello would become the father her son had never had. But that didn't seem likely because she hadn't even first told Mello that she had a son. The only person alive who knew was Reem, the cat who was truly her heart and had fed her and looked out for her when they was kids back in Brooklyn. Eva trusted Reem with her life and her secrets, and she knew he would never betray her in any way. Life had betrayed her enough on its own. She recited a rhyme she'd read somewhere that seemed to signify her destiny from the moment of her birth.

> *Monday's child is fair of face,*
> *Tuesday's child is full of grace,*
> *Wednesday's child is full of woe,*
> *Full of woe, full of woe, full of woe . . .*

That was her. A Wednesday's child. Eva's mind and heart were both heavy when Mello slipped up behind her and took her by surprise. He scooped her up from her ankles, ran his hands up her legs, then cupped her hips and pushed his hard dick against her as he embraced her and nuzzled her neck softly.

"What you doing?" he asked sleepily.

"Did I ever tell you that I was born on a Wednesday? Yeah. I'm a Wednesday's child. Full of woe."

"Well you one fine-ass Wednesday for a Saturday morning."

"I thought you was sleep," she said, leaning back against him.

"I was," he mumbled. "But then I missed you." He kissed her collarbone with warm lips. "Why you up so early?"

Eva shrugged. "I couldn't sleep. Too much stuff running around in my head. I think I worry too much."

Mello grinned. "You aint gotta worry about me, Mami. I'm hood certified, baby. I gets mine in."

Eva smiled. "I know you can handle yours, Mello. It's Fiyah who's got me kinda worried. He just got home and he's already making stupid decisions. His head is in a worse spot than it was in when he left. Life is short. He needs to elevate his game. For real."

"You ain't gotta worry about your cousin, baby. He's a grown-ass man and that niggah looks well fed and well fuckin' rested to me. Hey, I'm out here grinding two jobs just to pay for this shitty little room and you crackin' your hustle 24/7 too. Fiyah ain't under no stress, baby. He's kickin' back and relaxing harder than both of us put together."

Eva nodded. She could feel Mello, but still . . . she felt Fiyah too.

"He just had a hard-ass life, that's all."

Mello bitched. "Shit, we all had it hard. My moms used to sell rock when I was a tyke. My pops was one of her best customers. All kinds of scary fiends ran in and out of our crib around the clock. I got shook just by closing my eyes at night. I was too scared somebody was gonna roll in the joint and stick us up while we were sleep. If my moms hadn't died when she did, all of us woulda prolly got killed living up in there. *That* shit was hard."

Eva thought about her own life for a second then said, "Yeah. Parents can really fuck you up if they ain't careful. That's why you really gotta have your shit together and be stable before you try to raise a kid."

Mello turned her around in his arms and started kissing her neck.

"Well, we ain't gotta worry about nothing like that right now, baby. But I do want some kids one day. I love kids. I want a whole house full of them jokers."

Eva swallowed hard. She prayed things would fall into place and her son would have a father like Mello some day. That was her greatest wish for her baby, and she asked God every day to one day provide her son with a man in his life who would love him like he was his own.

Eva was torn up over her own role in her baby's life. Whenever she saw young girls out pushing their babies in strollers her heart would break. She didn't know what their situations were, but they were all young single mothers living in the hood, so they couldn't have had it easy. Sometimes Eva felt real guilty for not getting her son and struggling with him like other young girls did. Some got on welfare, others had baller boyfriends who sold product and kept their shorties laced in jewels and name-brand baby clothes. Other chicks had mothers who helped them raise their kids so they could still go to school and make something out of their lives.

But Eva had none of that. And besides, she didn't want to struggle and make her son struggle with her. Why short-change him like that when there was an angel named Miss Threet who was giving him all the love and care he needed? All the love and care she had?

"Where you at, girl?" Mello joked as she stood like a statue while he planted soft kisses all over her. He raised her wife beater and let his lips trail down her toned stomach until they reached the waistband of her thong. His strong hands cupped her curvy hips as he slipped his tongue in and out of her navel, then dipped lower and pulled her elastic band with his teeth.

He dropped to his knees as his fingers kneaded her thighs. Eva felt slickness seeping from her lower lips as his hot breath tickeled her stomach. She raised her arms and slipped off her wife beater, letting her big juicy titties bounce free. Her nipples were stiff and beautifully centered on her firm, round breasts and Mello moaned as they jiggled above him.

He slid his hands down to her ankles, brought them up the back of her thighs, and over her ass. His fingers curled around until they cupped her thick melons and Eva moaned and her pussy squirted as he opened his mouth and placed long wet licks all around one breast before taking it into his mouth and sucking on it to a silent rhythm.

Eva reached for his dick and held it as it throbbed in her soft hands. She stroked it through his boxers, then freed it and jerked it up and down, her hand closing over the head with each motion as she squeezed it and massaged it until Mello moaned.

"Let's fuck right here," Mello whispered when Eva tried to pull him over to the bed. He pushed her little thong string aside and lifted her left leg until it was resting in the crook of his arm. Pressing her backward, he guided his dripping head into her moist hole, then bent his head and licked her pretty nipples at the same time.

Mello sighed as his dick slid in and out of her, Eva's pussy getting hotter and wetter by the second. He held her ass in both palms and massaged its fluffy meat, loving the weight of it in his hands. Reaching underneath her body, he felt his dick pumping and driving deeply into her. He held her pussy in the palm of his hand and shuddered as his dick pile-drove into her squishy flesh.

He rolled her ass cheek around with his palm, moving her the way he wanted her to move. His fingers crept up to her crack and he played with her asshole before inserting his long middle finger straight up in there.

Eva bucked back on him and arched her spine. She leaned forward and bit down on his nipple, sucking it hard, then she cried out as he pummeled her harder, forcing her to cum in big fat pleasure waves.

Her body vibrated on Mello's rigid dick as she tried to catch her breath. He held back for her, plunging in slow but not deep, until she was ready to take what he was slanging once again.

With her pussy extra wet, Eva opened up to him even wider, and Mello dug her out with his entire muscle. He ran his hands up and down her arms and around her back and cupped her ass. Stroke after stroke her juices squirted out and his balls contracted as the head of his dick banged up in her gut. The window was cold on Eva's back as her man spurted his seed deep inside of her, cumming in big waves as she clamped down with her pussy muscles and milked every drop of love he had for her right out through the tip of his dick.

"I luh you, Eva," Mello panted and slobbered into her hair as he came.

Eva pressed her face to his chest. His heart pounded on her lips.

"Thank you, baby," she whispered, and she meant that shit. "Thank you."

Chapter 14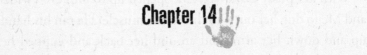

Serena hurried up the stairs of the six-floor apartment building. She had on a plain brown sweat suit and a pair of brown Gucci sneakers. Her short stylish hair was covered by a brown and beige scarf that she pulled down low on her forehead. Even though she wasn't even eighteen, Serena held on to the banister and pulled herself along like she was much, much older. Every fuckin' inch of her was hurting, and underneath her jacket she'd caked a thick gob of Vaseline over the B brand that was finally starting to heal on her right breast.

Brody was a dangerous man, and Serena was nervous. If she'd been spotted coming here, or if somebody even hinted to Brody that they might have seen her around this building, she knew what would be up. She'd be another New York City casualty. Her battered and broken body would be found in a Dumpster somewhere. Beaten. Tortured. And just like the other chicks he had discarded before her, shot up full of dope.

Serena stood in front of an apartment on the fourth floor. She rang the bell with quick, short jabs. Like a terrified mouse, she glanced over her shoulder about fifty times and when the door was opened she let her black, swollen eyes do the talking for her.

Bullet stood there with a surprised look on his face. He was a handsome cat. Tall and built. Not as big as Brody, but not as fearsome either. Bullet was missing that whole psycho thing that Brody always had lurking in his eyes, and as Serena stood before him, she implored him for help without words.

Bullet didn't speak either. He looked at the gorgeous young girl that his brother had turned out and was using as a punching bag, and his mouth hardened. Slowly, she raised her eyes so he could see her face. She let her scarf slide from her head, and then he saw it all. He winced at the bruises. At the amount of damage that those big, rock-breaking hands had done. Bullet couldn't stop himself. A gangsta at heart, he also had a mother. And a sister, and two nieces. He reached out and touched her battered face. Then he took her hand and gently guided her inside. He kissed her palm, then closed the door behind her.

Brody and his boys were watching a hot XXX flick in one of Bricks's bunkers when Bullet showed up. He gave the secret knock and almost immediately a black door the size of a double-wide garage was raised on its tracks. Bullet entered the room, which was large enough to hold six luxury cars. The bunkers were straight-up tight, and had every amenity one might need for the task at hand. They were all air-conditioned and well decorated, and this one contained a king-sized bed and two leather couches, carpet on the floors, and a small kitchen and bathroom area off to the side.

There were three other sheds just like this one in the back of Bricks. The one they were in was used to film some of the grimiest porno flicks on the underground market, and the others were used to burn and copy the tens of thousands of bootleg CDs and DVDs that made the black-market trade such a lucrative business.

Brody had a team of street hawkers, organized by Island, who hand-sold pirated units to the masses every day. They owned and operated scores of street tables in every borough of New York City. All were manned by persistent urban salesmen. And all were highly lucrative and kept Brody's phat pockets lined with bank.

Bullet glanced at the screen. They were watching a skin flick they had just recently filmed right there on the bed. He remembered it so well because it was so fuckin' brutal and so fuckin' graphic. And because it was one of the few flicks that his brother had actually starred in.

A lot of people didn't know it, but athletes and ballers had a fetish about underground porn. Some of them paid good dollars to get hooked up with a hot bitch on camera. They usually wanted to do some perverted shit to the girl that emphasized their power. Like pissing all over her face or in her hair, making her lick their assholes, or by using their fists in a way that made her endure a lot of pain while she was being submissive.

Bullet had seen all that shit. He loved pussy just as much as the next niggah, and there were times when he blew a bitch's back out as he slammed her pussy bone real good. But he wasn't into some of the shit these other cats dug. He especially wasn't into the shit that his brother got off on, and looking at Brody on the big screen now jerked his blood pressure up higher than it already was.

Fuck music was playing in the background and Brody was dogging the young bitch. He had his joint so far up her ass that she screamed with each thrust. It wasn't about sex for him. It was about dehumanizing the ho and torturing her. He held her down by her neck and used one huge arm to scoop her middle up so that her ass was high in the air. He slapped her jiggling flesh and pinched her hard with both hands. Everywhere he touched her he left a bright red splotch on her light skin. That niggah yanked her titties like he was milking a cow. He placed both hands on her ass cheeks and spread them so wide he coulda split her from one end to the other. Then he leaned over and placed both elbows in the small of her back, and pressed down hard. He was still slanging dick up in her as he tried his best to break her little spine in half. Suddenly Brody had some kinda prod in his hand. Bullet remembered walking out the shed on this part, with the young girl's screams echoing in his ears. Yeah, the dumb ho was screaming fuck me daddy, gimme more, more, more, but you could tell she didn't mean that shit. She'd been paid long dollars to play to the cameras, and that's exactly what she was gonna do even if it killed her.

Bullet watched his brother watch himself on the screen. Brody had a crazy little smile on his face. Like he was proud of his performance and was really into that shit hard.

"Yo, man," Bullet interrupted. He broke up all that concentration on Brody's dick game on purpose. Wasn't shit sexy about it no way. He busted the look of annoyance that crossed his brother's face, but Bullet was fuckin' annoyed too. "I need to holla at ya for a minute, bruh."

Brody stormed over toward the kitchen on his brother's heels. The niggah had the crazy look in his eyes but Bullet didn't give a fuck. He used to look up to Brody and they used to be real close. Every fuckin' day of jail time Bullet had ever done was behind some shit he'd gotten into because of his brother. He'd been a loyal lieutenant and had followed Brody's lead in all the drug-slanging, bitch-banging, and rival-hanging shit his brother cooked up. Bullet had crossed the line and slumped cats that he really liked and was cool with over his brother. All because they were blood and he was loyal down to his bones. But shit was changing. Brody had become crueler and more vicious over the years. Especially while he was on lock. He'd been lucky to get outta jail at all after all the convicts he'd buck-fiffed and smiley-faced up in the pen. Their own mother was even leery of the niggah now. She wouldn't even let him in the crib unless Bullet was there with him. And even then she kept her teenaged granddaughters away from him by making sure they stayed in a locked room until he left.

"What the fuck, niggah?" Brody held his arms up. "Didn't you see I was doing something?"

Bullet laid it straight out for the maniac.

"Look man, you need to chill with some of this shit, bruh." He gestured to the half-naked broads who were lounging on the sofas zooted out of their minds. "I'm just looking out for you, man. One of these bitches gone amp up on ya ass one day if you don't slow ya hand roll. You feel me?"

Brody narrowed his eyes. "What the fuck did you just say?"

Bullet squared up to his brother. They stood toe-to-toe, looking just alike. Except one was truly concerned, and the other was straight fuckin' crazy.

"We got a moms, B. We got a little sister too. How you can beat these bitches so far down is a mystery to me. I'm your brother so I'm telling you, man. You need to chill with some of that shit."

Brody moved so fast there was no time to react. He turned halfway left and bent slightly at the knees. He came up fast and hard, swinging his massive hand around in a vicious back-handed arc. His ring ripped straight across Bullet's cheek, drawing blood.

"Muhfuckah!" Brody raged. He lunged at Bullet again, and it took every man in the shed to jump on him and wrestle him down. "Don't you *ever* tell me what to do to my bitches! I'll roll ya fuckin' dome like you *one of those* bitches!"

Bullet just stood there. He didn't even touch his face. He just let the blood flow unchecked. He had seen his brother black out on many people and on many occasions. But they were blood. *Blood.* Just like the warm liquid that was now dripping down his face. Bullet knew his brother was off, but he never thought Brody would cross that invisible bloodline when it came to him. At least now he knew that he'd been wrong.

"I wish them old drunk bitches would shut the fuck up!" Fiyah muttered, tapping his pencil on his notepad and staring out at the rain. He was sitting in his small bedroom trying to lay some lyrics on paper, but Milena had company in the living room and they were making all kinds of noise.

He bumped out a beat on the windowsill, then scribbled a few words in his notebook. He paused and listened close to the beat in his head. His fingers drummed furiously, trying to capture the right flow. Then he wrote a couple more words before throwing his pencil against the wall.

It was too fuckin' noisy up in there.

Milena and her loud-ass friends! They were smoking weed

and drinking beer and shaking their asses to some live Big Daddy Kane.

Fiyah tried again. He muttered his flow, listened to the silent beat, then re-mouthed the words, fucking them up.

"Yo, Ma!"

Milena didn't answer, but he could hear them laughing.

"Ma!"

No response, but the laughter got louder.

Fuck!

Fiyah stormed out of his room but slowed his roll at the doorway of the living room. There were a bunch of Hispanic women in there. They were shaking their wide asses, jiggling their stomachs, and winding their hips to the beat. Fiyah started to say something smart, but one look from his mother and he checked himself.

She walked over to him holding her drink. "I have company, Fuego," she said. Milena looked nothing like her friends. With her slim body and youthful face, she looked twenty years younger than every other woman in the room. "I told you, we get together once a month now. We started it when you were in jail and we're not gonna stop just because you got out." She sipped from her glass and the ice cubes clinked. "And we don't really wanna see no men while we doing it neither. Why don't you go somewhere? Better yet, the rent is damn near due. Be a man and go make some money."

"It's raining out there, Ma."

"And what? A little water is gonna kill you? I walked those streets in the rain many nights when you were locked up, Fuego. Just to keep a fuckin' roof over our heads. I got wet plenty of times too. And the water didn't kill me neither. It just washed away my sins."

Fiyah stared at her. Something had changed in his moms.

She'd never been a soft woman, but she was harder now. Even harder than she'd been back in the day when she was into her drugs. He gave her a long look, then walked back into his room. He picked up his notepad and his pencil and looked out the window. The rain was stopping. Fiyah pulled on a hoody and stuck his pad and pencil in the front pocket. Then he walked out his room and into the living room. He brushed past one of his mother's fat-ass friends as he went by, and she reached out and pinched him hard on the ass.

"Sexy *culito*!" she giggled as Fiyah slammed outta the apartment with the sound of contemptuous female laughter ringing loudly in his ears.

Chapter 15

Mello walked down the streets of Harlem taking in the sights. With all the urban stores and pretty girls, it was easy not to see the darker, seedier things that made the hood he loved strike fear in the hearts of outsiders.

Up ahead of him a young wanna-be baller came out of a Spanish store carrying a bag of groceries. The chocolate-faced boy had a real bad limp and a peasy head. A group of cute but hard-looking teenaged girls passed by him and the young'un's head whipped around on his shoulders. He stepped dead in a big rain puddle, and when he tried to jump out the water he jumped right into Mello.

They bumped and the boy dropped his bag of food. Mello grinned and waved off the boy's "my bads." He scooped up a can of Carnation Evaporated Milk and tossed it toward the kid, who caught it in the bag.

The kid limped down Lenox Avenue for several blocks. He came up on a numbers spot where a crew of hardhead boys were standing around trying to get into some shit. They spotted him and the littlest dude in the bunch tried to roll on him. The kid limped on faster, and the crew followed him. Talking shit right on his heels.

Fiyah came around the corner on his way to his spot. He scoped out the kid, and then the small, boisterous crowd that was following him, and saw the fear in the boy's eyes.

"Whattup, Lil Man?" Fiyah said. He walked up on the kid like he knew him, and threw his arm around the kid's shoulder. Fiyah had been heading in the opposite direction, but he figured what the fuck. He turned around and gave the crew of hardheads a deadly look, then walked off with the limping boy under his protection.

Fiyah wasn't new to Harlem and he knew how hard it was out on these streets. It didn't matter how young those kids was. They would stick a blade in a niggah or pop ya ass off in the blink of an eye. He knew the trick was to show them that G code. That look that said I will slay your ten-year-old ass and then wait for ya daddy to go get his tool.

It worked.

"Thanks, man." The boy looked at Fiyah like he was a superhero for real, and after walking beside the kid as he limped home to give his grandmother her groceries, Fiyah walked back in the other direction. He stopped at a small area across from his crib that had a little bit of grass and a couple of garbage cans that bums set on fire in the winter to keep warm. The lot used to have a house on it, but it had been condemned and torn down by the city years ago.

Fiyah found a few soggy pieces of cardboard and sat down to let his words flow. And they did too. Flowed like sweet water. His lyrics came out in a clever mixture of Spanish and English that pleased the fuck outta him. He wanted his shit to sound perfect for Friday night, and he placed each word deliberately, erasing and rewriting if something was even slightly off.

Time passed as Fiyah got his shit off in his little notepad. He got carried away and wrote some more, until he could no longer see the lines in his little book. He stuck the notepad into his hoody pocket and held his pencil like a mic. He spit his awesome flow out loud and practiced his stage moves until his delivery and performance were perfect.

Fiyah was so into his imaginary set that he lost track of the time. He glanced at his watch and cursed. Panicked, he ran through the old lot and toward his building, so bent on getting to the crib that he never even noticed when his notepad fell out of his pocket and tumbled down to the grass.

Fiyah was sweating when he stepped through the door of his apartment. The television was playing on a Spanish language channel, and Milena was lounging in her chair. The living room was trashed from her company. A cigarette dangled from her fingers and a tall can of beer was wedged between her trim thighs.

She turned her head as Fiyah walked in.

"Your ass is late. Your parole officer just left. He said to tell you this is strike one. He said the next time he comes through after curfew your ass better be here."

She took a long pull on her cigarette, then went back to watching television like it wasn't no thang. Fiyah walked into his bedroom, patting his pocket as he searched for his notepad. A look of panic crossed his face. He glanced at his watch and then ran back out into the night.

It was dark as shit in the abandoned lot. Fiyah retraced his steps with his hands patting the grass in a wide arc. He found it! It was in the damp grass halfway between the cardboard he'd been sitting on and the sidewalk. Relieved, he stuck the notepad down in his back pants pocket. But as soon as he turned to go he got hit from both sides.

It was Bullet and that man-ass Rolo.

Them two big goons squeezed him on either side like bookends. Fiyah braced himself because he had a good idea of what was coming next.

"What it do, Fiyah?" Bullet said. His voice was low and vicious.

Fiyah shrugged. Bullet sounded fed. He had a long nasty cut down his face that Fiyah could see even in the darkness. "I'm chillin' man."

"In the muhfuckin' dark?"

Fiyah shrugged. "It's quiet out here. I like to keep the bullshit to a minimum when I'm doing my thang, ya dig?"

Bullet nodded. "Oh, okay, 'cause my brother Brody. You remember Brody, right? That big niggah who can brody a li'l niggah like you for your life? He's waiting for you. Go get ya cute fuckin' cousin and bring her to the crib on Lexington and don't be fuckin' late. Ya heard?"

"Man, fuck you."

Bullet snatched Fiyah's chest so hard he couldn't breathe. "Listen up, you dumb little bitch. You mighta been in the joint with my brother but you ain't seen one of his ass-fuckings yet. That niggah say he wants your cousin? Then bring him the bitch and be done with it." Bullet released him and Fiyah staggered backward. "You better have that ho at the crib in a quick minute."

Rolo caught Fiyah from behind and yoked him hard, slamming him backward across her iron thigh as Bullet poured his fury out on Fiyah's face. They fucked him over real good, busting his lips and almost breaking his jaw. Fiyah had taken ass-whippings in the past, but they were putting it on him so good that this one was one of the worst.

By the time they got tired his left eye was so swollen he could barely see out that shit. Fiyah staggered back across the street to his building. Blood was running from his nose and it felt like a couple of his teeth were loose. Even though he was in bad condition, Fiyah counted it as all good. He could survive a beat-down. What scared the fuck outta him was the thought of Brody coming after him with a burner. Ready to dead him in a split second.

Fiyah literally crawled up the steps in his building. He didn't know what the fuck it was gonna take to convince Eva that she needed to get down some kinda way with this program, but for his life, and for hers too, she was gonna have to play the fuckin' cards they'd both been dealt. Because this time the beast had sent a dyke bitch and his brother to deliver his message. The next time that psycho muhfuckah would be coming to bite them himself.

Eva had finished up her shoot early and taken the train down to Brooklyn. Brownsville was congested with all kinds of people and walking through the projects always brought back sad memories for her, although she forced herself to hold on to the thought of what was good about the place. Her son was here, and he was happy and healthy. Eva thanked God for that and she always made sure she came around in the late afternoons when Miss Threet might have him playing outside.

On the few occasions that Eva had come to building 420 in

the spring and summer and her baby wasn't outside on a nice day, she had called her old friend Sherri out the window then stood there talking to her long enough for Miss Threet to hear her on the second floor and peep out her own window.

Always, always, Miss Threet seemed glad to see Eva. She would come outside and tell all her foster kids to go over and say hi to Eva and give her a big hug, especially Cameron, and then she'd hold long conversations with Eva, asking about her dreams and what she had planned for her future.

"Do good things and go real far," Miss Threet would always say to her. "Life only hurts until it starts feeling good, baby. Everything that is back here for you, will be right here waiting after you make something of yourself and reach some of your goals, Eva. Just keep praying and asking God to bless you, and ask Him to bless me and all these beautiful children I got here with me too."

Looking at her son brought great joy and great sadness to her heart. Eva was so happy and grateful for the way Miss Threet was raising him and how she seemed to love him so much and how her baby seemed to love Miss Threet right back. He was always shy with Eva, and she told herself that was only because he didn't know her. But he was hers, there was no disputing that. Those twin strawberry-shaped birthmarks under their chins was their secret connection, and Eva looked forward to the day when she could come totally clean with Miss Threet and tell her the truth about the baby boy she had rescued from the laundry mat early one morning four years ago.

She was tired by the time she climbed back on the number three train back to Harlem. Mello was spittin' spoken word at the Corner Pocket Poetry Café tonight, but Eva had already told him she had something to do and wouldn't be able to make it down to see him, so they had agreed to hook up the next day. It was dark in the apartment when she unlocked the door, and she crept into the living room on her toes. Her aunt Milena was asleep in her chair with beer fumes coming off her in waves. A lit cigarette hung between her fingers. Eva cursed under her breath as she took it and put it out in the lid of a mayonnaise jar that had taken the place of an ashtray.

Creeping into her bedroom, Eva tried hard to be quiet. She hated coming home late and waking Rosa up in the middle of the night. That shit was traumatic. When she was Rosa's age she'd been awakened many times in the dark of night. Either by loud, drunken voices, or by painful adult hands. Either way Eva remembered being terrified and disoriented as she came out of her sleep. She wanted Rosa to sleep straight through the night with nothing but sweet dreams to remember in the mornings.

Standing in the darkness, Eva peeled off the cute little dress she had worn to work. Her bare breasts stood out prominently in the moonlight, and her flat stomach and round ass were ever sexy in her bright orange thong. She switched on the small fan that was on her nightstand, aimed it at her bed, then flopped down on top of her covers to enjoy the breeze.

She turned her head and her eyes fell on a picture of her and Fiyah when they were kids. It had been taken at South Street Seaport and they were both licking from the same strawberry ice-cream cone. Eva smiled as she remembered that day. Her father had taken the picture and sent it to Milena when she was in rehab. Some of her best memories of growing up were when Fiyah lived with them in Brooklyn.

Eva turned her head back and Fiyah was standing in her doorway. There was blood on his face and craziness in his eyes.

"Get fuckin' dressed."

"What?" Eva jumped to cover her body. Her breasts were

too full for her small hands, and she snatched her dress off the floor and held it under her chin. "Why didn't you knock? What the hell happened to your face?!"

"*You* happened to my fuckin' face. Get dressed."

"What you talking about, Fiyah?"

"Get the fuck dressed now, Eva!"

"Stop fuckin' yellin! Rosa's sleep! What the hell is going on?"

Fiyah crossed the room and got up in her face. "Ask me one more question, Eva. Go 'head. Ask me one more fuckin' question."

Eva was stunned. She didn't know who the fuck this cat was who looked like Fiyah. This cat was off the charts, and his whole grill had been busted.

She turned her back and started pulling her sundress over her head.

"Nah. Don't put on that old-lady shit. Put on some club clothes, goddammit. Something tight that a niggah's gonna really like. Get some of them fuckin' Birthday Cake shorts you be sportin' for that poser-ass Mello."

"Poser? You's a fuckin' poser!"

Fiyah barked on her. "Put some muthafuckin' shit on!"

Then just like Eva had feared, Rosa woke up.

"Eva?" the little girl said. Her voice trembled in the night and Eva's heart cracked. The last thing she wanted to do was put a single ounce of fear in Rosa's heart. India's murder had already left enough of that there.

"Go back to sleep, Rosa," Fiyah told the child. "Everything is okay." Then he grilled Eva again. "Get fuckin' dressed, Eva. I mean that shit."

"To go where, Fiyah? I ain't going nowhere unless I know where the hell it is."

"We going to a party."

"Where at?"

"At my manz crib. Across town on Lexington Avenue."

Eva cursed. "Oh, so you taking me over there so you can dish my ass off to Brody? Hell fuckin' no, Fuego! You ain't selling me out like that!"

"Eva, all you gotta do is play along with him for a hot minute. Ain't nobody asking you to have a baby for that niggah!"

She tried to push past him and get out the door, but Fiyah moved faster. He swung her around by one arm and she went sailing onto her bed. Then he dove on top of her and held her down. "Bitch you wanna live?" he said, his eyes wild, his mouth inches from her face. "You wanna eat? You wanna grind? You wanna fuck, Evita? Then do what the fuck I tell you to do!"

"Why? So that mothafuckah can put his brand on me? So he can fuck me up and scramble my brain and put lumps all over my fuckin' head?"

"All that swagger is for them *other* bitches!" Fiyah exploded. "Them dumb hoes! He ain't gone do none a that shit to you and he already told me that! Brody just wanna take care of your stupid ass! You ain't gotta stay with him long, Eva. Just chill for a quick fuckin' minute. He'll give you any fuckin' thing you want! Jewels, clothes, a brand new whip, you name it . . ."

"I don't want *shit* that maniac got! I see how he takes care of his bitches. He shoots them up with dope then fucks them up with both fists!"

"Don't play yourself, Eva. Brody is feeling you. Them other bitches don't even count. You're the one who's gonna have all the status. He'll bump all them guttersnipe chickens off the throne just to get with you."

"He can keep his birds. He just can't have me."

"You don't get it. Me and him had an understanding, Eva. That cat's about to come at my throat!"

"And so what? You just said fuck me? You get down with a fuckin' beast in jail and then toss me off just so he can eat?"

"You *owe* me!" Fiyah exploded. "*My* life was on the line, not yours! I went to jail for your stupid fuckin' ass! If it wasn't for you I wouldn'ta fuckin' been there! You *owe* me!"

Eva got real quiet. Guilt rose up in her heart because Fiyah was right.

"You *owe* me," Fiyah repeated, his voice a little calmer. "We used to be some slick-ass Bonnie and Clyde muhfuckahs back in the day, remember? Robbing and scheming. Getting over to get doe any possible way we could. Well Clyde got his ass locked down on The Rock, and Bonnie grew some ass and became a fashion model. Which one of us ate off that?"

"Let me pay you back some other kinda way, Fuego. Brody's got his hands too deep in the drug game. You know what kinda stumble I took when I was a kid and how hard it was for me to make it past that. I been clean for years, Fuego. Rasheena and Jahden did me so bad that I can't even be around nobody who deals with dope no more. That shit would kill me. Please. I'll pay you back, I swear. But let me find some other way."

They locked eyes, but there was nothing but stone in Fiyah's gaze.

"This is *el Barrio,* baby," he said, his voice low and cold. "We *all* got dues to pay. I paid mine, Evita. But you still fuckin' owe. Now grab your *shit,* and get fuckin' *dressed.*"

Eva jumped bad. "Well can I get some fuckin' privacy, then? Unless you wanna be looking all at my ass and shit!"

Fiyah stood up and headed out. "Just hurry the fuck up and change."

Eva slipped into a pair of jean shorts and a tank. She grabbed her purse from the dresser, then kneeled on her bed and raised her window. She climbed out onto the fire escape and braced herself for the hang-fall. She'd done it many times before back when she lived in Brooklyn and was still robbing and drugging. It was how she used to get outta niggahs' cribs with their wallets in her hand.

But this time Eva was window-dropping for a whole different reason. Crouching down, she looked back at Rosa before closing the window once more.

She put her finger to her lips . . . *ssshh* . . .

In the living room, Fiyah was fed. Pacing the floor past his snoring mother, he wondered what the fuck was taking Eva so long. He stormed back to her bedroom and stood outside the door. "Yo, Eva! Hurry the fuck up!"

He opened the door a crack and saw Rosa sitting up in the bed. She was alone.

Fiyah cursed.

"Where's Eva?" he demanded.

Rosa glanced at the window and put her finger to her lips . . . *ssshh* . . .

Chapter 16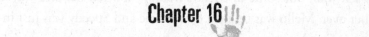

Eva's red heels clacked on the concrete as she ran through the pissy alley. All kinds of bums and fiends were lurking in the shadows, but she didn't give a fuck. Right now her greatest threat was Fiyah. Somebody she had trusted with her life on many occasions. Somebody who was trying to fuck her life up right now.

As soon as she rounded the corner and came upon the brightly lit avenue she pulled out her cell phone. She was breathing so hard her fingers kept slipping and missing the digits.

"Hey, baby," she said, trying to sound cool. "Change of plans. Can I chill at your crib tonight?"

Eva listened to the voice on the other end of the line.

"Cool. I can swing by there. Yeah, I'm straight, baby. I'ma hop in a cab. I'll be there in a few."

Fifteen minutes later Eva was sitting in Harlem's Corner Pocket Poetry Café. It was a hip hop set known for smashing poetry and street-inspired spoken word. Mello's friend Speedy was emceeing on the stage and Eva paid her cover charge and got her hand stamped.

She was planning to just ease over and grab a spot against a back wall, but some of Mello's homeys spotted her and waved her over. Mello was up next on the mic and Speedy was just introducing him.

"I ain't got enough words in my vocabulary to describe this next cat up, so I'm just gonna let him get deep into his flow game and blast y'all asses with a lyrical smack down! Born and raised right here on the streets of Harlem, let's give it up for Ramel 'Ice Mello' Williams!"

Mello stepped up on the stage looking fine as fuck. His juicy-ass lips and muscular body had panties all over the room on soak. His skin was butterscotch smooth under the stage lights and his hairline was freshly shaped. As plenty of chicks sat around staring at her man, tongues hanging out and pussies dripping, Eva wanted to cry.

This muhfuckah was so good to her. So damn good. Never could she imagine that after all the grimy shit she'd done . . . all the lying and the stealing, the drugging and the hoeing . . . that a real live man like Mello would not only want her, but he would love her so good like he did. Eva felt safe with Mello. Not even thoughts of Rasheena could hurt her when she was in his arms. But still . . . Eva fought not to give in to that nagging feeling. That crushing guilt that told her that not only didn't she deserve to live a life with Mello, but she wasn't gonna get the chance to live it either.

She sat there cold and filled with dread and fear as her baby heated up the mic. Dudes clapped and yelled, and females hooted and screeched as Mello laid his philosophical game down in a way that everybody could feel it.

The crowd jumped to their feet and gave him big props when he was finished, while Eva just sat there trembling. She stared into his strong handsome face with tears in her eyes. Mello looked at Eva as he was leaving the stage, and blew her a kiss from his sexy lips.

She smiled slightly, then rose and made her way toward the hall before the line got too long for the single-stall ladies' bathroom. Moments later, she was startled as Mello slid up next to her and whispered hotly in her ear.

"Hey, shawty . . ."

She turned to him with a bright smile. "That was a real live piece," she complimented him, even though she had been so deep in her pain that she'd barely heard a word he said. "You really put it down out there."

"You liked it?" he asked, biting down on her earlobe and then grazing her collarbone with his tongue.

Eva held her head back to give him more access. "You know I did." She allowed herself to enjoy his tongue for a quick moment, then she pulled away. "Baby, we gotta talk."

He nodded. "Yeah, you said something came up, right?"

Just then the bathroom door opened and a short thick sistah stepped out. Mello took Eva's hand and pulled her inside. He closed the door and locked it, then started kissing her neck again.

"Mello . . ." Eva breathed softly.

"Yeah." He cupped her breast and rubbed her thick nipples. "Whassup?"

"It's Fiyah . . ."

Mello lifted her up and set her on the edge of the tiny sink. He pressed his hard body into hers and moaned as his dick leaked crystal drops of pre-cum in his boxers. There was an In-Sight advertisement on the wall behind Eva. On it was the cover from Noire's book *Candy Licker*. The poster also featured a short poem, and Mello began whispering it hotly in Eva's ear.

"Can I lick that candy girl? Come let me taste . . . the sticky part of your world . . ."

"He's been running with that cat Brody . . ."

Mello licked around the inside of her ear. "Lemme lick that candy . . . lick it till you sweat . . ."

Eva moaned. "They were locked up on Rikers together . . ."

Mello dropped his kiss down to her breast. He caught her stiff nipple between his teeth and swirled his tongue around it right through her shirt. "Make that sweetness overheat . . . get it as hot as it gets . . ."

He slid his hand down the back of her shorts and cupped her phatty ass cheek.

"Fiyah said dude saw me on a visit and started wanting me . . ."

Mello stabbed her in the stomach with his hard dick. His fingers dug their way toward her pussy. "I wanna be your candy licker . . ."

He unbuttoned the front of her shorts and tongue-fucked her mouth.

Eva moaned, then pulled away and whispered, "Fiyah made a deal with Brody, baby. Fiyah got some kinda hook-up in the joint, and as a trade off . . . Brody got me."

Mello stopped suddenly. His body went cold.

"Fiyah tried to snatch me up and take me across town to Brody's crib. He said them cats ain't gonna stop until Brody collects what's due."

Mello took a step back and stared at her. Eva's lipstick was smudged and her thong was showing through her unbuttoned shorts. Without a word, he turned away and slammed out the door.

Eva zipped her shorts and ran out behind him. She didn't catch up to him until they were outside on the street.

"Mello, wait! *Mello!*"

He turned around, and the look on his face made her shake with fear.

"You fuckin' playing with me?"

"What the fuck are you talking about?" she yelled. "I didn't even do nothing!"

"So that's how your family rolls? Your own cousin tossin' you off like a fuckin' bird or a chicken? I'll *cancel* his fuckin' ass . . ."

Eva ran behind him. "Mello, *wait!*"

He turned again. "Wait, hell. You ain't nobody's fuckin' property Eva. Not mine and not your weak-ass fuckin' cousin's neither."

"I know, baby. But a lot of stuff went down in the past that you don't know about!"

Mello smirked. "Like what, Eva? What the fuck don't I know that could make me swallow some shit like this?"

Eva breathed hard. There was no way in fuck she could tell him everything. Not everything. "It was my fault that Fiyah got knocked. He went to jail because of me. That gun was my business. If I hadn't passed it to him he wouldn'ta had it on him. My cousin took the fall and never even thought about snitching. He did it because he loves me."

"I luh you and you don't see me trying to peddle your ass off to no maniac."

"I know. But me and Fiyah were into a lot of stupid shit when we were younger. Both of us fucked up a lot. But when it really counted Fiyah went down alone. When he coulda taken me down with him. I guess I do owe him something for that."

Mello chuckled. "So what you expect me to do? Turn my back and let that niggah trick you off, and when Brody tosses you then I'm supposed to act like shit is all good and nothing happened?"

"No," Eva cried out. "I ain't saying that! I just don't want my cousin to get hurt."

"See that's where we different. I don't give a fuck *what* happens to his grimy ass."

"Mello . . ." Eva moaned. "Baby please don't—"

"Sorry, Mami. Your cousin gets no respect over here. He rolled around on a bunk with Brody and now he gotta handle that shit. He shoulda took the dick-down in the joint. Instead he carried his debt out on the streets and dumped it in your lap. Let that bitch pay the costs like a real fuckin' man!"

Eva sniffled. "And me? What about my ass? I gotta pay the costs for every shitty thing I did in my life too?"

Mello shook his head. "Nah, baby." He reached into his pocket and took a key off his ring. "You, I got covered. Go to my crib and rest. I don't know about your cousin, but your shit is gonna be straight. Believe that."

Bricks was almost on fire by the time Mello and his boys arrived. He walked straight over to the VIP section where Brody was reigning supreme in his special booth, holding court with his crew.

Fiyah was sitting on Brody's left, and even from a distance Mello could see the little pussy was shook. Mello rolled straight up on him and smashed his bitch-ass without saying a word.

For the second time in one night Fiyah was on the receiving end of an ass-kicking. Mello came straight from the streets and beat him down with his bare hands. Brody's boys jumped like they wanted to make a move, but Brody checked them with one raised finger. Mello's goonies stood tall and on the ready too, and nigs on both sides were heavily strapped.

"Chill," Brody said. He backed his cats up with a look. "Let this fool handle his."

He nodded at Mello's crew, then kept on watching as Mello and Fiyah went at it in a brutal fashion. Tables were knocked over and drinks were spilled, but in the end Mello was standing on his feet like a winner, and Fiyah was fucked up and bleeding from his nose, and once again on the floor.

"You's a *pussy*, man!" Mello raged over him. "A straight-up bitch! You give a *fuck* about your fam 'cause you too busy looking out for ya *self*!"

Mello pulled his murderous gaze off of Fiyah and put it dead on King Brody. He held it there hard for a few seconds before raking it across the rest of Brody's crew.

"Fiyah . . ." Mello's words were directed at the man who was wheezing and rolling around on the floor, but he grilled Brody again with straight contempt. "Man I don't know how you gone get squared up with this grimy muhfuckah right here, but it ain't gone be through Eva." He spit down at Fiyah and barked, "Both of y'all best stay the fuck away from her. Your weak ass ain't got the muscle to dish her off!"

Mello turned back to King Brody and made shit real clear. "I don't give a fuck what you offered this chump-bitch, or what he promised you. Eva don't belong to him. And she sure as fuck don't belong to you. She belongs to *me*. Anybody want her? Then step up on some of this shit right here and try to get her."

Brody was amused like a muhfuh. He nodded at Mello with big respect in his eyes. He'd enjoyed the show and appreciated all the violent entertainment.

Daddy Dre ambled into the area. Fiyah was still rolling around on the floor holding his ribs. Dre gave him a disgusted look and persuaded Mello and his boys to go chill at the bar so he could treat them to some free drinks.

Fiyah struggled to stand as Mello walked away. His whole face felt like a mass of swollen meat. He touched his nose and lip and blood was all over his hands. He pulled himself up by the edge of the table, and tried to fall back into his booth seat again.

Brody checked that shit.

"Nah, muhfuckah," he said, throwing out a straight arm and blocking him. "Stand ya fuckin' ass up, homey. You can't be getting fucked up like that in public then think you gone cozy up next to me. It ain't happening."

"He didn't fuck me up," Fiyah muttered, humiliated.

Brody threw his head back and laughed. "Oh he fucked you up all right, ese. I know that kid real well. He's from the streets. You *better* watch ya back 'cause Ice Mello ain't no fuckin' joke. You gotta respect a cat who rolls up to handle his. It shows he's hardbody and got loyalty. A gangsta like that would never pass his fam off on no deal. He'd go down in the gutter fighting for her first."

Brody's face got hard. All the laughter was gone.

"Here," he said, reaching into his waistband. He tossed Fiyah a gat with a shiny silver handle. "Mello is holding a heavy tool and he ain't got no problem using it. You can believe that shit. Strap up, homey. And make sure that crazy niggah don't get you first."

Chapter 17

A whole week had passed and Fiyah was still sore as fuck. The red lumps and bruises on his face had darkened to blue and his ribs still hurt bad if he moved the wrong way. Fresh from the shower, he came out the bathroom wrapped in a towel. He stepped into his room and checked out his face again before brushing his hair and getting dressed.

A lot of shit had gone down in a short amount of time but tonight was Friday and it was Fiyah's night to shine. That is, if he lived long enough. He walked out of his room and ran into Milena, who was coming out of the kitchen.

"You finally washed your ass and put on some clothes?"

his mother sneered, dragging on a cigarette. "You been hiding out in your room all week. You might as well get out there on the street and deal with your problems 'cause you can't hide from them in here forever."

"I wasn't hiding, Ma. I was writing. Creating shit. Working on my flow."

"What you should be working on is a *job*, Fuego. Try that shit. You eat here and use up all my water and electricity. Where do you think I get the money to pay for all this shit? Huh? Where do I get it?"

"I don't know, Ma. But I'ma have a little something for you soon. That's real. I promise."

She waved him off.

"You're just like that shiftless-ass father of yours. Can't keep a job and full of all kinds of promises that don't help pay the damn rent."

"I said I'll get you something, Ma! Damn! What's up with this shit? You been riding me ever since I got the fuck home! Eva's been gone all week and I don't hear you bitching about her! I been right here with you and you can't stop fuckin' with me! What's wrong with you?"

Milena dragged on her cigarette. She crossed her arms and stared at her son with bitter sorrow in her eyes. "It's still about you, huh, Fuego? From the time you was a kid it's always been about you. Did I make you like that? You're a selfish ass. And when you get it in your head that you want something for yourself, nothing and nobody else matters."

"That ain't true, Ma. I care about all of y'all. You, Rosa, and Eva. I'm about to make shit happen for all of us. I promise."

Milena smirked. "There you go again. I'm through with you and all your tired promises. I've heard them all before and you never deliver."

Fiyah opened the front door and stepped out. Tonight was *his* fuckin' night. Not even Milena was gonna rob him of that.

"I'm sorry, Ma."

He bounced.

Fiyah entered Bricks like he owned that bitch. Reem had left his name on the guest list, and unlike a slew of other cats who were standing outside begging the bouncers to get in, he had no problems sliding past the velvet ropes at all.

He strolled through the crowd feeling strong and determined. He was tired of running, tired of being scared, and tired of getting his ass kicked. Tonight he was ready to face the music in more ways than one.

Bricks was packed out with ballers and fine honeys. Reem was on the stage emceeing the reggaeton competition, which from the sound of things had already begun. Fiyah scanned the crowd. He spotted ill Nino with his entourage balling in the VIP section, but King Brody's usual booth was empty.

His cell phone vibrated in his pocket and Fiyah pulled it out. He had a text message from the King. It was real short too. Only one line. *Where's the bitch?*

Shook, Fiyah looked around, but he couldn't spot nobody. He walked over to the bar and stood next to his old friend Sasha as she waited for an order of drinks to come up.

"Sash, slap me with some Yak, baby."

She gave him a shot and Fiyah downed that shit in two gulps.

Daddy Dre walked up and patted Sasha on the ass. He nodded toward Fiyah's empty shot glass. "That one's on me, baby."

He looked at Fiyah. "'Bout fuckin' time you got here. Reem thought your PO mighta got hold of ya ass."

Fiyah nodded. "Oh, *somebody's* gone be on my ass tonight. I can feel it."

"Then bust your nut real quick and break out. Go stand where Reem can see you. These cats been spitting nursery rhymes all night and my customers ain't handling it well."

Fiyah moved toward the stage with his balls all up in his chest. This was his moment and all he could do was pray he lived through it. ill Nino was in the house and so were about ten A&R's from various major labels, including Daddy Yankee's. If somebody was scouting for Hispanic talent then they had come to the right fuckin' joint tonight, because Fiyah's time had arrived.

The new-jack reggaeton rapper on the stage had just finished his set. It was weak and played, and the crowd booed like a muthafuckah to show just how much they didn't like it.

Reem spotted Fiyah waiting, and waved him up on the stage.

"Aiight, show some love for our next performer, a hardbody homeboy fresh off the tiers of Rikers Island! My son, Fuego 'Fiyah' Perez! Give it up, y'all!"

Fiyah took the stage and immediately he started earning his name. His shit was so hot that cats watching from the bar started sweating. He waxed lyrical on they asses, every single move, every single gesture, was perfectly choreographed and timed. The audience was feeling him. They was responding. They were practically nutting on his dick.

He spotted Dre standing off to the side pointing at his watch, but Fiyah ignored his ass. Fuck that PO and fuck King Brody too. This was his moment, and Fiyah was busy fuckin' up heads, to include his own. Then suddenly two things happened at once. ill Nino stood up from his seat in VIP to get a better look at the wonderment on the mic, and King Brody stepped into Fiyah's frame, surrounded by his crew.

Fiyah stumbled. Just a little bit. But that was all it took to throw him off his well-rehearsed game. But then the beat changed and his game became nonexistent. Ice Mello had barged up on the stage behind him, tryna steal the show.

> We get it in, my team pack the club out!
> Straight to the bar, no Cris, Yak the cup out!

Fiyah's head whipped around and his mouth fell open. Ice Mello was standing there spitting crack into his own fuckin' mic.

> Niggahs talk slick, we pull straps and bug out!
> Step on the kicks? We might black the fuck out!

Fiyah was stung. It was a total bitch-slap. He stood there and watched, helplessly infuriated as Mello moved to the edge of the stage and shit all over his flow. The chicas in the crowd were screaming and pulling up their shirts, and Mello grinned and rapped to their panties as he put on Fiyah with his words, the same thing he had already put on him with his bare hands. A muhfuckin' beat-down.

> Mami's in the dugout,
> Big breasts and butt out . . .

Mello's rap game was toxic. It filled the air with his personal brand of funk, and even as he stood there looking and feeling stupid, Fiyah had to admit that shit. The kid was everything they'd said he was. Larger than life. His flow game was furious, brilliant.

> No names needed,
> That takes the fun out!

Fiyah stood there on boil, gripping a dead mic. He felt dumped on, like he shoulda been wiping shit off his face. It was reggaeton night. Not fuckin' hip hop! This cat had violated an unwritten club rule that demanded retribution, so when Mello started in on his third verse for his final kill, Fiyah stole up behind him and power-smashed him over the dome with his fuckin' mic.

It was the fight of the century.

Fiyah caught a glimpse of Brody and his boys knockin' people down in the crowd as they moved toward the stage charging toward him. Fuck Mello. These cats were coming to clock his ass out and he knew it. But then a group of pissed-off cats from Spanish Harlem rushed the stage and caused chaos to descend on the club. It took Dre, Reem, and a whole cast of muscled-up bouncers to drag Fiyah off the stage and to protect Mello from the mad reggaeton-loving muhfuckahs in the crowd.

Dre pushed both of them down the hall and out the side door. Fiyah and Mello grilled each other for a quick second, then both of them broke the hell out.

Out on the streets, Fiyah took off running toward home, furious as shit. Mello took off running too. In the opposite direction. Grinning like a muhfuh. Hyped as hell.

The crowd was still wildin' inside Bricks. Spittin' urban rap on reggaeton night was a good enough reason to toss shit up.

Brody stood guzzling straight Bacardi as he watched Dre and Reem push the two rappers down the hall and out the side door. His eyes stayed locked on Fiyah's retreating back until he was gone from view. Brody twirled a toothpick in his mouth and looked relaxed and comforted by the atmosphere of random violence that was in the air.

He leaned into his younger brother. "Follow that bitch," he ordered.

"Fiyah?"

"Nah, follow ya fuckin' dick, stupid ass!"

Bullet boiled. "Man, fuck you. You follow him."

"What the fuck did you say?"

"I said fuck you, B. I ain't no nervous bitch you can bend over and ass-fuck. You need to chill the fuck out with that shit."

Brody grunted, then smashed his glass into the side of his brother's head. It was a fast and vicious move that was meant to be disorienting and humiliating, and it worked because Bullet was definitely both. Blood ran down his face and he staggered. Brody slammed him up against a nearby pillar and got up in his face.

"You lucky I dig your fuckin' moms, man. Or I'd smash your bitch ass up for real."

Bullet slumped over in pain and embarrassment as Brody released him and stormed off into the wilding crowd. His eyes burned like deadly lasers into his brother's body. It took all his control not to pull out his tool and blast that psycho-bitch in the back of his dome. Instead, he leaned against the pillar trying to recover as he stared at his brother and wrestled with his mounting rage.

"You gone get done right, son," Bullet muttered under his breath. "Your fuckin' time on the throne is 'bout to be up."

• • •

Fiyah was just about to duck into his building when he glimpsed a strange car pull up at the curb. "Muthafuck!" He ran up the stairs as fast as he could, and jabbed at the doorbell, sweating out his panic.

Downstairs in the lobby, Parole Officer Daniels had just come through the door. He paused to finish his cigarette, then flicked the butt on the black-and-white tiled floor and stepped on it. He glanced at his watch, whistling good-naturedly. He was a big man and he moved slow. But he moved all the fuckin' time, and that's why he was so good at catching his parolees sleeping. He took the steps up to the Perez apartment and rang the bell. When nobody answered, he rang it again.

Fiyah answered the door with a towel around his waist. His skin looked damp and there were a bunch of old bruises on his face that had started to fade. He had a smaller towel in his hands that he rubbed around his head like he was trying to dry his damp hair.

"Where were you? I called three fuckin' times."

Fiyah shrugged. "I was taking a shower, man."

"For a whole fuckin' hour?"

"What can I say? I'm a clean cat."

Daniels looked down at Fiyah's feet. He still had on his socks.

The PO shook his head. "Nah, you're a fuck-up, Perez. A fuck-up. But you only get three strikes, and then I get your ass. If not tonight, then tomorrow night. Idiots like you always violate. I can set my watch to that shit."

Daniels turned to leave.

"One more thing. The next time you take one of your beauty baths, make sure you answer the damn phone."

"Can't." Fiyah shrugged. "Phone's in the kitchen. And it ain't cordless."

Back in his room Fiyah stepped past the pants and sweaty polo shirt he had just stripped out of in a hurry. He peered out his bedroom window and saw his PO walking out the building. A midnight-black SUV pulled to the curb in front of the PO's car, and the back door opened. Two big feet swung to ground.

King Brody.

"Oh shit!" Fiyah ran out the room, grabbing his gear off the floor as he passed. He jetted into Eva's bedroom where Rosa was sleeping, and hopped into his pants. Opening the window he climbed down the fire escape and jumped down to the alley on the side street below. Fiyah pulled his shirt on as he ran, and despite the deadly consequences, he never looked back.

Bricks had officially closed for the night, although there was a lot of drugging and gambling and fucking going on in the downstairs rooms. Reem walked ill Nino and a couple of his Bottom Half Boyz outside where their Lincoln limo and driver was waiting at the curb.

Reem gave ill some dap. "Yo, that shit was fucked up in there tonight, man. My son Fiyah lost his head."

"Yeah, but I peeped his game. I know he's nice."

Reem nodded. "Fiyah got some crazy shit with him, but he just got bum-rushed up there. Don't focus on the fight man, keep your ear on the flow."

"Oh yeah," ill agreed. "Ya boy's a contender. But so is his backup singer."

"Ice Mello? That boy is the hard truth. He spits it like nobody else. I didn't know you was down to tour with another hip-hop artist, though."

ill Nino grinned. "What? You scared he might throw some shit all over your shine, Raw?"

Reem laughed. "Man, get the fuck outta here. Ain't a rapper out here who can bite off none of this."

"Cool. Let's sleep on this till I get back next week. In the meantime, tell your little homeys to fall back. This is Harlem, man. Cats get blasted out here over small shit. We wanna keep the battle on wax, not on the streets."

ill Nino and his entourage got in their whip leaving Reem standing on the street. He chilled there with his hands in his pockets as a few drunken stragglers stumbled down the block and a small army of young promoters handed out flyers to anybody who would take them. A young Puerto Rican kid tried to push one off on Reem.

"After-hours party, homes?"

Reem dissed him. "Man get the fuck outta here."

Chapter 18

Fiyah hid in the shadows and back alleys of Harlem all night long. Fear and rage kept his mind turning. Rage because of Eva and that violating-ass Mello. And fear because he knew King Brody's patience had run out and that meant his time was just about up.

From the rooftop of a nearby building, Fiyah staked out his crib all day long. He needed to get inside and get his shit, but he also knew Brody was watching and waiting for him to show his position so he could take him down.

Every few hours a shiny late-model whip driven by one of Brody's manz roared down the street blasting loud music as gangstas waved shiny gats out the windows.

Fiyah leaned on the roof's railing and peeped all the happenings. He saw the young boy with the limp going on another grocery run for his grandmother. At four o'clock Rosa came home from dance practice and skipped up the front steps of their tenement. The people of Harlem were moving about doing their regular thang. They didn't know or give a fuck about the fact that shit was hot on the streets and had gotten extra critical in Fiyah's life.

Day turned into night and it started getting late. The rooftop was shitty. With its endless variety of used condoms, crack vials, and dirty needles, it was a certified pebble beach. Fiyah had already taken a piss on the opposite side a couple of times, and now he was hungry. He'd figured out what to do hours ago, and after Rolo's whip passed by for the fourth time, he left the roof and darted across the street and into his own building.

Quietly, Fiyah climbed the stairs and snuck down the hallway to his mother's apartment. He unlocked the door and slipped inside. Silently, he moved down the hall and froze outside of Milena's bedroom.

Fuck noises were coming from behind the partially closed door. Fiyah peeped into the darkness and made out the forms of his mother in there with some cat who was banging the shit outta her. He could only see the guy's shadow, but he could tell he was big. The dude was handling Milena like she was a ball of meat. His hands were around her throat as he thrust into her with powerful, back-breaking strokes. The noises his mother made were killing Fiyah. She screamed in pain and pleasure at the same time, and allowed the big guy to twist her up, feet to the ceiling, ass in the air, anyway he wanted to.

"Aah-aah-aah!" Milena hissed into the darkness as the dude flipped her around. The smell of pussy was strong in the air, and Milena's firm breasts rose and fell as she was slammed and bounced around on a big thick dick.

The man reached his arm back and swung downward, slapping Milena's bare ass so hard she arched her back and cried out like a kid who was getting a whipping. He palm-stroked her harshly like this, his hand cracking violently down on her ass as the noise exploded into the air. Fiyah just was about to lunge into the room and rescue her when his mother let out a deep-throated scream. "I'm cumming! I'm cumming! Fuck me! Fuck me harder! I'm cumming!"

Squeezing his eyes against his rage, Fiyah forced himself to move on. He crept past the room and eased open the door to his bedroom. Inside, he grabbed a gym bag and tossed his notepad and a few other items inside, then got down on his knees and fished around under his bed with both hands.

A *slide-click* sounded, and something cold was pressed to the back of his head.

Fiyah turned slightly and found himself looking down the barrel of his own gun.

King Brody, butt-naked with Milena's pussy juices coating his dick, had him on lock.

The gangsta laughed. "You looking for something, homey?"

Fiyah froze and put his hands up over his head. Rage coursed through his blood. This niggah had been sniffing around the crib not just for Eva, but for his fuckin' *mother*!

Brody backed off a little. "Hands down, niggah. I ain't gone shoot you yet. Come on in the kitchen, man. Your moms can hook us up something to eat right quick while me and you talk a little shit."

Minutes later Milena stood in a sheer robe at the stove while Fiyah sat across from Brody, who sat there naked with his long legs stretched out like he was right at home. The semiautomatic was sitting on the table between them. Locked and cocked and ready to pop.

"You got a banging-ass family," Brody told Fiyah, grinning as Milena walked past on her way to the refrigerator. Milena wouldn't meet Fiyah's eyes and he didn't wanna look into hers neither.

Brody saw the mother-son guilt and shame, and laughed. He reached out and slapped Milena's pert ass. "You got a fine-ass chocolate cousin who can't nobody seem to fuckin' find . . . and that sweet little Rosa too. What is she? Eight? Nine? She's 'bout to be fine as hell one day soon."

He laughed and turned his attention back to Milena. "But your mother, ak. This old bitch is hot, man. I mean *hot*. Got a super-juicy dome game and gives it up real deep from the back . . ." He shook his head like it was unbelievable. "Tappable ass must run in your family, yo."

Fiyah flinched. Enraged at his mother and fighting to hold himself back.

"Whattup, son? I say something you didn't like? You swelling up or something? What? I gut-fucked your *mother* and now you wanna grab this gat and twist my skull back? Go 'head. Try that shit. This your crib and you a man, right? You holding ya own shit down?"

Brody spun the gun on the table.

"Then go for it. Lunge, muhfuckah. But you better move fast and you better aim right. 'Cause if you don't my boys'll be all over this fuckin' firetrap in two minutes. And when they leave it's gone be a forensics feast up in this bitch 'cause it won't be nothing but dead bodies left to tell this urban tale."

He laughed again, then sat back in his chair.

"Chill, muhfuckah. Your moms just sucked my dick dry, ese. We practically family now. Besides, I ain't the one you should be gunnin' for. You ain't even handled that low-level action with Mello yet. What makes you think you can fuck with a big-dicked, heavy-balled muhfuckah like me?"

Brody stood up and slammed both hands on the table. His dick swung in front of him and hung down like a deadly brown snake. "It's time for you to start putting in work, son. There ain't but two men in your mother's life. Which one of us is really fuckin' her? I tell you what. You wanna keep your entire family out of a bloodbath? Then do yourself a big favor. Grab ya fuckin' nuts. Gangsta up and take that gun you sitting there itching to snatch, and get out on those streets and hold your shit down. You wanna square up with me? Handle that beef with Mello and bring me Eva. Before I go get that bitch myself."

Fiyah sat frozen with rage and fear.

Brody left the gun sitting on the table and took his time walking naked down the hall toward Milena's room. Laughing all the way.

Fiyah stared at the gat for a long moment.

His mind flashed back to the sex sounds he'd heard as he came through the door. He pictured Brody dog-fucking the shit outta his mother. Yanking Milena's hair and blowing her back out. He grabbed the burner and jumped to his feet, his fury totally unchecked. He started toward the hall then stopped suddenly, his stomach pained by what he saw.

Straight ahead was the room Rosa shared with Eva. Brody had bypassed Milena's bedroom and gone in there. Fiyah watched helplessly as the naked kingpin leaned over Rosa's sleeping form and planted a long kiss on her cheek. Fiyah glanced down at the tool in his hand. When he looked back again Brody had stood up and was facing him with a come-get-it look on his face.

Fiyah stood frozen. His arm desperately wanted to raise the hand that held the gun, but his heart wouldn't let him. Rosa stirred in the bed. She called out for Milena saying she was thirsty, then turned over and went back to sleep.

King Brody stood there waiting patiently for Fiyah to get his courage up. But Fiyah was battling himself on the inside. Brody liked killing people. If Fiyah made one wrong move his whole family could get took down.

Brody strode down the hall then stopped outside of Milena's room. He grinned at the loaded weapon hanging uselessly in Fiyah's hand, then shook his head, twisted the doorknob, and went inside.

As soon as the door closed Fiyah raised the tool. He gripped it in both hands, all kinds of scenarios playing out in his mind. He could bust up in his mother's room and pop one off in Brody right now! He wanted to do that shit so fuckin' bad! He could actually see that clown's dome cracking open like a fuckin' smashed egg. Killing Brody would bring Fiyah the most immense satisfaction of his life. It would give him back his fuckin' future and restore his fuckin' manhood.

But it would also cost him, and prolly Eva, Milena, *and* Rosa, their lives. Fiyah wasn't prepared to have his entire family buried, which is why he was back in the kitchen and still gripping the loaded tool when Brody came out his mother's room dressed. The King walked past Fiyah like all he was gripping was a lollipop, and got ready to bounce.

At the door, Brody turned around and challenged him once more. "You gone use that shit, or what? Flex niggah! You got a gat, so *flex!*"

Fiyah didn't move.

"Damn," Brody said over his shoulder, laughing coldly. "It stanks like pussy up in here. Goddamn house full of bitches."

Even after the door slammed shut Fiyah could still hear that maniac laughing. He twirled the gun in his fingers and aimed it at the just-closed door. His hands were shaking like the gun weighed a hundred pounds. Furious but defeated, Fiyah dropped the gun to the table and sat down and banged his head. Hard. Three times.

Somebody banged on the door and Fiyah sat upright again. On guard, he picked up the gat and moved cautiously toward the door.

"Oh shit," he said, then stashed the piece down the back of his pants and covered it with his shirt. He opened the door, breathing hard.

Fiyah sighed as Parole Officer Daniels stood there watching the last glimpses of Brody as he walked down the stairs.

"Associating with known felons?"

Daniels shook his thick head.

"That's two, Perez. Three strikes and you're out."

The next day Fiyah hit the streets in search of Mello.

Brody's burner was a comfort in his pocket, but fear was still heavy in his gut. Fear for himself and for his family. A gorilla like Brody was always good to his word. If Eva didn't get with the program then all of them would surely get sprayed. Fiyah thought about the way Brody had leaned over and put his grimy lips on Rosa, and he had to force himself to bite down on his rage. He had to find Eva. Brody had already fucked his moms, and now he was tryna fuck his whole family. He couldn't allow that shit to happen.

It was Sunday and he remembered Eva telling him that Mello mentored youths at the Corner Pocket Poetry Café. Gripping his gat through the pocket of his hoody, Fiyah threaded through the slow-moving after-church crowd of street shoppers.

"Hey yo!" somebody called out, and Fiyah looked left. The young chocolate-faced kid with the limp was walking parallel to him across the street. He nodded when he caught Fiyah's eye, and Fiyah nodded back.

"Yo, wait up!" the boy called out.

Fiyah ignored the kid and kept stepping.

The kid ran into the street, limping and dragging his bad leg. He caught up with Fiyah and stared at him with admiration.

"You the one who got those dudes off my ass the other day."

Fiyah shrugged. "Oh yeah?"

"Yeah, you don't remember? Them chump bitches only brave when they swarmin' with a crew. They was planning to jump me over there by the park. They fell back 'cause you rolled up."

Fiyah shrugged again. "Yeah. That's cool."

"So where you strollin', man?"

"I'm handling my bizz, young'un. And leavin' yours alone. Step off, little papi."

"C'mon, man. If you handling street bizz you gonna need somebody at ya back. Every gangsta does. I owe you one so I gotcha back, man."

Fiyah flinched as the kid raised his shirt and flashed a gun that was tucked into his pants.

"Yo, man, what the fuck you doin' with that shit?"

"I handles minez too, dude."

Fiyah looked down at the kid's gimp leg and shook his head. "You look like you been in enough street battles. Get your ass on home to ya grandma and put that tool away."

Fiyah stepped off walking strong, leaving the kid behind. He had bigger shit to concentrate on, and he didn't even notice when the kid let him get ahead a little bit, then started following him again.

Mello's homeys was congregating outside the Corner Pocket Poetry Café when Fiyah rolled up. A Mister Softee truck sat at the curb playing that special ice-cream music that made kids come running from miles around.

Fiyah peeped Mello standing in the midst of a bunch of young heads. He watched as dude counted all the kids then went over to the truck and bought ice cream for every one of them. Licking cones, the kids followed Mello through the doors of the café and that's when Fiyah made his move.

He rolled straight up on the corner cats, and two of them yanked out tools before he could tell them he was coming in peace.

"Yo, y'all can put all that firepower away, homes. I ain't tryna get nothing poppin'. I just need to holla at ya manz Mello real quick."

A big dude with crazy eyes stepped up. He pulled a tool from the back of his waistband and swung it hard, cracking Fiyah down to the ground.

"Who the fuck you be?"

Fiyah climbed to his knees, shaking his head. Blood flew from a gash that had opened up on his temple. "I'm Eva's cousin. Fiyah. Tell Mello I'm out here."

A short dude with a Black & Mild blunt behind his ear started laughing.

"Oh, I know this niggah, y'all! This the cat Mello fucked up the other night at Bricks, yo. Mello *stole* this bitch! He slapped his dick all over dude's mic!"

Fiyah ignored the noise. Still on his knees, he looked up at the big cat who had pistol-whipped him and said, "That's me, baby.

Yeah, Mello fucked me up. Now, I'm about to move slow because I got some heat on me too, and I don't want nobody to get hurt. I'm gone pass you my tool, just so you know I'm straight."

Fiyah reached into his pants and came out with his burner. He gripped it by the barrel and held it out toward Mello's goon.

Dude snatched the gun and pocketed it.

"Feel him up," he told his boys.

Fiyah held still and took the thorough pat-down.

"Now you got my shit and you smashed my dome. So we cool, right, ak? All I wanna do is see Mello. I need to talk to that cat right fuckin' now."

Fiyah walked into the café and found Mello sitting at a table near the stage. He was leaning forward on his elbows and listening intently as a young Hispanic kid threw down on a spoken-word piece that had a beastly flow.

"Yo, that was the shit, Roberto. You got real talent, man. I'm proud of you. Okay, who's up next?"

"I'm next," Fiyah said, standing near his shoulder.

Mello looked up. Seeing Fiyah, his face turned hard.

"Get outta here, man. You fuckin' with my community time," he said coldly. "Come back later."

"Where the fuck is she, man?"

Mello grilled Fiyah with bitter contempt in his eyes. "Yo, little dudes," he said to the young'uns. "Check this out. We 'bout to take another quick break, aiight? Go wash ya hands, sons! Ain't gone be no sticky shit all over my mic, ya heard?"

He turned back to Fiyah. "Man, why the fuck you in my ear?"

"I gotta get with Eva. I need to know where she is."

Mello shrugged with disrespect. "Fuck you. Eva's with me. In my back fuckin' pocket. I already told ya bitch ass. You wanna get with her? Then get past me."

Fiyah sighed. He wiped his hands down his face and looked at Mello with bloodshot, exhausted eyes.

Mello laughed. "Damn, dude. Brody got yo ass shook! *Hard*. What the fuck you really come here for?"

"I came here to get mine in."

"And you really think I'm just gone give her up to you? You think I'ma just break out and tell you where she is?"

"Hell yeah. If you don't wanna get caught in the cross fire, then you should."

Mello got amped. "Muhfuckah you smell any fear coming off me? I'm covered from all angles. But what about you? Everybody in Harlem knows what the fuck is out there hunting for you, homey. And your bitch ass let that predator loose on *Eva*? Man, fuck you. Step the fuck outta my space!"

"It ain't even like that no more, man. I wanna help her—"

"Nah, you wanna help *yourself*! It's all about *you*, dude. Look at ya tired ass! Brody coming at your throat, and like a bitch you out here running scared. Your life ain't worth shit compared to hers. I ain't gonna let you sacrifice my baby—"

Fiyah was fed. There was no way to make this cat see the bloodbath that was gonna go down unless he found Eva and convinced her to act right. She didn't have to do it forever. Just long enough to satisfy Brody until the next chick caught his attention.

"You got me wrong, Mello. All wrong. But it's cool. You just keep Eva on lock. And when she sticks her head up and finds out her whole family has been planted in the ground, see if she's still willing to toss that phat ass in your direction."

While Fiyah and Mello went at it inside the café, the boy with the limp stood outside watching for signs of static. Two corner boys out slinging trap spotted him and made a move. It was Sunday and business was slow. Fuckin' with a gimp kid would help the time pass faster. They rolled on the boy, who was standing there staring into the Corner Pocket Café looking jumpy and scared. He froze when they got up on him, shaking like he was about to piss in his fuckin' pants.

"Yo, lil' nig," one of the trap boys said. "This my fuckin' block. What you doin' on it?"

The limp boy yanked up his shirt and whipped out his tool, and before that shit could clear his waistband, the second corner boy beat his gat-draw and popped one off in his neck.

The kid went down hard, and one of Mello's boys scoped the action from across the street and came running.

"What the fuck you doin', man?!" he barked on the young trap boy. "You just shot a fuckin' kid!"

Dude took off running. "He pulled out a gun, man!" he called over his shoulder, then him and his friend fled the scene, feet flying as they disappeared down a nearby alley.

Fiyah had just gotten his piece back from the bouncer and was standing in the doorway when he saw the boy go down. Mello pushed past him from behind as he came running outta the café, along with most of the young boys who had been inside. Cars had stopped and the streets had descended into panic as some pedestrians ducked behind cars and others rushed over to the spot where the boy had fallen.

Fiyah ran toward the crowd and cursed when he saw the gimp boy laying on the ground. Sirens sounded loudly, very close by, and he thought about his parole status and ducked deeper into the crowd.

"Call an ambulance!" somebody screamed, and one of Mello's manz knelt down beside the boy. An old black woman took off her church shawl and pressed it against his wound as she recited the Lord's Prayer in the child's ear.

One of the bouncers from the Corner Pocket Poetry Café picked up the gun the boy had dropped the moment he was shot. He turned it over in his hands then cursed loudly as he saw the orange safety ring. He stared down at the kid's motionless body in disgust.

"This shit ain't even real! It's fuckin' plastic! A toy fuckin' gun!"

He passed the shit to Mello, who nodded. The gun was a fake. It was a good-looking fake, but the shit would never shoot a damn thing. Not even water.

The police rolled up on the scene and niggahs started scattering. Mello walked out into the street, heading back to the café, but a young black cop checked him and drew his gun.

"Drop your weapon! Drop that shit right now!"

Mello put his hands up in the air, the toy gun pointed toward the sky.

"Stay calm, officer. It's just a toy. The kid pulled it out and got popped by accident . . ."

The black cop was a rookie from Westchester and he wasn't takin' no chances down here in the deep hood.

"Drop the fuckin' gun now!"

Mello got swallowed up by the boys in blue. Despite the loud, angry protests from the witnesses in the crowd, the cops had their gats trained on him and ready to spit.

Cautioning himself to stay calm, Mello tossed the fake tool to the ground. The moment he kicked it away about ten cops rushed him, tackling him to the ground. Mello grimaced as his face was slammed into the concrete pavement over and over again. Shit went real dark for a moment, but when he managed to open his eyes he saw one thing real fuckin' clear. Fiyah was using the commotion as his cover and was darting away from the crowd. He took off walking down the street, fast as shit, in the opposite direction. As Mello got roughed up and tossed around by a crew of Harlem cops, he caught one last glimpse of Eva's cousin as he jetted toward safety. Fiyah glanced over his shoulder at the beat-down Mello was taking, then kept right on walking, never slowing his roll.

Chapter 19

Living with Mello was everything Eva had ever dreamed of. When she was snuggled under the covers with his strong arms holding her, nothing could touch her. No longer did fear drive her into nightmares at night, twisting her up inside with guilt and torment. Mello stood on guard for her like a faithful watchdog. His love was what Eva had been missing her whole life and still . . . her life felt so good she wondered if it could last.

Sitting cross-legged with her back against his headboard, Eva gazed out the window at the brick wall that was Mello's New York City view. His crib was really just a big closet in a reconstructed warehouse on the very edge of Harlem, but to her it was like living in a palace.

Her man was overdue on coming home and Eva couldn't sleep without him in bed with her. She'd been with him for over a week and they'd stayed up late every night sexing the hell outta each other and whispering all kinds of plans for the future they wanted to have. Her baby had been outta the drug game for years, and Eva was proud of him for making his money the honest way. They had talked about moving into a bigger place, and with Mello doing so good on both his jobs, Eva hoped they'd be able to make that dream a reality real soon.

And she was bringing something other than her body to the relationship too. The Birthday Cake clothing line had blown up sky-high and as their featured model she was swimming in gigs. Suddenly ads featuring her face and body were popping up everywhere, and her income was rising along with her visibility. There were several international accounts on the books already, and the young urban, hip-hop set living in places like China and Jakarta were demanding to be outfitted in the stylish gear that was cut in different sizes to accent feminine curves no matter what the wearer's shape.

Eva could have never dreamed that she would come this far in her once-fucked-up life. She had a good career and somebody actually loved her! The starving little girl who used to chew on folded squares of toilet tissue, and who had stood on street corners turning tricks before she even had her first period, was actually loved. But sometimes she thought Mello was too good for her. On her really dark days Eva could get bent over. Gripped with guilt and shame. All of the low-down stunts she had pulled. All the shiesty shit she had done. It was all stuck in her memory and it haunted her, even though in her heart she knew all of it wasn't her fault.

There'd been a couple of times when she had tried to tell Mello about some of the things she'd done in her past. But crazy shit would creep into her thoughts and mock her at the worst possible times. Mello might have his head between her legs, munching her pussy out deliciously, and Eva would look down at herself and freak the fuck out. The vein she used to shoot up in was in the crease of her groin. She would swear that shit was bulging and pulsating, her track marks thickened with scar tissue caused by overuse and infection. That was why she never shaved her pussy hairs, but at times she was convinced that Mello was noticing that shit while he was down there and was wondering what was up.

There were other things that got in her head too. Although a lot of her scars had faded, nobody could get rid of every single bad thing they'd been through in life. Mello's lips would be leaving tender kisses on her breasts, arms, and thighs, and Eva would lay there squirming. Not because it felt good, but because she was afraid he'd wonder about the lash marks Rasheena's belts and cords had left on her skin that no amount of cocoa butter could make go away. She'd had to make up a lie because she used makeup to cover things up during her shoots, so she'd told Mello her crazy grandmother had whipped her with switches when she went down south in the summers. It was easier than admitting to being abused by her own mother.

Eva knew the day would come when she would have to come straight with Mello. They were planning a future together and he had a right to know about her past. But could she tell him everything? Would he still want her if he knew she was a former chickenhead who had done more scandalous shit than a little bit? Would he keep loving her if he knew she'd given birth to and abandoned a baby boy?

It was late and Eva was tired, but all this shit was heavy on her mind. Brody was hunting for her and she knew he'd already fucked Fiyah up and put all those bruises on his face. Fiyah was lucky that was all they'd done to him. He was probably bent tryna figure out where she was, and Aunt Milena was probably just as bent from watching Rosa all by herself.

She couldn't hide in Mello's room forever—this Eva knew. But in order to have peace between her man and her cousin, she needed to kill all the static and find a way to get them to feel each other on some common ground. She'd been thinking about something for days that might work out, but she didn't have the skills or the connections to pull it off by herself.

She checked the time on her cell phone and saw that it was after three a.m. She knew Reem was a night nig, and was probably still up writing songs or working on his flow. Staring down at her cell phone, she punched a number and waited while it rang.

"Reem? You up? It's Eva."

"Whattup, baby girl!" Reem sounded wide awake.

"I know it's late but I need some help, Reem, and since Mello ain't home yet this is a good time for us to talk. Now, I know you up on all the beef going down between Mello and my cousin. It started because of Brody but it's bigger than that now. But check this out. I wanna squash this shit between them but I need some help."

Reem was hyped. "Don't worry about it, baby girl. Just tell Reem what you need done."

"You know the Birthday Cake clothing line is blowing up, right? Well I got a text today that said my boss wants to shoot another marketing video. The line is booming in a lot of Hispanic markets and she's looking for a hot fusion track. Something Hip Hop, but reggaeton too. Can you put Mello and Fiyah down on that? Make 'em put their mic skills together so they can stop hatin' each other and be done with the bullshit?"

Reem seemed to like what he was hearing, and Eva had mad trust in her boy.

"Sounds like a plan, shawty. Let me run it past ill. See when we can get them nigs to have a conversation and maybe get some studio time."

Eva lay back on the bed and stared hard at the ceiling wishing Mello would hurry up and come home. She was counting on Reem to work his magic on two hardheads who wanted to tear out each other's throats. It wasn't gone be no easy feat, talking them cats into the same room, but Eva had faith that her friend Reem could pull it off and get the job done.

Mello didn't bust up in the crib until sometime the next morning. Eva had been worried outta her mind all night, but she could tell her man was heavily stressed the minute he hit the door. He moved real slow, like he was in pain, and his whole shit was all fucked up.

"What happened!" Eva cried. He had left the crib looking damned good in his fresh Sean Jean gear and spotless AF1s. Now his shirt was ripped, his lip was swollen, and there was a hole in one knee of his pants. He went straight to his mini fridge and gulped out of a carton of orange juice like he was dying of thirst. Then he took a cold piece of pizza off the tiny table and set it on a paper plate. His platinum chain caught a glint from the light and sparkled around his neck. He pushed a button to open the tiny microwave, then finally looked at her. "Hold up. Lemme nuke this shit for a sec."

"Hold up *hell*!" Eva blurted out. "Where you *been*? Tell me what the hell happened to you!"

Mello took a big bite of pizza and said, "Your fuckin' cousin happened to me."

Eva looked puzzled. She reached out and touched the cut on his lip tenderly. "Fiyah did this to you?"

Mello thought about the way Fiyah had dipped from the scene while he was getting his ass kicked, and got heated all over again. "I told you that cat is grimy, Eva. Fuckin' punk-ass bitch!"

"But what happened? Y'all got into some shit? I heard on the radio that somebody got shot on the Avenue yesterday. Did somebody shoot my fuckin' cousin?"

"Nah, but somebody shoulda popped him one. He rolled up at the café's youth set with a gat and a baby sniper packing a fuckin' water gun. Hell yeah he shoulda got shot. The kid took one for him instead."

Eva was crushed. "How the fuck you gonna say something like that, Mello? You saying my cousin deserves to get shot down in the street like a dog?"

Mello stopped chewing. "Hold the fuck up. Am I hearing you straight? Fiyah's got the baddest psycho muhfuckah in Harlem looking to tap your ass, and there's a twelve year-old kid laying up in Harlem Hospital with a hole in his neck. I went to jail over a toy fuckin' gun, and spent twenty hours in a pissy cell getting stomped out by a bunch of NYPD Blue Boys, and you grillin' me just 'cause I talked shit about your cousin? You sound crazy, baby. Real fuckin' crazy."

Eva threw her hands up. "Okay! Cool! Fiyah fucked around and made a lotta bad moves. But you ain't gotta take that shit out on me, Ramel! He's family, goddammit! *My* fuckin' family. What am I supposed to do, just shit on him and keep it moving? What the fuck do you want me to do?"

"You can start by keeping your ass right here in my room and letting your cousin take his punishment like a fuckin' man."

Eva overflowed. She jumped bad real strong because for the very first time Mello had really hurt her feelings and she wanted him to know that shit.

"I tell you what, Ramel. You might not give a fuck about your little bit of missing-in-action family, but I got mad love for my cousin. No matter what the fuck he does wrong, that's not gonna ever change. Never. And I'm getting about tired of sitting up in this box all day too. You get out there on the streets every day and you *do* shit! You see people, you talk to people, you eat what the fuck you wanna eat. I missed a whole week of my life ducking and hiding and fucking around in here with you. If I feel like going out, then you can believe I'm gonna step."

Mello gave her a long, cold look.

It was so long, and so cold that Eva actually shivered under his gaze.

"Fuck it then. I ain't into keeping chicks where they don't wanna be. Run out there on the streets and catch up with your sherm-ass cousin. Ask him to keep Brody and his crew off your ass. I'm done."

Eva snatched her phone off the bed. She grabbed a ponytail holder from the nightstand and tied her hair back, then she slipped on her shoes and picked up her purse. Without saying another word to Mello, or even looking at his black ass, she bounced.

The streets of Harlem were a blur as Eva walked briskly away from Mello's crib. All kinds of noise was bouncing around in her head, and once again she felt like that unwanted little girl from a cold tenement apartment in Brooklyn. The little girl who had abandoned her baby in the dark of night, and who was now getting caught up in foul karma as the one person she truly loved practically abandoned her too.

Tears were in her eyes as she brushed past people on the sidewalk. She'd heard Mello calling her name as she ran down the steps of his building, but she had igged his ass and kept on going. Her phone was vibrating in her purse and she ignored that too. Let him blow it up. She wasn't about to answer that shit.

She was turning down Lenox Avenue when she heard a horn honking. Eva looked over her shoulder and saw Mello's whip pulling up alongside of her.

"Eva!"

"Fuck you!" she said, turning her head and dissin' him. She walked faster, her ass bouncing hard under her little pink skirt.

He honked some more.

"Eva! Yo, your aunt been tryna call you! Rosa is sick!"

Oh, that was some dirty-ass shit.

"That's low, Mello!" she screamed over her shoulder. "That some low shit even for a fuckah like you!"

"Check your phone, Eva. Something ain't right with Rosa. Your aunt was crying. She wants you to come home, baby. She needs you."

Eva stopped in her tracks. There was no way in hell Mello would lie about something like that.

She turned around and looked at him. He was leaning across the front seat with panic in his eyes. Eva pulled her cell phone from her purse. She had six missed calls. Five of them from Milena.

"Get in," Mello urged, and Eva jumped her ass in the ride quick and fast. Her heart was pounding as Mello pulled out into traffic and headed toward her crib. She tried to call her aunt back but the phone just rolled straight to voice mail. She checked her messages too, but all she could hear was Milena screaming and crying into the phone. In fuckin' Spanish.

"Oh, God," Eva prayed out loud as Mello wove the ride in

and out of lanes and around sharp corners. She couldn't remember praying this hard since that cold dark night down in the Howard Houses laundrymat. But on that night she was high and terrified and alone. This night she was with a real man. Somebody she knew loved her and would always have her back, no matter the cost. Everything was gonna be all right. Her crib was right up ahead. Not even five minutes away. Eva put her hand on Mello's arm and held on.

Chapter 20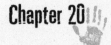

"**W**hat the fuck happened in here?!" Eva shouted the minute her aunt opened the door. The apartment had been wrecked. Shit had been tossed all over the place. Dishes, clothes, curtains. Somebody had dragged all the cushions off the sofa and cut them shits wide open.

Milena sank into Eva's arms. She looked raggedy. Her face was bruised and swollen and alcohol was heavy on her breath.

"He beat me," Milena moaned. Eva looked into her mouth and pulled back, horrified. Her aunt's two front teeth had been fist-cracked. There was nothing but jagged little shards left sticking out from her gums.

"*Fiyah?*" Eva said in disbelief.

"No. Fuego is in jail! His parole officer arrested him on a violation. It was Brody! He wanted me to tell him where you were." Her face broke apart again as she cried loudly, "But how the fuck was I supposed to tell him what I didn't even fuckin' know?"

Eva felt her blood run cold.

"Auntie," she said quietly. "Where's Rosa?"

Milena nodded toward the bathroom and sobbed. The door was closed. "She's in there. Brody put her in there. He was terrorizing us. Torturing us. Me *and* Rosa. He came here to kill Fuego, but Fuego got away. Me and Rosa was left here by ourselves and Brody almost killed us!"

Eva felt feverish. Like all this shit couldn't be happening. She glanced toward the bathroom just as Mello was backing up out of it.

Rosa lay limp in his arms as he called out her name. "Rosa! Wake up, baby girl. C'mon, Rosa. Open your eyes."

Eva crossed the room in a panic.

"Lemme see her," she said, her eyes scanning Rosa's small body for some sign of trauma. The girl was dressed in a short pink nightgown that smelled like vomit and old pee. Eva cried inside as the smell triggered memories of her own rank days.

"Rosa?" she said softly, patting the little girl's cheeks. "Can you hear me?"

Rosa was in and out. Her eyes would open for a few moments, and then fall closed again as her head slumped to the side and drool slid from her mouth.

Eva got closer. "Rosa?" she said, her voice shaking. She slapped the girl's cheeks harder, then lifted her eyelids and stared at her pupils.

"*Rosaaaaaa!*" Eva screamed. She shook the little girl's shoulders as the child opened one eye and grinned at her. Rosa scratched her arm weakly, then fell off into oblivion once again.

All the signs were there, yet Eva still didn't wanna believe it.

She turned to her aunt. "What the fuck did you give her!" she demanded, rage burning in her entire body.

"It wasn't me," Milena cried weakly. "I didn't give her nothing. I swear. It was Brody."

Mello looked puzzled.

"Eva, what's up?" he asked. "What's wrong with her?"

Eva cried from her gut and her knees wobbled with grief.

"She's high, Mello," she gasped. Anguished tears ran freely down her face. "She's fuckin' high! Rosa's nodding!"

Mello sat down and stared at the limp little girl in his arms with disbelief.

He sat her up. "High? On what?"

"Smack. Heroin," Eva moaned.

Mello was quiet for a quick moment. Rosa's chin had fallen to her chest. Her lips were turned down at the corners and she bobbed slowly downward, then got it together slightly and sat back up.

"Nah," Mello said, shaking his head in denial. "*Duji?* How you know it's that?"

Eva pushed Rosa's braids over her shoulder. She touched a vein in the girl's neck that appeared swollen and red, and said in a soft, hollow voice, "Because I used to shoot that shit myself."

They didn't have time to wait for no ambulance. Paramedics wouldn't come this deep up in the hood without a police escort anyway. And that could take all day to arrange.

Mello ran to his car with Rosa in his arms. He buckled her into the backseat then he sped off, honking his horn at the city traffic as he tried to make other drivers get the fuck outta his way. Even at the rate of speed he was driving at, he couldn't stop himself from taking quick peeks at Eva. What she'd said upstairs in the apartment had fucked him straight up. Rosa was sick. Eva said the girl was so high it could kill her, and getting her to the hospital was his primary mission. Even though Mello knew it wasn't the time or the place to get with Eva about her past, he couldn't get that shit outta his head. *I used to shoot that shit myself.* Those words had come straight outta Eva's mouth. Out of the mouth of the girl he loved.

He ran a red light and slammed on the brakes as a young boy walked his pit bull puppy out in traffic. Mello had no choice but to wait, and he couldn't help but glance at Eva.

She sat there with her eyes screwed closed and her fists clenched tight. Her lips were moving and he knew she was praying her ass off. Praying for Rosa.

"Eva," he blurted, unable to keep his mouth on lock. "You used to get high?"

He nosed the car back into traffic and resumed his high-speed drive.

"I was a junkie, Mello," she said, sounding miserable and empty. "I was a ho too. I had a baby when I was fourteen and I left him in a laundrymat."

Mello was struck down. His whole body went numb and his stomach lurched violently. His head was buzzin'. He felt physically sick. But the moment he looked over at Eva . . . at his baby . . . at the fine-ass chick who had won his heart, nothing else mattered except her.

"T-that's cool, Eva," he said. She had been a kid when all that shit happened. It was in the past and she didn't owe him no more explanations neither. "I don't care what you been through, baby girl. I still love—"

The sound of screeching tires cut the air. A burgundy Expedition came hurling toward them. A loud crash and the cracking of breaking glass. Suddenly the windshield was flying toward him in shards, and all Mello could do was lunge across the seat for Eva and duck . . .

The impact ripped the hood off Mello's car. The engine block was thrust toward the steering wheel. The smell of burning oil was in the air, then Mello closed his eyes and his thoughts drifted skyward with the smoke . . .

The first person on the scene was an elderly Asian man named Daniel who owned a fruit stand on 125th Street. He saw a young black woman crawling out of the mangled car through the shattered passenger window, then lost sight of her in the thick smoke as she ran toward the back door of the car.

Immediately he went for the driver. It was a young black man, and he'd been knocked unconscious by the impact. Even with all the blood on his face, Daniel recognized him. His name was Ramel. He worked a vendors' table on 125th Street and he came into Daniel's store to buy Fuji apples almost every day.

Ramel was trapped in the wreckage. He must have been leaning sideways in his seat when he was hit because the left side of his body had absorbed a lot of the impact in the crash. The kid had probably been lucky, Daniel knew. The steering wheel had been driven forward, and it would have gone right through the young man's chest had he been facing the dashboard at the time of the collision.

A woman's screams cut into his haze, and Daniel ran around

to the other side of the car. To his horror the young woman who'd climbed out the window was now getting out of the backseat. She was screaming into the air and clutching something in her arms.

Daniel caught a quick glimpse inside the back of the car. A little girl was in there. She was slumped over, laying across the backseat. Still strapped in her seat belt. She looked just fine. Except her head was missing.

The screaming young lady was carrying it in her arms.

What happened next was so graphic that it scared the piss outta Daniel. He was a sick old man, and he'd long been considering returning home to the peace of his own country. What he was seeing right now was giving him the best damn reason to leave sooner rather than later.

A black Escalade pulled up next to the car. Two men jumped out and were joined by the three occupants of the crashed burgundy Expedition, one of whom appeared to be a sizable girl and had a large, bloody cut on her forehead. Together, they rushed the screaming young lady, grabbing her so roughly that she dropped the little girl's head. It rolled toward the gutter and came to a standstill at Daniel's feet.

As the crowd on the street watched in disbelief, the screaming black lady was dragged into the Escalade. The little girl's blood was all over her clothes and still dripped from her hands. All five of her kidnappers jumped into the Escalade with her as she fought and screamed, and Daniel covered his toothless mouth in fear and horror as the big SUV spun its tires and sped its occupants far away from the scene of their ferocious crime.

Chapter 21

Black Girl Lost ... Again

Hands were all over her in the back of that Escalade. It was wide open like a limo back there, and a series of punches and kicks rocked down on her that were so brutal that Eva prayed for death.

But anything, even taking a beat-down, was better than the image that was frozen in her eyes. Eva balled up on the black carpet and screamed. Far more from the heart-stopping sight of Rosa's decapitated head than from any physical pain that Brody's goons could inflict upon her in this crazy life.

The whip sped down the streets of Harlem, and they talked shit and beat Eva until the car came to a stop. A fist landed hard on her right eye and she was dragged from the car by her hair. She cried out as her bare back scraped across the floor, and then banged against the vehicle's metal step-up. Eva twisted herself back and forth and flailed her legs, until she realized that her right ankle was flopping around like it was boneless and hurt worse than anything else on her body.

Eva had no idea where she was. They tossed her into a big room with a cement floor and concrete walls. The room was cool but damp. There was cardboard on the floor and several machines that she'd never seen before. But there *was* something there that was real familiar to her. CDs. Thousands of them. Some in printed covers, others stacked two to three feet high on small tables.

She was inside one of the print bunkers that Brody ran. Mello had called them press and kills.

Eva stared from the floor as Brody walked in. He was dressed in a black wife beater and some jeans, and his bald head gleamed under the bright light.

He squatted down beside Eva and grinned.

"Hey lil bitch," he said softly. "So you finally decided to come check me out, huh?"

Eva just shivered. Her body was a ball of agonizing pain, and the craziness in Brody's eyes scared the shit outta her.

He reached out and touched her hair and Eva yelped like a small dog.

"You scared of me?" he asked, grinning. "Why?"

Eva just lay there on the cold floor.

"I remember the first time I saw you," Brody whispered. "You was visiting Fiyah on The Rock and I knew you was something special. You was wearing these little jeans that were so fuckin' *tight* . . . I promised myself, one day your fine ass was gonna be sittin' right on my face."

He reached out to touch her and Eva flinched again. Without warning, he ripped her earring from her earlobe, and warm blood cascaded down her neck as her flesh tore.

"So I got down on a little sumpthin' with your cousin," Brody kept right on talking like didn't shit happen. "You know, a little business got handled between men. Fiyah was all for that shit. A dick up the ass will make a niggah cool with a whole lotta shit! But when it came time for that bitch to show and prove . . . he did every fuckin' thing he could think of to keep us apart. Now, why do you think that is?"

The pain in Eva's ear was practically unnoticeable. She hurt so bad in so many other places that her earlobe didn't mean shit. She knew she was going to die in that room. This wasn't the fuckin' movies and wasn't no hero gonna blast up in there and save her ass. Eva felt her own death coming, and after the miserable life she had lived, she was cool with it.

"Is it because your cousin thinks I'm too hard for you?" Brody said, his fingers playing in the bright blood that was running down her neck. "Or could it be because you walk around with ya ass in the air like you too fuckin' good for me?"

Eva didn't answer. She'd made up her mind. No matter what this beast did or said, he couldn't hurt her. Eva thought back to all the miserable days of her childhood. She remembered how she used to be able to make herself float and go limp. Become invisible and impenetrable. She tried that now. As she lay defenseless under Brody's evil glare, she let herself go limp and willed her soul to break free.

She felt the transition. The act of her spirit separating from her body. Eva felt light. The worst had already been done to her. There wasn't shit else this bastard could do to hurt her. At least that's what she thought until she saw what Brody was holding in his hand.

He laughed as Eva's eyes grew wide. He was loving her terror. Getting off grand on that shit. "Oh, yeah," he said as she stared at what he was holding out toward her. "Your cousin told me about that monkey that used to ride the fuck outta ya back. He said you liked that shit so much you used to do all kinds of nasty shit to get it."

Brody held Eva's fear up in the air. He pushed the plunger and released a few air bubbles, then he smushed her face into the ground with his big, rough hand, and kneeled with his knee pressing into her temple.

"He said you liked to hit that main vein. The one in ya neck." He guided the tip of the needle toward Eva's jugular. "Rosa liked it there too, ya know. She liked it there." Brody reached under her skirt. He dragged his hand between Eva's legs and dug around in her pussy. "And she liked it right there too."

Short bursts of panicked air were all Eva could squeeze from her throat. She lay there panting, terror clogging her chest. Her worst nightmares were about to be repeated and there was nobody who could save her. She squeezed her eyes closed tight. And when she felt that old familiar sting, and then that powerful rush of fear as it coursed through her veins, she screamed.

There was no day and there was no night.

There was only darkness and pain. Twisted anguish and joyous fear.

Eva lay on the cold cement floor naked from the waist down. Her broken ankle was cuffed tight. A chain had been looped over a ceiling beam and her injured leg was suspended in the air, way over her head.

Brody had brutalized her. Every time she moved, she hurt. Deep lashes had cut into her pretty brown skin, laying open her flesh in some places down to the bone. He'd pumped her up with fear too. The fear that she'd once both despised and adored was now an ever-present specter in her world. Eva nodded and she drooled. She picked at her open lacerations and let her soul fly free.

Sometimes she was alone, and other times she was not. Rosa spoke to her often, and India did too. She heard other voices in the darkness. The cries of a small baby and the drunken curses of a long-lost mother.

Time passed by in a haze. She was violated painfully. With objects, fingers, and other body parts. Brody fucked her in brutal, degrading ways. He inserted himself into every part of her body that he could, and he made sure he hurt her each and every time. Eva rode the pain and bore it well. She had suffered much worse before and she comforted herself with the fear that suspended her in a stupor, dulling her senses. Brody was generous with his fear. At least in the beginning. Eva's mind stayed in a tunnel. In the darkness of a project clothes dryer she prayed to God and suffered for her sins. There were some clear moments too. Moments where she fully understood that Brody controlled her fear. And once more, after so much fuckin' time, fear had gained control of her body.

It didn't take long for her to start jonesing for it.

He made her cook it herself now. And find her own damned vein too.

Brody liked seeing her squirm on a string. The first time he left her alone for too long, sickness gripped her and Eva shit all over the floor. He hosed her down like a dog. He laughed hard as fuck as she begged for that shit. He grinned as she spread her lower lips offering him pussy, top, ass, anything. Then he left her there sick and alone, wet and trembling in agony, begging for that fear.

Brody made sure she suffered as much as possible. Every few hours his belt would rise and fall on her stomach and breasts as she vomited bile and shivered on the frigid concrete. Her broken ankle turned black. Her toenails paled and curled backward as her flesh died from lack of circulation. All the muscles in her body stiffened. Her nose dripped. She prayed to God. *Please. Please, dear Lord. Give me what I love. Give me what I fear. Give me what I need!*

He left her alone for the next two days. And when he came back she was sicker than she'd ever been in life. When the door was finally raised up on its tracks Brody had to beat back flies and wave his hand in front of his nose at the shitty smell.

Eva lay there spread-eagle, one leg still up in the air, her eyes half open. Her lips were caked and parched, and black rats had bitten and chewed on her flesh all through the night.

"Fuckin' bitch prolly dead," Brody said, unconcerned, but when he kneeled down next to her he saw she was still breathing. She was still jonesing too.

"Here," he said, holding out a package before tossing it across the room, just beyond her reach. He sat on a small stool and watched as Eva used the last of her strength to retrieve the dope. She stretched her arms and scooted her torn body across the cement, and when her broken ankle swung on the chain, she moaned deeply from the excrutiating pain and had to rest and catch her breath before she could try again.

The bitch was determined—Brody gave her that. She dragged the package toward her with her big toe, then scooped it up in her hands like it was made of gold. He tossed her the dirty works that had been used on countless fiends before her, and watched as the once-beautiful Eva cooked brown skag with grimy, trembling hands.

Eva prepared her fear like an old pro. And truly, she was.

There was enough for three hits in the package and she knew exactly what she was doing as she pulled back the plunger and filled the syringe with every drop of cooked fear in her spoon.

By the time Brody realized what was up it was too damned late.

"That's too fuckin' mu—!" He lunged toward her and warned, but Eva's deft fingers had already found her sweet spot. She depressed the plunger and pushed the dope into her groin as fast as she could, and by the time Brody managed to tear the syringe from her hands, Eva had already hit herself with a lethal amount of fear.

Brody went fuckin' bonkers. "Stupid bitch!" He kicked her in the head, the face, the back. He swung his fists, and then grabbed his belt and swung that too. Exhausted, he dug his boot into Eva's stomach sending clear liquid shooting out her nose and mouth.

Eva just lay there. She didn't feel a thing. Her life was a tragic collage passing slowly in front of her eyes. She saw the closet she used to get locked in and the bathtub with the fat water bugs crawling out the drain. She reflected on her near starvation. That odd feeling of having a stomach bloated full of chewed toilet tissue, yet still being weak from hunger. She remembered those early days of desperation, when, forced to feed her own habit, she had to get out on the cold streets and sell her body to any man who had the cash she so desperately needed.

As Eva spiraled into that forever tunnel of darkness, her fear slowly turned to joy. She saw her friend India, and her baby sister, Rosa, whose life she had entrusted in Eva's care. Miss Threet came into view. She was sitting on the bench in front of building 420, surrounded by mad little kids. Eva's curly-haired baby boy was one of them. His name was Cameron, and he was staring at Eva with a birthmark under his chin and love in his big brown eyes.

Life only hurts until it starts feeling good.

Eva looked up with a smile on her face. Mello's hands were on her. Tickling that weak spot right behind her knees. She grinned at her baby. He was it, and she was his. Brody still raged over her, but she was way beyond his reach now. *"Thank you, baby,"* Eva whispered, although her cold lips never moved. She felt Mello's weight pressing into her from behind. His strong arms scooped her up from her ankles to her waist, holding her in his protective embrace. "Thank you, baby." She whispered it again, and she meant that shit. "Thank you."

Chapter 22

Fiyah was the last person released from Rikers for the day. He'd spent a week on lockdown, fuckin' around with his stupid parole officer. Daniels had showed up at the house the night the little gimp kid had gotten shot, and the first thing Fiyah had thought was that Mello had given his name up and they were gonna try to somehow railroad his ass and hang the shooting on him. When his PO started making noise about his failure to sign off on some fuckin' kind of parole document and turn it in, he thought dude was joking.

But he wasn't. That cat was dead serious. His dick had

been hard for Fiyah since the day they met, and he was on a mission to see to it that Fiyah went back to the joint to serve out the remainder of his time.

It was pure luck that Fiyah had landed a judge who had a little bit of sense. She'd taken a look at the same violation charge that the judge at Central Booking had signed off on, told him to sign the document in her presence, and tossed the whole case right out the door.

"Man," Fiyah had bitched and whined when his public defender told him his charges were being dropped. "I been fuckin' around out here for almost a week! I shoulda never been locked up in the first place! Who the hell can I sue?"

"Actually," his public defender had laughed, "you aren't in a position to sue anyone, but the judge did chastise your parole officer for being 'overly enthusiastic.' "

Fiyah was given a MetroCard to get on the train, and that was the end of that. No apology, no explanation as to why these clowns had detained him behind some simple-ass "failure to sign a document" charge.

It was dark when he made it back to Harlem. The trap boys were out grinding but the foot traffic on the streets was real light, even for a weekday. Fiyah approached his mother's apartment and looked up at the windows like he always did. Every room in the crib was dark, and something about that bothered him as he climbed the stairs.

"Yo, Ma!" he called out as he stepped into the apartment. The smell of rotting garbage snaked down his throat and forced him to cover his mouth. Milena was a neat freak and never in his life, even during her heavy drugging days, had Fiyah seen his moms's crib so fucked up.

He stepped deeper into the living room and that's when he

saw her. Milena was balled up in a knot on a cut-up sofa cushion. In the middle of the living-room floor.

"Ma!" Fiyah yelled. He rushed over to her and shook her shoulder. "Ma! What the fuck is up! Wake up, Ma. What the fuck is up!"

Milena rolled over on her side. Her grill was swollen and dented and her front teeth were shot the fuck out. Fiyah saw a crazy big noogie on her forehead where somebody had clocked his moms in her dome. Milena looked up into the eyes of her only child and wept.

"Fuego . . ." she wailed. She reached her arms out to him and knocked over a half-full can of warm beer. "Rosa . . ." She shook her head, unable to say the rest. "Rosa . . . Rosa . . . Rosa . . ."

Fiyah rocked his mother in his arms as fear slowly spread through his body. He knew something vital had changed in their lives. It felt like the old days. Back when Milena had been on a mission drinking and drugging all over Harlem. He let her cling to him. It had been a long time since she had hugged him or had let him touch her at all. But all around them were empty bottles of beer and rum. There were endless ground-out cigarette butts all over the floor and his heart almost broke when he caught a glimpse of the fresh track marks on his mother's arms.

"What happened to Rosa?" Fiyah kept asking her softly. But each time the drunken Milena tried to tell him she would burst into tears. She cursed herself for being an addict and a selfish mother. She pulled at her own hair as she wailed in Spanish that everything that happened was her own fault for having a weakness for bad men and evil drugs.

Milena went on like this for hours. Clinging to her son and alternating between fits of extreme grief and bouts of debilitating guilt. It was well into morning by the time Fiyah got the story out of her. And even then a lot of things were still unclear to him. But one thing he understood without a doubt. Little Rosa was dead. Right now she was laying all by herself somewhere in a cold morgue, where Milena had been forced to go identify her head.

Excruciating pain shot through Fiyah and tears fell from his eyes. He had loved Rosita. They all had. She'd been a part of their family even before India was murdered, and it killed him that he hadn't been there to protect either of the sisters from their horrible fate.

"What . . ." Fiyah asked his mother through the haze of his tears. "What happened to Eva? She was in the car too, right? Did she get hurt? Where is she now?"

Milena had burst into fresh tears at the sound of her niece's name. "*Evita . . .*" she wailed. She clutched Fiyah tighter than she ever had before. "*Evita . . .*" Milena moaned. "They took her, Fuego. People said they took her outta the car right there on the streets in front of everybody."

Fiyah went cold. "Who took her, Ma? What are you talking about? Did somebody take Eva to the hospital? Is she hurt?"

Milena sighed and tried to ball up in a knot again. The truth was just too painful for her to face. "A man saw her," she muttered. "The Chinese man who sells fruit on 125th Street. He said Eva wasn't really hurt, but her boyfriend Mello almost died. And Eva . . ." Milena trembled and squeezed her eyes closed tight.

"What, Ma?" Fiyah urged. "What the fuck??"

"Eva got snatched, Fuego. By Brody and his friends. They put Eva in Brody's car after the accident, and ain't nobody seen her since."

Mello's injuries had been quite severe, but he was young and strong and the doctors said he would definitely recover. He'd taken a big hit in the accident and had sustained a serious brain concussion. In order to keep him still so that his brain could cease swelling and begin to heal itself, Mello had been sedated with strong tranquilizers for four whole days.

On the fifth day he had begun to stir and come awake, but his broken left hip had been so painful that they'd shot him up full of medication and he'd gone gratefully back into oblivion.

But on the sixth day Mello was wide awake and riding his pain. He had cuts and bruises all over his face and his neck, and his left shoulder had been dislocated by the impact. His boys had been coming up to the hospital nonstop, checking for him and making sure everybody was handling him with care.

"Where's Eva?" was the first thing outta his mouth as soon as he was able to form words. The young nurse's aide who was attending to him had stopped fiddling with his tubes and gave him a look that showed she was uncomfortable.

"I'll go get a doctor," she'd said as she scurried out of the room without answering his question.

Mello was in intense pain, but he wanted to know where his baby was, and he wanted to know right then and there. "Where the fuck is Eva?" he roared as loud as he could. His voice bounced weakly off the walls and fell back on his ears. He reached for the call button and pressed that shit over and over again. Finally the door to his room burst open and the scary white nurse and two doctors came in.

"Mr. Williams," the older doctor said soothingly. "I see you're awake and feeling a little better, yes?"

Mello felt dizzy. He'd used up all his energy doing all that hollering.

"My girl was in the car with me. Her little sister was too. Where are they? My girl's name is Eva Patterson. Is she okay? Did she get hurt too?"

The doctor spoke slowly, like he wanted to choose his words carefully.

"There was no Eva Patterson brought into the emergency room," he reassured Mello. He deliberately failed to mention Rosa's horrible death. And of course he was aware that the woman in question had been taken from the accident scene by unknown persons. The police had come by several times to interview Ramel, but he'd been too heavily sedated to talk. "I'm told the young lady who was in the car with you seemed to have sustained very minor injuries."

"Where is she? Has she been up here while I was sleep?" Mello asked, his voice growing weaker. He was tired. Fuckin' exhausted. Every inch of him felt like he'd been stomped out. All of his bones felt cracked and broken. "I need to call . . . I gotta make sure my baby's straight . . ."

The doctor watched as Mello dozed off, overtaken once more by the medication.

"We'll keep him under for the rest of the night," he told the nurse. "Let the poor kid get a little more rest. He'll have enough to deal with in the days ahead."

Mello slept a deep, solid sleep. But not even the drugs could stop his heart from crying out for Eva in his slumber. Trapped deep in the recesses of his dreams, he ached for her and yearned to hear her voice. He was dying to hold her hand and see her face. And he swore that he would. Just as soon as he could keep his eyes open and stand up on his feet.

The next morning Mello was awake before the sun came up. He eyed a phone sitting on his nightstand, and pain cut through him as he reached out to get it. Gritting his teeth, he lifted the phone with his good arm and sat it on his stomach.

He punched in Eva's digits, and listened as the call went straight to her voice mail.

"Yeah, it's Birthday Cake and I'll give you a slice so you can slurp your plate! You've reached Eva Patterson, premiere model for Noire's Birthday Cake Urban Wear. I'm probably out doing big things right now but if you want to leave me a message just wait for the beep and . . . hell, you know what to do! One luv! Peace!"

The next number he dialed was Speedy's. His boy answered on the third ring, but Mello could tell he had been knocked out sleeping.

"What it do?" Speedy grumbled.

"I don't know. You tell me," Mello answered.

"Oh shit. You up, niggah? I been up there looking in ya grill for hours every fuckin' day. I been talking all kinds of shit to you and you ain't talked none back."

Mello chuckled a little bit.

"Yeah. I'm up, dude. I'm up. Yo," he said quietly. "Where the fuck is Eva?"

Speedy coughed real quick and then said, "I don't know, man. Don't no fuckin' body seem to know and the cops don't act like they care."

Mello listened as Speedy ran shit down to him raw. His boy knew he'd been banged up, but he still gave it all to him. The good and the ugly. Speedy knew a niggah needed to have all available info so he could sort shit out. Wasn't no need in holding nothing back. Mello was a big boy and it was time he got up outta that fuckin' bed and handled his.

"Come get me" was all Mello said when Speedy finished talking.

"Man, you all broke the fuck up! Now I told you. We been out there looking for her. We got eyes everywhere, man. The moment she pops up—"

"Come and fuckin' get me!" Mello yelled. He threw the phone down on the floor and started pulling tubes from his arms and hands. He even pulled one outta his dick. By the time Speedy showed up twenty minutes later, Mello had already cursed out two nurses, threatened a doctor, and signed himself out of the hospital.

"Mr. Williams!" a young resident cried out as Mello limped down the hall, supported on both sides by Speedy and Gita. "You're in no condition to leave! If you walk out of here now, we won't be responsible for what might happen to you!"

Mello just grunted and kept right on moving, shuffling like an old broke-down man. He wasn't giving a fuck about himself right about then. His mind, his heart, his soul was on Eva. *She* was who he was responsible for, and he was about to get out on the streets of Harlem and find her.

"**W**e been all over the fuckin' place," Speedy told him. Gita was driving and Speedy rode shotgun. Mello was stretched out in the backseat. Groaning and grimacing every time the whip hit the slightest bump. "That niggah Brody been laying low. He ain't showed his face in Bricks at all. His brother Bullet stays somewhere in Harlem but don't nobody outside of they click know where Brody rests."

Mello held on to the arm rest and tried to stay cool. He'd called Eva's phone until her voice mail was full. Where the fuck could she be?

"What about her fuckin' cousin? Fiyah. Anybody get with him?"

"That fool got knocked the day before you crashed your shit up, man. I heard he got took down on a parole violation. Stupid-ass fuck."

Mello nodded. He was gonna find Eva. Find her or die trying.

His first stop would be at her aunt's crib. He'd find out what the fuck Milena knew, then come up with the rest of his plan from there.

"Stop right here," he told Gita as they pulled up outside of Eva's building. His boys jumped out the whip and came around to help him get out, and Mello leaned on them gratefully and breathed through the sharp pain.

"Nah," he said, checking them as they tried to help him to the door. "I got this. Y'all chill down here for a minute."

"Niggah," Speedy said, "who the fuck you think you is? The Incredible Hulk? Yo ass got pins in ya fuckin' hip and you can't even sit up straight. How the hell you gone get all the way in that building by yourself? And then up the fuckin' stairs?"

Mello shrugged. He'd asked himself the same questions. But it wasn't even six o'clock in the fuckin' morning yet. The sun still hadn't come all the way up. If he rolled up on Eva's aunt at this time of morning with his goonies checking behind him, she might clam the fuck up and not tell him shit. He couldn't risk that. He shook Speedy off and dragged his bad leg as he limped slowly toward the building. If he wanted to find Eva then he would have to approach Milena on his own. And that was exactly what the fuck he was about to do.

It took him forever just to get to the front stoop. And once he was there, he had to rest for a few before he could open the door to the vestibule. Mello was breathing hard and sweating. Never in life had he been in so much pain. But he kept moving. Inching his way to the staircase where it was gonna take a fuckin' miracle for him to get up those steps.

The first two steps were the worst. He almost blacked out right then and there. The shit was just that bad. He held on to the banister and leaned his weight onto his good arm. This way he was able to slide his bad leg out, then lift it up without jerking his hip too much. He'd gone up three-quarters of the steps. Sweating and moaning, determined to get to Milena, when he saw feet at the top of the landing.

Mello froze, all pain forgotten. One foot looked soft and brown. The other was black and shriveled. Like it had gotten frostbitten or something and was rotting away. Mello cocked his head to the side, trying to figure that shit out. He took another step up, and then another. Something glinted on the blackened foot. He was in the midst of taking the third step when he realized what his eyes were seeing. A gold toe ring. He'd bought it from Cartier and slipped it onto her toe with his very own lips.

He heard his cry, but it seemed so far away. He staggered quickly up the few remaining steps, falling forward in his haste, and the only pain he was conscious of was the stabbing pain in his heart.

"*Evaaaaaaaaaaaaa . . .*" Mello screamed. He fell on top of her, clutching her stiff, mutilated body to his chest. His mind refused to believe what his eyes were telling him as he hugged her, patted her hair, and wept tears of pure love and devastation that sprang from the very bottom of his soul.

Inside the apartment Fiyah had just risen from the sofa cushion he'd been laying on with Milena. She'd clung to him all through the night, refusing to let him leave her, not even to take a piss.

He'd been holding that shit for hours, and now, just before the sun came up, he eased away from his sleeping mother. He stood up and stretched his arms over his head, and was walking toward the bathroom when a sound so fucking tortured, so blood-curdling, shattered the silence of the morning and sent him running toward the door.

"*Evaaaaaaaaaa . . .*"

Fiyah heard the brokenhearted cry as he flung the door open wide. The scene before his eyes was overpowering, and at first he couldn't move. But then a scream tore from his throat as he realized what he was seeing, and he couldn't stop himself from falling to his knees.

"*Evitaaaaaaaa . . .*" he screamed, crawling toward his cousin on his hands and knees. Eva's eyes were open, staring blankly. Her body looked rigid in Mello's arms and her beautiful brown skin was turning gray. She had on a shirt and her bra was showing, but that's all she wore. Her skin had been cut into, and blood-crusted lashes were all over her. Guilt and rage tore through Fiyah with a force that was strong enough to stop his heart. Mello was clutching her in his arms, and rocking her like she was a baby.

Fiyah reached out for her, his heart pounding with grief, but a bitter, hate-filled look from Mello checked him cold.

"Don't fuckin' touch her!"

Fiyah shrank back, stunned silent.

"You dished her off, bitch. And now she's fuckin' *dead.*"

Fiyah climbed to his feet. The whole world had turned dark before his eyes. He turned around and staggered back into the apartment where Milena was sitting up on the cushions looking disoriented.

"Fuego?"

"Don't go out there, Ma," Fiyah said, his voice cold and empty as he headed toward his room to get his gat. "Eva's dead."

Chapter 23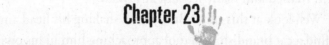

Fiyah walked from Harlem all the way downtown to Lexington Avenue.

His mind was so full of guilt and grief that he didn't even feel the sidewalk under his feet.

He stood outside of Brody's crib dripping with sweat. The sun was up and beaming down on him. His gat hung heavy in the front pocket of his hoody, as he took the stairs up to Brody's joint, two at a time.

He tapped on the door using the butt of the pistol, then stood to the side as somebody barked, "Who is it?"

"It's Fiyah," he said calmly, holding the burner at his side.

The door swung open and Bullet stood there in a pair

of boxers. He scoped the gun in Fiyah's grip and the rage in his eyes, then slowly moved aside and let him in.

Fiyah walked into Brody's joint fully aware that he would never walk back out. He could hear Brody and his crew chillin' in the living room and he headed that way. They were sprawled on the leather couches, eating breakfast and watching cartoons. Brody looked up and saw him coming. His crew jumped to it like trained dogs. Tools were brandished in a flash, every one of them trained and ready to bark at Fiyah.

"Well look at this shit," Brody said, shaking his head amazed to find a cat brandishing a tool approaching him in his own living room. "This dick-headed bitch rolling in here with a fuckin' burner when I got my own brother manning the door. 'Sup with that shit, Bullet? You stupid-ass fuck . . ."

Still cool, Brody set his plate of food down on the table and leaned back in his big, king-sized chair.

Fiyah walked right up on the big guy, and pressed the gat to his dome, expecting to take at least five rounds at any moment.

"Eva's life wasn't the trade-off, Brody. Yours is."

Brody put his head back and laughed. He waved his hand at his boys who were ready to let their burners spit. "Put ya tools down. This niggah don't flex. Not even with a fully loaded gat."

He looked up at Fiyah as his boys settled back down. "It's about time you got here. Did you see the little present I left for you outside your moms's door?"

Fiyah shrugged. He refused to let Brody see his pain. "I got a little present for you too, ak. It's time for your fuckin' ass to get *brodied.*"

Sliding the gun across the top of King Brody's head, Fiyah pulled the trigger and bust a cap straight down the middle of Brody's body.

Nobody moved except Fiyah and Brody.

Brody slumped over, dead where he sat, and Fiyah tossed his gun down on the table next to Brody's plate. He held his hands in the air, surprised that he was still alive and on his feet.

Bullet moved into the room and froze Brody's crew with one look.

Fiyah stared at Brody's brother and four of Brody's most trusted lieutenants without an ounce of fear in him. He had done what he came to do and now he was ready to die.

"Well? What the fuck y'all niggahs gone do?" he said with a shrug.

Bullet took a step up on him. A glass of orange juice was in his hand. He walked past Fiyah and over to the dead body of his brother and stood looking down at him. Bullet's deadly gaze traveled from Brody over to Fiyah, and back to King Brody again.

Without warning, he smashed the glass over Brody's motionless head. Then he slung the lifeless body of his older brother out of the chair, and claimed his seat.

"We gone finish grubbin'," Bullet said, shrugging his massive shoulders. He picked up a piece of bacon off of Brody's plate and stuffed it into his mouth. Then he snatched Fiyah's gat off the table and tossed it back at him. "The muhfuckin' King is dead. Long live the King."

• • •

Wednesday's child is full of woe,
Wednesday's child is full of woe,
Wednesday's child is full of woe . . .

They buried Eva on a Wednesday.

Milena was in no condition to make funeral arrangements, and Rasheena was off somewhere on a mission and couldn't be found. There was no one else for Fiyah to call. Until Reem tossed a name at him that he'd never heard before.

"Get in touch with a lady named Miss Threet. I know her. She lives in Howard projects in Brooklyn, and Eva knew her too. I don't know how to tell you this, ak, but she's raising Eva's son."

Fiyah had rocked on his feet. "Eva's *son*?"

Reem nodded, then told Fiyah everything that Eva had confided in him.

"You got a little cousin, man," Reem said. "He's around four now. Miss Threet used to take in homeless kids when me and Eva was coming up. She was good to everybody, and Eva trusted her to raise her son."

Reem shook his head and there was sorrow in his voice for his lost friend. "Eva always talked about getting her baby back, yo. That's what she was living and grinding so hard for. She was trying to get herself situated and get up enough ends to one day walk into building 420 and be a mother to her son."

Fiyah's mind was heavy with grief and disbelief as he rode the train out to Brooklyn and found the lady Reem had told him about. Miss Threet had broken down and cried when she learned of Eva's death. Fiyah told her Eva had been in a real bad accident, and kept the grimy parts of her death to himself.

"I never could stand that Rasheena," Miss Threet said. "I remember how cold Eva used to be in the winters. The child never had enough clothes to wear or enough food to eat. I tried to help her as much as I could. I even went to talk to her mother one day, but that fool pulled a knife on me and told me that Eva was a bitch and a tramp." She pursed her lips, tears in her eyes. "Of course you could see that wasn't true. The girl couldn't have been more than eight or nine at the time. I watched Eva, though. Gave her what I could give her whenever it was possible. I saw what her people were doing to her. I knew what they were turning her into. That's why when I found that naked little baby down in the laundry room early one morning I took him in and I kept him. I knew all along who he belonged to. I'd seen Eva sitting out there on the bench crying as I walked up, and when I came out carrying her baby in my arms this real big smile came over her face, then she turned around and ran like the dickens."

Fiyah asked to see Eva's son, and almost broke down when a little curly-haired boy came out of a back room with a brown face and Eva's distinctive birthmark under his chin. Fiyah stared at the child as Miss Threet kissed him and smoothed his hair. He looked just like Eva, and it was heartbreaking to see her beautiful brown face on his little body.

"I was worried when she moved to Harlem, but she came down here all the time, you know," Miss Threet said. "She sent money too. Wrinkled tens and twenties with no note or nothing in the envelopes. I knew it was her, though. I knew that child was trying her best to do what she thought was right by her son. She was always trying to get a peek at him, and whenever she showed up I made sure to bring Cameron outside so she could get as full on her baby as she wanted. I figured I was just holding him for her, you know? Keeping him safe until she got her life in order. I always expected her to come and get him one day. I could see how much she loved him. I guess that's not gonna ever happen for her now. It won't happen for Cameron either, huh?"

Tears flowed freely down Fiyah's face. He was stunned by what the old lady was telling him. But he was also feeling a spark of joy that there was still some part of Evita that was left for them.

"What are you going to do with him?" he asked. "With Eva's baby?"

Miss Threet shrugged. "I'm gonna keep on loving him and feeding him. Eva left him in my arms so I know she trusted me to do him right. I'm gonna keep her trust."

Fiyah was devastated. Eva's son was his *family*. But in his heart he knew he couldn't take care of a kid, and Milena's life was on the fucked-up path again. Taking the best part of Eva and putting him in that kinda gutta environment would be like killing her all over again.

"You can come and see him, you know," Miss Threet offered. "I'm not holding the boy hostage. Just giving him what his mama would have wanted him to have. I'm sure she would've wanted him to have you too. After all, you are his family."

By the time Fiyah left Brooklyn he was busted up inside. He rode the train uptown with a stomach that was heavy with grief but hopeful for Cameron too.

Miss Threet arranged for a double funeral. For Eva and for Rosa. There were cars lined up and down Lenox Avenue as the good people of Harlem came out to show their respects. An organist played "Keep Your Eye on the Sparrow" as mourners walked past the caskets and cried. Both caskets were closed. They had to be. The bodies of Eva and Rosa were in no shape to be on display to the world.

Milena and Alex sat in the front row and were comforted by Miss Threet and her friends. Alex had rushed back to Harlem with a quickness, and had spent hours crying with Fiyah and with Mello too.

Reem and ill Nino sat up front too, watching as Fiyah leaned over Eva's casket and placed a gentle kiss on the lid.

Mello sat in the front aisle in a wheelchair watching Fiyah too, grief blending with his rage. "Just hold on," Miss Threet told him as she came up and patted and rubbed his back over and over again. "Hold on, son. It only hurts until it starts feeling good."

Mello cried out. "This shit ain't gone never feel good!"

"Oh, it will, baby," Miss Threet promised. "God won't allow us to hurt forever. One day you gone feel good again. One day."

But right now all Mello could feel was the pain. Speedy rolled him over to the casket and he gazed at the smiling picture of Eva that had been blown up and placed on a large metal stand. He had taken this picture himself, the first time he'd ever seen her, and Eva's bright smile had been just for him.

Fiyah came over and looked up at the picture too. His face was a conflicted mask of grief and remorse. Then he looked down at the tears in Mello's eyes. The last time they'd spoken Mello had been laying on the floor outside his apartment with Eva's cold body clutched in his arms.

"Yo, man," Fiyah said, his voice low and deep. "I'm sorry."

Mello igged the shit outta him, and then Fiyah said it louder. Much louder, because he wanted to make sure Mello really heard him. "Yo, I said I'm sorry, Mello. I took Evita away from both of us, and it's nobody's fault but mine."

Mello turned toward him then. He looked up at Fiyah with a tearful gaze that was colder than the most bitter winter. "You got that shit right, you bitch-niggah. You got that shit right."

Chapter 24

Four Months Later

Mello took his time walking down the streets of
Harlem. It was a fall day, but kids were playing
stickball in abandoned lots and it was hot enough to pass
for summer. He walked past a group of young girls who
were laughing and jumping double dutch. He caught a
glimpse of Eva in a smiling brown face, and for the first
time in a while he grinned inside.

Mello paused near a tenement stoop. A little kid who
looked about five years old was sitting on the steps, coloring in a jumbo-sized coloring book.

The little boy looked up with a curious expression on
his face. He pointed at the sling Mello still wore on his
arm.

"What happened to your arm, Mister?"

Mello stared down at the kid.

His hip and his shoulder were both healing, but his one-handed jumper would forever be shot.

"I had an accident, lil man. I got hurt."

The kid looked doubtful. Like he didn't believe him.

"Did you get shot or something? All five of my brothers been shot before. My brother Dame got shot in his throat. He can't talk no more but he can still draw. Can you draw, Mister?"

Mello shook his head.

"Nah, little man. I never could draw."

Mello moved on for a few blocks, then stopped outside of a storefront shop. The sign on the door said BOTTOM HALF BOYZ, and after taking a deep breath, he walked inside.

Inside, Mello spotted Reem. He was spittin' in a booth while the sound engineer and a few of his boyz did their thing on the console.

"'Sup." Mello nodded.

Reem peeped him and signaled the engineer, then came out of the booth with a grin on his face. He dapped Mello out, then gave him a hug, being careful not to get too close to his bad arm.

"You aiight?" Reem asked, stepping back and checking his boy out.

Mello nodded. "I'm straight, man. I'm straight."

Reem nodded back. "Good. 'Cause she woulda wanted that, you know. For you to be aiight." Reem looked over Mello's shoulder just as Fiyah came out of a back room.

"Just like she wanted y'all to get down on this track. We talked all the time, me and Eva. She was excited about this shit, man. So y'all cats be cool. Aiight? Put all that bullshit beef in a box and let's get this one in for Eva."

Fiyah walked into the room and Mello stared him down. Harlem was small, yet they hadn't run into each other on the streets since Eva and Rosa's funeral. Mello's eyes told Fiyah that he hadn't missed his ass neither.

Reem busted the vibe crossing the room and held up his hands. "Aiight now. Be easy, my nigs. This my muhfuckin' spot and I don't want no shit outta y'all. Ya feel me?"

Reem turned to walk into the booth, but checked himself when he saw that neither Mello nor Fiyah had moved an inch.

"What the fuck? Y'all still standing around bumping eyeballs? Man, get y'all asses in that fuckin' booth. Time is money, gentlemen. Let's get it in!"

Mello turned around and followed Reem into the booth. When he got to the glass door he paused and looked back, then held the door open for Fiyah.

"You coming?"

Fiyah hesitated. So much had happened. The guilt still lived on his face.

He nodded and pulled out his little notepad.

"Yeah," he said, moving forward and following Mello into the booth. "Yeah."

Inside the booth, Mello and Fiyah got busy laying down the track. The beat was sick, and both men were prepared to ride it.

Fiyah glanced at Mello, and put his shit out there.

"I ain't doing this for you."

Mello stared at him. Hard. "And I sure as fuck ain't doing it for you."

"I know."

Mello nodded. "Cool. Then let's lay this shit all the way down and let's do it right."

Fiyah nodded, then muttered under his breath, "This is for Evita."

"Yeah," Mello said out loud. "For Eva."

Mello led off as they got it in right there in the booth, busting the track up.

You hear my *warrior*-cry!
Picture ya vision through a *warrior's* eyes!
It's hard to see past the pain to more glorious times!
Eva said to channel my aggression, put it all in a rhyme
And on the day it manifested they caught on to the vibe!
I'm the last of my kind, the rebel called *Ice Mello*
Instincts and quick reach was forged in the ghetto!
Where the blocks is hot, but the nights they could get
    very cold . . .
I'm focused, but on my shoulders lies a heavy load . . .
And on my road to success I paid a heavy toll
Feels like I'm battling myself for my very soul
You hear it in the songs . . .
You see it at the shows . . .
Now it's time for this chapter to come and close
So now I start anew
I'm tryna walk it through
Taking steps, bridging gaps, so we can mend the wounds!

It's like *Fiyah* and *Ice*!
Glory and *pain,* inspired my life!
I know its trife, but we live by the roll of the dice!
Decisions were made, consequences were paid
How much would you sacrifice?

Flipping pages in his notepad, Fiyah broke in with the second verse.

Everybody knows *Fuego* spits flame!
Best with the pen game and that shit can't change
My destiny's to shine, Eva gave me the recipe,
Although sometimes I let the hood get the best of me
Flow so ferocious I give it to 'em in doses
Known to spit fire on whoever comes the closest
Better take notice to what's happening 'round here
Talent, young, hungry and passionate 'round here
Yeah, too many end up in coffins over the money
It's a new day and I choose my *fam* over money!
And through the tribulations
Hard times and hatred
I put it all in the song and found my salvation
And I can wrestle with the demons and the dark
Long as I got Evita in my heart!
And deeply seated in my thoughts
I keep it *caliente,* you know I got the spark!
We're coming full circle now, we headed for the charts!

It's like *Fiyah* and *Ice*!
Glory and *pain,* inspired my life!
I know its trife, but we live by the roll of the dice!
Decisions were made, consequences were paid
How much would you sacrifice?

And at the end . . .

There was face-painting and party clowns, and a big red bounce house with mad little shoes scattered around outside. Mello stood watching as Reem stood on a picnic table wearing a T-shirt with Cameron's picture on it and spitting into a cordless mic.

> *We gotta celebrate!*
> *It's ya birthday, son!*
> *Uncle Reem's on the mic, gonna show ya how it's done!*
> *We got cake and ice cream, we feeling alive,*
> *We partying for Cameron 'cause my man is five!*
> *So when I say happy, y'all say birthday . . .*

"Happy Birthday!" all the little kids screamed as Cameron released a bundle of multicolored balloons and blew out the sizzling candles on his fifth-birthday cake.

They were celebrating on a grassy field in Brooklyn's Prospect Park, and Mello grinned and snapped endless pictures as mad lil shorties crowded around Cameron trying to get up on that first piece of cake.

"All right now!" Alex yelled out as she laughed her ass off and tried to calm the kids down. "Everybody's gonna get a big piece, I promise. Gone!" She shooed the kids back a safe distance, then picked up a large knife and guided Cameron's hand as she helped him cut his birthday cake. "Back up, babies! Back your little butts up," she giggled. "'Cause we 'bout to eat some *cake!*"

Mello snapped a few more random shots, including some of Miss Threet hugging Reem as she laughed in the midst of all her foster kids. Then he zoomed his lens on the birthday cake and focused on the colorful image that had been carefully emblazoned there.

Eva.

Her smiling face stared at him from the center of her son's rectangular sheet cake. She looked sexy and vibrant, exactly the way she had in life. Mello gazed down at the image of his baby. For the past nine months he had struggled with her death and fought to remember her in the light of beauty, and not as he'd seen her last, in the rigors of her horrific death.

It was still hard for him to block out all those memories, but hanging out with Cameron was slowly helping him to do just that. Playing with the young'un, talking to him about his mother, just loving on the little kid and sharing all of his memories of Eva so that one day they would be Cameron's memories too, really, really helped a lot.

"Okay!" loudmouthed Alex yelled again, "Cake is cut! Who gets the first slice, Cam?"

People always talked about how Mello had stepped up and taken responsibility for Eva's son, but Eva's girl Alex had really stepped up too. She'd come back to Harlem after wrapping up her singing gig, and had opened up a small studio above a barbershop where she was giving voice lessons to neighborhood kids.

Mello had been surprised as hell when Alex called him screaming and laughing one Saturday morning urging him to listen as Cameron sang his ABCs. It had been live. Lil man had put some funk on that everyday children's tune, jazzing up his ABCs with a little urban flair, and in a voice that was way too dope to be coming from such a little kid.

Looking around the huge park at all the playing children and strolling families, Mello couldn't help but yearn for Eva. She was missing out on so fuckin' much. Alex and Fiyah had decorated the party area, stringing colorful balloons and cut-out clowns and party streamers everywhere they could. Miss Threet had brought all her foster kids out with her and a whole crew of other kids who lived in her building were there too. Some of the kids had spent the morning running across the grass flying kites, while others played kick ball and freeze tag, and even more ran around flinging bright yellow Frisbees up in the air.

Fiyah's mother, Milena, was sitting on a blanket watching the happenings from sad and guilty, but also happy eyes. Mello had heard her tell Alex that she wished Rosa could be out here playing with all these kids, and just hearing the little girl's name had sent Mello's grief slamming back to the surface. He'd been forced to go crouch behind a tree until he could stop the tears from falling from his eyes as he relived that fateful car ride and the last time he had seen Rosa and Eva alive.

He'd gotten his shit together in time to take pictures of Cameron before he cut his cake, but grief could still do him like that. Charge up on him and batter him out of nowhere. It might start with just a familiar word or phrase. Or a song might come on the radio that Eva used to like. Sometimes he'd get hit with a big dose of her when he ate one of their favorite foods, and there were other times when he woke up in the middle of the night and could swear to God that he smelled her scent.

To help get past his pain, Mello spent most of his free time focusing on Cameron. Between him, Reem, and Alex, the little boy had almost every book and every toy you could think of. They took turns picking him up from Brooklyn on the weekends, and Mello looked forward to chilling with his shorty and schooling him on all the things Eva would have wanted him to learn.

Eva's soul was all tangled up in his memories when Mello felt a tug on his pants leg.

"Here," Cameron said, holding out a party plate with a thick hunk of cake sitting on it. "It's the biggest piece, Mello. I cut it for you."

Mello was touched. He looked down at the cake. It was a huge center slice and it held the image of Eva's bright smile. He sighed deeply, then looked down into the eyes of the small boy who was offering it.

"Yo, man, c'mere," he said, closing his camera lens as he took the plate and sat down with his legs folded under him. He glanced up at the sunny sky and sent his baby girl a silent message that he knew, even way up there in Heaven, she really needed to hear. *I got him, Eva. Cam's gone be straight, baby girl. I got him.*

It damn near blew Mello's mind when he heard Eva respond

in his ear, clear as day, like she was sitting right there beside him. *Thank you, baby. Thank you.*

Mello swallowed hard. One day, he knew, life was gonna get better. It could only hurt until it started feeling good. Grinning at his lil shorty, Mello pulled Cameron down beside him, and together they sat in the green grass and shared a sweet piece of Eva's beautiful smile.

About the Author

NOIRE is an author from the streets of New York whose hip-hop erotic stories pulsate with urban flavor. Visit the author's website at www.asknoire.com or email the author at noire@asknoire.com.